The River

House

by Shawn Maravel

D1714529

Other titles by Shawn Maravel

Cover illustration by Erika Plum with @erikaplumcreations

Author photo by Erika Plum with @erikaplumphotography

Find Shawn Maravel on Facebook and Instagram:
@shawnmaravelauthor

This book and my literary career are dedicated to my mother, Barbara Baumgarten. Your legacy inspires me every day to carry myself with more understanding, acceptance, grace, and humility. You live on in all that I do, and I hope that when they see me, they also see you.

The River

House

Shawn Maravel

Chapter One

Jocelyn Larsen hadn't seen the river house in over a decade. The exterior paint, once a cool slate blue, was now sun-bleached and covered in mildew. The trim, front deck, and stairs leading up to the house were no longer crisp white, but a shabby ivory. Crab grass and dandelions grew unapologetically in the long winding gravel driveway where two rental cars were parked. The gardens that flanked the house, or rather, where Jocelyn remembered them to be, were overgrown and lost among the weeds. She could just make out what remained of the pickleweed she and her grandmother had planted what felt like a lifetime ago.

Closing her eyes, she took a deep breath, inhaling the familiar scent of a faded childhood. She could hear the gentle lapping of the Rappahannock River on the beach at the edge of the property, and it delivered more peace than she had anticipated.

In the last fourteen years, plenty had changed about Jocelyn as well, though the years had been much kinder, generous even. Her golden hair cascaded in loose waves down her back, reaching the top of her jeans. Her once girlish face hardened with feminine maturity. Her prominent cheekbones were softened by a supple complexion. Her lips were full, and her steel gray eyes reflected a hint of green, borrowing the hues of her pale green tank top. She was a far cry from the little girl who had once retreated to her grandparents' bungalow every summer, and the home was just as unrecognizable.

This house, she thought somberly, hadn't been loved like it should have. She was ashamed to admit that it had been years since she'd really even thought about the place for longer than a moment. Life had picked her up and carried her away. She had lost herself so easily in far more complicated distractions. Budding career goals, the demands of a fast-paced life in Austin, and trying to force relationships to work that should never have started in the first place.

On the outside, Jocelyn could pass for a woman who had figured it all out. A natural beauty, a graduate of the University of Houston with an MBA, a homeowner at thirty-four, and up for promotion at the recruiting firm Bradford and Bend. But on the inside, she felt more lost than even the old river house appeared.

The last time Jocelyn had stepped foot on the property, she had freshly turned twenty, her head full of plans, her focus on grander things. Her family had only visited the house in Farnham a handful of times since their move to Texas fourteen years earlier, and those years had been very different from her childhood. She had been teetering somewhere between a girl and a woman. Growing up, she considered, more quickly than she should have. She had spent more time on her phone wishing she were back in Texas with her friends than she did enjoying a tranquility that had once cradled her heart and mind so effortlessly.

Without realizing what she had done, Jocelyn had managed to misplace her affection for the house entirely, and she now felt the reality of her betrayal crushing in around her. How had life taken such a turn, she wondered as she watched her parents ascend the steps leading up to the house.

Grace, Jocelyn's mother, was strong and athletic in build. It was a sobering sight to see a woman she had always considered to be a pillar of strength in her life appear so delicate, clinging to her husband Calvin's hand as he led her up the steps. Her hair, a natural mix of gold and silver, fell loose just past her shoulders. She was exquisite, even at the age of sixty-four, embracing her gray hair, her fresh face masked in grief. Her beauty was timeless and natural, not fighting the hands of time, rather owning them.

Calvin, only a few years older than his bride, was handsome and distinguished with a medium beard and a faded military haircut that was nearly all gray now. He carried himself as a soldier would, though he had only served a few years active duty before working as a civilian contractor. He was steady, though Jocelyn knew him to have a tender side, especially when it came to her mother.

As her parents entered the house, Jocelyn let her thoughts wander for a while longer outside, not quite ready to be flooded with the memories that undoubtedly awaited her inside.

When her grandfather had died and her grandmother was moved into an independent living facility in Texas, nothing remained to draw her thoughts back to Virginia. With the loss of affection and magnetism to the place that had once been a symbol of peace and clarity in her life, she realized she had lost so much more as a result. Now, nearly a month after her grandmother's passing, faced suddenly with mortality, her grasp on her own life felt unexpectedly upended.

Jocelyn pulled herself back to reality and shifted her attention to her brother, Andrew, who was working to unload the remaining belongings from the rental cars.

"Need a hand with those?" she called over.

Andrew poked his head out from the open trunk and replied, "Nah, I've got it. Thanks though."

Age had been equally fair to her brother. His hair had darkened to a mousy blonde and his eyes were a gray blue. His hair, usually cropped short, was grown out and styled with a messy kind of indifference to match the beard he had been growing over the past month. As a warrant officer in the U.S.

Army, it was a luxury he was able to enjoy only during leave time. His build was strong and lean, and his boyish smile softened the hard lines of his face. He was handsome in an effortless kind of way. Only two years older than Jocelyn, it was no wonder the two were often mistaken for twins.

Andrew's wife, Claire, worked expertly to corral their three small children as they took turns making a beeline for the beach. Wyatt, the oldest at seven, was a spitting image of his mother. Though his hair was light like his father's, contrasting with Claire's dark shoulder-length waves, they shared the same warm brown eyes, olive skin, and full lips. His inherited dimples often got him out of trouble, though his father's unbridled spirit often landed him right back into it. He was a quiet boy with an old soul, but having fun trumped all other priorities. Though he did his best to help his mother look after the twins, his desire to test his own boundaries was threatening to win out. The girls, Vivian and Elizabeth, were difficult to tell apart. At four-years-old, they didn't quite understand the magnitude of the weapon they wielded. They had their mother's thick dark hair and their daddy's steel blue eyes. It wasn't hard to imagine they would be a handful once they were old enough to start showing an interest in boys. According to Claire, this stage had already begun, and Andrew was in fierce denial.

"I'll meet you guys inside," Claire called back, Elizabeth…or Vivian, Jocelyn couldn't tell which, was dragging her sister-in-law towards the beach. "I might as well let them get it out of their system," she called over, defeated.

"You've got this, Babe!" Andrew replied, fumbling with the bags he insisted on carrying alone.

"I'll come join you in a bit!" Jocelyn offered.

Taking a deep breath and exhaling slowly, Jocelyn turned her attention back to the house. With a heavy heart, she collected her suitcase and went inside.

The interior of the house, though worse for wear, was exactly how Jocelyn remembered it. Off to either side of the hallway were bedrooms. She knew the one on her left to be the master with an ensuite and a walk-in closet. The other was the same size but had a smaller closet and a shared bathroom that could also be accessed at the end of the hall. To the left, behind pocket doors, were the washer and dryer, and past that were the steps that led upstairs to two more bedrooms. Upstairs, each room had its own private bathroom and a small walk-out deck off the back bedroom.

Walking past the dining room, Jocelyn found her parents looking out the window of the living room that stood adjacent to the kitchen. The view that looked over the Rappahannock River was timeless and unchanged. Though the years had passed mercilessly for the raised bungalow and the waters that flowed beyond the edge of the property were new every day, the view was exactly the same.

Calvin tucked Grace against his side, rubbing her arm affectionately. Their love had traversed a lifetime together. A love story written for those who still believed it possible to belong to a single person and they to you. He held her as she shuttered under an onset of emotions that she had taken great care to control on the drive down.

Watching them with affection, Jocelyn knew her parents had been designed to get one another through any storm that life threw at them. High school sweethearts who had defied all odds, they had set an unreasonably high expectation for what love should look like. As she looked on, she couldn't help but wonder how she would ever get through life if she never managed to find such a love.

Pulling her eyes away at another onset of unbridled turmoil, she scanned the room. Sheets were draped over the furniture, protecting the antique pieces from the dust and dirt that settled on the surface. She knew the furniture beneath the sheets to be eclectic, a collection of yard sale and thrift shop finds; nothing of sentimental or monetary value. Collectables and framed photographs littered the walls, marking some of the countless adventures hosted there. Pictures from her own childhood as well as her mother's, starting with the very first photo that had ever been taken on the property. Her grandparents stood proudly out front, holding up a set of keys in one hand and each placing the other on her grandmother's growing belly, beaming with pride over the purchase as well as the pregnancy. The home wasn't just a time capsule of her own youth, she reminded herself, but of her mother's as well.

Jocelyn turned her attention back to her parents. Her father's knowing embrace and ability to deliver comfort without words had helped to sooth her mother. They stood together, gazing out the window with an air of peace about them as the memories and comforts of home flooded them both. Jocelyn moved over to join them and took her mother's hand in her own.

"I'm so sorry, Mom," she began, resting her head on her mother's shoulder. "I should have made more of an effort to help you look after the place."

The guilt of her regret was crushing.

"There's no need to apologize," Grace assured her. "We moved you halfway across the country. Sometimes moving forward means you have to leave the past where it is."

Jocelyn planted a soft kiss on her mother's cheek. "Well, I'm here now," she assured her.

While the list of chores was long, Grace decided what she needed more than a clean house was time to reflect on the life that had blossomed there. It had taken the better part of the morning to retrieve and sort through all the boxes from the attic. The contents of which were now fanned out on a quilt that

Claire had spread out on the patio beside the murky pool. From there they could keep a watchful eye over the children as they splashed excitedly at the water's edge on the beach a few yards away.

Calvin and Grace skimmed the file folders, retrieving paperwork for the house they would need as well as a few large boxes of family keepsakes Grace's mother had saved. Claire helped Jocelyn and Andrew thumb through albums and boxes of loose photos, and they were all transported back to moments in time they had all but forgotten about.

"Wow," Andrew exclaimed. "Was this you, Mom?"

Andrew held up the photo of a girl who looked to be no older than sixteen. Despite being drenched from the rain that fell down around her, she was stunning, with two long braids, tanned skin and a retro two-piece bathing suit.

"Sure was," Grace confirmed.

Andrew passed the photo to Claire.

"Beautiful," she stated before passing it on to Calvin.

"This was the first time I had joined your mom at the house for the summer," Calvin reminisced. "We had taken the canoe out to explore some nearby runs and we were caught in a summer storm. She drove me wild in that suit," he added, turning to deliver a sweet kiss to Grace's waiting lips. "Gram and Grandpa almost made me sleep outside. They were afraid your mom and I would—"

"Woah," Andrew interrupted. "I'm pretty sure we all know what they were afraid of." He shivered to illustrate his disgust.

Claire nudged his arm good-naturedly, unable to hold back her laughter.

Jocelyn shook her head with a smile. She knew that despite his theatrics, Andrew was just as happy as she was that their parents had defied the odds of terminal young love. For years she had looked to their story as a guide, trying desperately to make her first boyfriend fit into a mold he had been destined to break free of. She had dated one wrong guy after another to chase down a love like theirs and had only recently abandoned the fantasy altogether. Her last long-term boyfriend, Michael Turner, was a good man but far from the right one. Or maybe she was just being too hard on him. She struggled to know the difference anymore and was determined to give her heart a break from men until she figured it out.

"Oh, this one's a winner," Andrew exclaimed, tossing a polaroid over to Jocelyn.

In the picture, no older than seven or eight, Jocelyn's face was streaked with tears. Her expression was contorted with a mix of anger and fear, her fists clenched hard at her sides. Beside her stood a boy, his body soft and sunburned, his wide toothy laugh exposing gapped teeth. In his hand he held a dead crab over Jocelyn's head.

"Ugh, Jack Evans," she groaned. "What a dick."

"He was fun," Andrew retorted.

"Yeah, maybe to you he was," she flung the picture back at her brother. "I can't remember a single happy memory with him in it."

Jocelyn reached into the box beside Andrew and retrieved another photo. Five children; Andrew, Jocelyn, Jack and his brother and sister Will and Sarah remained suspended in time as they jumped together from the dock into the river.

"I do miss Sarah, though," she admitted. They were the same age and, as the only girls of the group, had been thick as thieves.

The five of them had spent nearly every visit together all the way up until she was about ten, Jocelyn recalled. Unfortunately, after they moved to Texas their families had lost touch. As much as Jack made a career out of torturing her, she was willing to admit that their time at the river house just wasn't the same without the Evans family. If I recalled correctly, their father Peter worked at the local water and wastewater plant while their mother Margaret homeschooled the three siblings. It was a life Jocelyn had envied growing up, especially when it came time to go back home. She often wondered what it would be like to wake up every morning to look out over the calm water and feel the cool breeze on her face. Life, it seemed, was slower by the river than it was in Alexandria, only a short drive from the bustling city.

"I'll be damned," Calvin exclaimed, unearthing a plaque from a memory box.

Glued to the wooden board was a green toy shovel. At the base the words, "The Girl with the Green Shovel" were engraved.

"I can't believe they saved this," he said with astonishment.

Reaching out, entranced, Jocelyn took the plaque in her hands. She remembered the day she had retrieved the seemingly insignificant beach toy as if it were only yesterday.

Jocelyn fought back tears and anger that formed a hard lump in her throat. For a six-year-old, she had built up quite a resilience to bullying, but Jack knew exactly how to get under her skin like a splinter.

When she and Sarah had asked to borrow his red shovel to build a sandcastle, he had agreed, only to, in one swift motion, shovel a pile of sand into her bathing suit.

"Fine! I'm going to find a green one!" she had declared, before storming off.

"I don't know why he's so mean to you," Sarah, said sweetly. "He's usually really nice."

Rinsing out her suit in the shallow water, sniffling back the tears that fought to break free, Jocelyn highly doubted the possibility. "Well, he's not very nice to me," she insisted.

Jocelyn looked over her shoulder and smiled as Andrew wrestled Jack to the ground. He was only eight himself, a year younger than Jack, but he was eager to use defending his sister's honor as an excuse to wrestle. Soon Will—who was a scrawny seven-years-old—joined in. Before long, the boys were all having more fun than they were asserting chivalry. Either way, she hoped that Jack's swim trunks would be full of sand by the end of the encounter.

Determined to best him, she stormed down the stretch of public beach, her eyes peeled for a miraculous green shovel. Nothing, she decided, was worse than making a fool of herself in front of Jack.

Above most everything, Jocelyn was strong-willed. She had never wanted anything more in her life than she wanted a green shovel in that moment. She searched near the garbage can, venturing even to peer inside, shifting a few discarded paper plates and empty soda bottles aside to see what might be hidden beneath them. Sarah joined her in the search, and they combed through the grounds of the picnic area, finding little more than scraps of food and litter of every variety. She had even stared a little too long at a boy's yellow shovel further down the beach. Even if she could convince herself that stealing was okay—just this once—Jocelyn knew that Jack would be rewarded in reminding her that the shovel wasn't green, so it didn't count.

"He built me a boat for my Barbies in Boy Scouts," Sarah said as they made another pass down the beach. She had been telling Jocelyn for easily ten minutes about all the great things Jack did on a regular basis. Uncaring about Jack's laundry list of good deeds that she doubted were entirely true, but unwilling to hurt her friend's feelings, Jocelyn mostly listened.

Sarah, despite her loyalties as a friend, looked up to her big brothers. Especially Jack. When she wasn't comforting Jocelyn after the mean things he did, she was trying to convince her that he wasn't all that bad.

"He even played rescue mission with me with my Barbies and his G.I. Joes," she added cheerfully.

"Your Jack and my Jack are not the same," Jocelyn insisted. "My Jack is a bully."

Sarah opened her mouth to dispute the claim but thought better of it. As much as she wished that Jack would treat her friend the way he treated her, he insisted on doing otherwise, and even she didn't understand the reason for it.

They continued along the waterline. Pieces of litter poked up along the beach, ugly reminders of the patrons who had been there before them. Various shards of plastic in all shapes and sizes were washed up among the seaweed, unrecognizable from the containers they had once belonged to. Straws, bottle caps, and broken flip flops were among the discarded debris strewn over the shoreline.

"People are gross," Jocelyn proclaimed.

"My mom always brings a garbage bag when we go to the beach," Sarah said. "We aren't allowed to leave until we fill it up."

Jocelyn still wanted that green shovel more than it made sense to, but searching in vain, putting all her effort into finding something that may not even exist, felt silly. She could end up wasting the rest of her day at the beach looking for something she would never find.

"Do you want to pick up litter instead?" Jocelyn asked.

"Sure, let's go ask my mom for a bag."

They began to make their way over to where Margaret sat beneath an umbrella, reading in her chair.

"I don't want to build a castle anymore anyway," Jocelyn lied.

They were picking up garbage among the long grass that covered the dunes when a small fleck of green caught Jocelyn's eye. Buried in the sand of the dune, shielded largely by the tall grass, Jocelyn unearthed the protruding handle of a green plastic shovel. The young girls' eyes met, both equally excited *at the discovery. Without words, they darted off towards the boys in the same instant, eager to show off her treasure.*

The boys had moved on to tossing a football around. Jack's red shovel lie discarded a few feet away. Jocelyn sashayed victoriously over to Jack, her face beaming with pride.

"I found it," she announced, holding up her prized green shovel.

Jack's face flashed with disbelief. With a shrug, he collected himself and turned to lob the football back to Andrew.

The feeling of defeat threatened to steal her joy, but she curbed it. Jack didn't ignore her often, she reminded herself, but when he did, she knew it was because she had won.

At the time, Jocelyn recalled, it hadn't seemed like a big deal. But the green shovel had only been the beginning. After that, her luck was unstoppable. The next weekend, while the other kids searched the yard for four leaf clovers, she had found one with five leaves. A few weeks later, she had discovered an abandoned ten-dollar bill in a parking lot. By the end of that summer, Jocelyn had earned the nickname, The Girl with the Green Shovel. Her grandfather had taken it upon himself to mount the shovel and hang it up in her room as a symbol of her good fortune.

Jocelyn studied the plaque for a moment longer, as if it held the key to unlocking all her deepest unanswered questions. Where had that little girl gone, she wondered. The little girl who settled for no less than what she wanted. She pursued one dream after another, she reminded herself. Her degree. A few semesters abroad exploring beautiful European cities. A once in a lifetime internship that had landed her an amazing job upon graduation, and a career she worked hard to excel at. But she couldn't claim that it had afforded her true happiness. Perhaps, she contemplated offhandedly, like with the green shovel so many years ago, she wouldn't find what she was searching for until she stopped looking for it.

The sun began its descent below the horizon, washing the sky in a brilliant pink and purple glow. The warm air was cooled by the breeze that came in from the river. Sitting on the back porch, mesmerized by God's beautiful watercolors, the family sat in silent appreciation. Even the children were settling down, gazing over the river, watching the birds make their final passes over the water's surface. Below them, the dark green water from the rectangular pool looked black and murky, but not even that could take away from the beauty that washed over the scene.

In the dim light of dusk, Jocelyn thought little else mattered outside of the relaxed weight upon her shoulders. A tension she couldn't remember acquiring but was unable to recall a recent memory untainted by. She sank lower in her rocking chair, curled up in a light blanket to keep the bugs away and closed her eyes, letting out a long sigh of relief.

"We need to sell," Grace said abruptly, breaking the silence.

Jocelyn's eyes shot open, her heart wounded at the thought of it. While her mother's proclamation shouldn't have surprised her, she knew instantly that she wasn't ready to let go of a place she had only just rediscovered.

"I hate that it took us this long," Grace went on. "I thought it would be harder to sell when Mom was alive, but now I see that was a terrible mistake." She closed her eyes, releasing a reserve of built-up tears. "I didn't want to let it go," she continued. "But what good has that done? I'm only preventing another family from having a chance to build new memories here."

Jocelyn felt panic overtake her. While she knew that her mother was right, she couldn't help but feel her heart continue to sink at the realization that her time in the house was coming rapidly to an end. She knew with absolute certainty that she needed to stay longer, if only to say goodbye.

"There are a lot of memories here," Calvin offered.

"But Texas is our home," Grace said firmly. "There's no reason to keep this house simply to possess it."

"I agree," Calvin said somberly.

"The place needs a lot of work," Andrew ventured.

"I agree. It will be quite the undertaking to get the house ready to sell, but I've been considering this for a long time," Grace admitted. "With the money Mom left me, we can breathe life back into this place. My parents paid the house off decades ago. Whatever we put into the renovation, I will see back and then some. This isn't about the money," she professed. "It's about knowing when it's time to let go."

"I wish I could help out," Andrew said with regret. "My month of leave is almost up."

"You've been such a help already," Grace assured him. "It's been such a blessing seeing all of you. We don't see you nearly enough since your move to Savannah."

As if in agreement, Elizabeth and Vivian both climbed into Grace's lap, curling up like two little kittens under each arm. Wyatt, momentarily thwarted by the absence of room to join in, recovered quickly and crawled into Jocelyn's lap instead, wrapping himself in her blanket. Jocelyn stroked his hair and rocked gently back and forth.

"I'll do it," she offered boldly. Though she was still trying to work out the logistics in her mind, she was determined to do whatever she had to in order to secure whatever time she could at the river house before it was lost to her family forever.

"You'll do what?" Grace inquired.

"I'll get the house ready for resale," she clarified. "I can request to work remotely for a few months. Of course, I'll have to check with Bridget, but I imagine she'll be willing to work with me."

"Are you sure?" Grace asked. "That's a lot for one person to take on, especially with everything you have going on at work right now. I don't want to hurt your chances of receiving that promotion. You've worked so hard for it."

The plan was still in its infancy, but the more she thought about it, the more excited Jocelyn became. While she had no doubt that the undertaking would certainly be overwhelming at times, she felt confident that it was exactly what she was meant to do. In that moment, she knew, Virginia was where she was meant to be.

"I'm positive," she asserted.

Grace squeezed Calvin's hand, anchoring her emotions, her face glowing with pride and gratitude she couldn't find the words to express.

Jocelyn raised her glass of iced tea and proposed, "Let's enjoy one last week together here. Then I'll get to work on fixing the place up."

Grace smiled sweetly. She nuzzled the now sleeping grandbabies in her arms and felt a sense of calm wash over her. "Thank you, Jocelyn." A stray tear trickled down her cheek. "You have no idea how much this means to me."

It was quite the undertaking. Of that Jocelyn was certain. But part of the drive to make the offer had so much more to do with her own restoration. She needed to repair herself as much as the old river house needed to be. She wouldn't be afforded another opportunity like this again. She could only hope that what she was seeking would be found on the other side of the renovation.

Chapter Two

Jocelyn sat cross-legged on her bed, tying her hair up into a messy bun. Her phone lay discarded on the nightstand atop a to-do list and her planner. Her room was in disarray, illustrating how much harder it was than she had originally assumed it would be to determine what she would need for an extended absence and what would have to stay behind.

The condo wasn't very big. Rather than opting for large and run-down and outdated, or glamorous and wildly out of her price range, Jocelyn had chosen a small new construction one bedroom home that met all her needs and was aesthetically pleasing. She knew the materials were cheap and cookie-cutter, but it was quaint, and clean, and overlooked the park. It wasn't her ideal location of course. She had hopes of moving out of the city someday, but for now the condo suited her needs just fine.

As many plans as she had for continuing to build a life there, the idea of escaping Texas was electrifying, even if only for a short stint. Jocelyn had put her education and career goals ahead of her personal life for so long, to lead with anything else felt carefree and reckless. While her determination had resulted in a great many professional achievements, in recent years she found herself fighting back the feeling that something was missing. She needed to step away, re-center herself, and return to her life with more certainty than she felt leaving it. Though the timing wasn't ideal, she couldn't help but think that this was exactly what she had needed to gain some perspective.

Upon her return to Austin, Bridget had granted Jocelyn's request to work remotely from Virginia. Afterall, while Bridget was sympathetic to the situation, she hadn't grown Bradford and Bend's clientele by 400% in ten years by being soft. She had a firm to run and clients counting on the best results. They were the top recruiting firm in Texas and well on their way to claiming the title of best in the country.

If Jocelyn was to remain competitive for the promotion, she would need to prove her worth by delivering a proposal that not only met, but exceeded Bridget's expectations. In three months, the board would meet to evaluate each of the teams' proposals. It was all the time Bridget could grant her to finish the repairs on the river house, and Jocelyn was determined to make it work.

With only two weeks of vacation time to settle in and get the renovations underway, she would be expected to work her normal hours the remainder of her time in Virginia. In addition, she would be required to return to Austin once before her time in Farnham was over. Her team would be presenting a mock proposal to Bridget before their final presentation before the board.

As conflicted as she was, this promotion had been years in the making and now she was close enough to touch it. It was hardly the time to let her growing uncertainty about the direction of her life upended everything she had worked for.

Jocelyn had spent the last week getting her affairs in order. She had her mail forwarded and provided her neighbor with a key to make weekly visits to the condo to ensure that nothing caught fire or flooded in addition to watering the handful of less-than-thriving house plants she kept throughout the condo. She'd also tied up all the loose ends at the office. All that was left was to pack.

As excited as she was to leave, Jocelyn felt herself growing anxious at the idea that she could be leaving herself vulnerable to being overlooked for the promotion. If harvesting the fruits of her labor wasn't incentive enough to strive for the job and remain on task, her competition for the position was sure to provide the remaining motivation she needed. Michael Turner, of course, was her strongest competitor. While Jocelyn could live with working alongside her ex, she was absolutely certain, if he were to receive the promotion over her, that her tolerance for his close proximity would surely expire.

As if on cue, Michael's name flashed across her phone screen with a brief yet frantic message.

Virginia?! You can't be serious!

Jocelyn cringed at the text. Despite an amicable break-up and managing to remain professional coworkers, she and Michael hadn't spoken for weeks outside of cordial office run-ins. However, she couldn't say she was surprised that he had an opinion about her sudden and unexpected leave of absence. He didn't make an effort to hide how he still felt about her. Whether it was intentional or a lack of skills in discretion, she couldn't say.

Rather than sending a reply, Jocelyn climbed out of bed, grabbed her phone, and abandoned it face down on the leather bench at the end of her bed. She glanced around her bedroom, knowing she wouldn't see the space again for several months. The late evening sun was setting, casting golden light through the two large windows facing the bed. In the corner of the room sat a gray armchair and a small table with a book she'd started reading months ago. If pressed, she couldn't even remember what it was about. How had her life become so busy, her work so all consuming, that even the prospect of reading for leisure required planning? Reading required relaxation, she reminded herself, and that was something she hadn't enjoyed in a long time.

She doubted she would be able to relax tonight. She had a busy day of travel ahead of her in the morning and she had yet to pack. Whenever she had tried, she'd just ended up with disorderly piles on every available surface in the bedroom and an empty suitcase in the middle of the room.

With her procrastination all but spent, Jocelyn began the task of fitting everything she would need inside a single suitcase. Seated on the floor between a pile of freshly folded clothes and her luggage, she began organizing her belongings into what she would bring and what would stay. She packed and unpacked her favorite mauve sundress several times, certain she would have no occasion to wear it, but unwilling to take the risk of leaving it behind. Decidedly, she left the dress in and tossed a pair of strappy rose gold sandals in beside it. Both, she doubted, she would have reason enough to wear on a construction site, but it was a gamble she was willing to make. In addition to packing her wardrobe staples, she included a few of her favorite bathing suits and excluded her raincoat. Rain, she decided, would call for lazy days spent inside and little else.

As she made a final assessment of her inventory, Jocelyn's phone chimed several more times in rapid succession and she groaned knowingly.

Maybe amicable was the wrong term to describe how she and Michael had ended things. More accurately, it could be said that he had agreed to give her space. He made little effort to hide that he was eager for her to realize she'd made a huge mistake. She imagined her leaving for Virginia would only confirm his worst fears. That she was really and completely over him. Which, she was almost certain was the case.

Comfortable didn't mean compatible, she reminded herself. At least for Jocelyn it didn't. Michael didn't challenge her. Being with him was easy. At first it had felt like a dream. But the dream grew stale and boring, and in time she had found that the ease in which they existed together was stifling. In their nearly two years together, they had never fought, though it wasn't for a lack of effort on Jocelyn's part. While she would normally never have imagined trying to pick fights in a relationship, she often found herself doing so with Michael.

His docile nature seemed to awaken a restlessness inside of her she hadn't realized she'd been harboring. In a relationship that unfolded robotically, she was desperately looking for a pulse. She was looking for passion. Something boiling beneath the surface that would keep her warm at night. A forever kind of love had to be about more than just friendship with benefits. She wanted the kind of love that could develop her.

Jocelyn closed her suitcase and rose from the floor. Before retrieving her phone, she walked over to the armchair and grabbed her book and tossed it on top of her luggage.

Taking a deep breath and falling back onto her bed, she unlocked her phone and read the messages Michael had sent.

Jocelyn, I respect your decision to go...but selfishly I want you to stay.

We can be happy together. I promise you that.

I miss you, Jocelyn.

I'm afraid that your leaving means you don't feel the same way.

Jocelyn wasn't unfeeling. Of course, Michael's words meant something to her. But the reality was, she needed to walk across the coals a bit. She needed to test herself. Test her endurance and find herself stronger on the other side of something she didn't have a plan for. Her whole life in Texas had unfolded in such a way that she questioned regularly if any of it had in fact been her doing at all. Had she simply been carried away by a current stuck in a daze, unsure of where she was anymore? She enjoyed her job well enough, her co-workers and her salary, but she wasn't thriving. Perhaps she'd had it too easy to recognize that she really did have it all. All Jocelyn knew was that she needed a change of scenery and distance from a life that threatened to suffocate her.

She couldn't bring herself to write the words, "I don't love you." As far as she was concerned, she had already made that point very clear when she had broken things off. If Michael couldn't accept that, then it wasn't her job to spell it out for him. She didn't owe him answers, nor did she think her reasons would soothe him, but she respected him too much to ignore him entirely.

My heart needs to grow fonder for Texas.

Distance will do me some good.

The three little dots to indicate Michael's typing appeared before Jocelyn could put her phone down. Despite herself, she waited for his reply.

And if it doesn't grow fonder?

She questioned whether it was worth responding. She knew as well as he did that after the brief absence she would be back in her condo and back at the firm as if she had never left. When she said she needed space, she meant it emotionally, not physically, and certainly not permanently. Didn't she?

***

As Jocelyn moved throughout the river house the following evening, making notations on her pad of paper, the list of repairs and upgrades grew. Initially, she had jotted down the few suggestions her family had offered. New floors throughout the house, new appliances, upgraded bathrooms and kitchen, and getting the pool back up and running were among the requests that her mother had made. Her father, ever a practical man, reminded her that the roof, HVAC, and water heater would need replacing as well. Andrew had suggested a simple landscape design, focusing mostly on removing what was overgrown and cleaning up what remained. For resale purposes, there was no need to go out and invest in new plants. Repaint and power wash *everything*, Claire had insisted. Nothing freshened up a place quite like a new coat of paint. It went without saying that the four different patterns of wallpaper throughout the house had to go as well.

While she didn't aim to create an insurmountable list, Jocelyn knew that details mattered when it came to the inspection as well as attracting the right buyer. Whenever she put the notepad down, it seemed another need presented itself.

When she stopped to make lunch for herself, she was greeted by a small gray mouse that scurried behind the pots and pans in the cupboard. She couldn't contain her scream and fled clear across the kitchen, leaping onto the opposite countertop. She reached cautiously for the pad of paper beside her and jotted down, "mouse traps." While sweeping up the porch as an excuse to get some fresh air, a sizable splinter lodged itself into the heel of her foot. Hobbling back over to the pad of paper, she added, "refinish porch." When she went to wash the dishes and was reminded that *she* was the dishwasher, she included, "dishwasher" to the growing inventory.

Once she was content with a modified and prioritized list, Jocelyn got to work researching and contacting local handymen for the various jobs ahead. Given the rural area, her options were limited, but she imagined, if the price was right and the reviews were positive, it wouldn't matter much who did the more technical work. Replacing appliances and equipment, while important, required skill, but not necessarily creative vision. The general contractor, she considered, was a whole different story.

Though there were only a handful to choose from, River View Construction stood out. The company had over fifty reviews, none of which were less than four stars. The photos of the work were immaculate and exactly the modern, clean-lined, airy beach style she was looking to incorporate in the renovation. Clearly the lead contractor had a keen eye for what worked well together and how to marry simplicity with character.

Jocelyn felt hopeful that the project would be a manageable undertaking with the right help. She could divide her attention between accomplishing the job and finding the time to uncloud her mind from the rat race she'd been running as long as she could remember. Though her work wouldn't stop officially, she could already feel the haze lifting as life on the river came into view. Even if only for a short time, she would enjoy the reprieve from city living and her stuffy office space.

After an alarmingly cold shower, moving the water heater up a few ticks on the priority list, Jocelyn headed outside to the porch with a blanket and her book to enjoy the quiet evening. Boats docked at neighboring harbors were silhouetted against a sky set on fire by the setting sun. Rocking the chair back and forth gently with her foot, she gazed at a view she imagined she would never grow tired of. Reflexively, she slapped at a mosquito on her leg and studied her surroundings. Turning to the notepad that had become something of an honorary appendage since settling into the river house, she jotted down, "screen in the back porch."

After taking in a few long breaths, she wrapped herself in a blanket and reached for her book, flipping to the first page. Waves lapped at the shore in the distance, their gentle serenade bringing her unwavering peace. Despite the work that lie ahead and the huge adjustments she would have to make in the coming weeks, the warm breeze and the familiar smells of the river told Jocelyn that she was exactly where she needed to be.

Chapter Three

Jocelyn had been weeding the garden out front for well over an hour and it still looked as overgrown and neglected as when she had started. With a garbage can full of unwanted plant life, her skin glistened with a generous sheen of sweat and her muscles ached from the tedious work. As she labored, she was reminded of how little effort was required of her to maintain the small patch of yard in front of her condo back in Texas and that the pool was never green. Though, the color and overall suspicious water quality might not be enough to keep her from jumping in later.

Her hair, woven into what was once a pair of neat French braids, was now frizzy and sweat-soaked at the roots. Wearing jean shorts and a cropped tank top, she still felt overdressed laboring away under the merciless morning sun. How, she wondered, could it be so hot at nine o'clock?

Unconcerned with her own appearance, it was the state of the house that Jocelyn was most worried about. Nearly a week had passed since her arrival and, apart from some mouse traps, a thorough deep cleaning and yard work, the list of repairs and renovations remained unaddressed. Scheduling the work hadn't gone as smoothly as she had hoped. Everyone she had called was booked out for a few days. It felt as if the sands of time were already working against her rigid schedule.

Just then, a large black pick-up truck with the logo "River View Construction" on the side rumbled down the gravel driveway and parked a few feet from where Jocelyn was working. From the passenger side window, a menacingly large

Rottweiler let out a powerful bark of greeting and despite herself, Jocelyn jumped. Clutching a freshly plucked bouquet of weeds to her chest, she discreetly worked to collect herself.

"Don't worry, she's harmless," Jocelyn heard a deep voice call over from the far side of the truck.

She tossed the weeds into the waste bin, brushed her hands off on her shorts, and rose to greet her contractor. When he rounded the truck and came into view, she became painfully aware of her disheveled state and quickly worked to tame a few flyaways with her dirt-stained fingers.

His black T-shirt and dark-washed jeans clung tightly to his muscular frame. His build was that of a man who was strong because he was hardworking, not simply because he worked out. Muscles, Jocelyn imagined, that had been built on days not unlike this one. He was handsome, though the word fell short as she took in his tanned skin and rugged good looks. His thick brown hair was cropped short, his chiseled jawline covered in a light beard, but it was his soft blue eyes and boyish smirk that left her defenseless.

She was sweaty and disheveled and had been graced by age, but Jack recognized her right away. Of course, this was Jocelyn Larsen. He knew her face as well as he knew the stilted home that had fallen to disrepair at her back. Though they had both changed a great deal since he had seen them last, their beauty was timeless respectively. Her expression, briefly awash with bewilderment, gave no indication that she recognized him in return.

When he had received the message from his secretary, Jack had his suspicions that the name and location for the job were no coincidence. He had known the property to be just shy of abandoned in recent years and had all but forgotten about it until he'd been contacted for the estimate. Now, it took every muscle in his body to fight the feelings that returned at the sight of the girl he had once resolved to never see again.

The memories of Jocelyn's sweet face and the intrigue that drew him towards her as a boy came rushing back as if they'd never truly left. It took everything in his power to compose himself with a carefree and discrete expression.

"You must be the contractor," Jocelyn declared, extending her hand in greeting. "Sorry," she said gesturing towards the layer of dirt beneath her fingernails. "There's so much to be done around here. I figured I'd get a head start."

Taking her hand in his firmly, Jack smiled easily. "Every little bit helps," he agreed. "Jack," he said, anxiously awaiting her recognition.

"Jocelyn," she offered, still seemingly unaware that they were far from strangers.

He wasn't one to play games with a woman. Surely not when she was a client. But Jack suspected this was the fresh start that he and Jocelyn were due after the less than harmonious childhood they'd spent together. He didn't expect anything to ignite between them, nor was he in a place to initiate such a flame, but he could tell that fighting back the nostalgic pull of young love wouldn't be effortless on his part.

"Mind if Lady joins us?" He gestured towards the truck where his faithful companion patiently awaited an invitation.

"No, not at all."

"Are you sure?" he asked.

Jocelyn felt heat enter her face again imagining the look of terror she must have expressed only moments before. "No. No. I'm fine, really. I love dogs," she assured him.

"I know she's not quite a Labradoodle," Jack joked, reaching for the handle to let Lady out of the truck, "but with her temperament, she might as well be."

Jocelyn knelt down as Lady approached and extended her hand for her to inspect. Lady, a lover of attention, closed her eyes in contentment as Jocelyn scratched behind her ear, Her tongue flopped out of her mouth with a broad smile, and she wagged her tail so that her entire backside shook.

Pleasantly surprised by the dog's gentle nature, Jocelyn mused, "Quite the diplomat you've got here. Does she always join you on the job?"

"As often as I can manage it," Jack replied. "Not all my clients can see past her breed though, unfortunately."

"She's beautiful," Jocelyn marveled. "So...majestic."

Rising to her feet, Jocelyn gestured towards the house. "Here, let me give you the tour." As she made her way up the porch steps, she began untying her braids, unable to stand the disorder of her appearance any longer. "Where did you get Lady?" she asked casually.

Her golden hair cascaded in loose waves, brushing the tanned small of her back. The muscles in her legs were lean, drawing Jack's eyes down the length of her body as he followed. When he noticed her bare feet, a smile spread across his lips. He remembered well that she had always been carefree as a child, and he was pleased to see that little had changed in that regard, though he could tell, by the way she ran her fingers through her hair, that she was insecure about her less polished appearance.

"She was raised on a farm," Jack replied. "Bred to enjoy the finer things in life when she wasn't turning out litters of puppies."

"I thought she might have had some puppies," Jocelyn replied. "I bet she was a wonderful mother."

"The best." Jack shucked off his shoes next to the welcome mat and brushed off Lady's paws. The subtle gesture wasn't lost on Jocelyn.

She pushed the door open and led Jack down the front hallway. He followed, already knowing every inch of the house by heart, picturing the infinite potential as he recalled each room.

"She was set to live out the golden years of her retirement on the farm," Jack continued. "But over the years I fell in love with her and she with me. I've done a dozen or so jobs over on the farm and every time I went, she'd always find me. Intrigued by all the noises I made and tools that I used. I considered getting one of her pups on more than one occasion, but the idea of training a puppy on a boat always felt like more trouble than it was worth. When the breeder saw how much we had bonded to one another, she offered to let me take Lady home and I didn't hesitate."

"A boat?" Jocelyn asked, crossing her arms over her chest with intrigue.

"A houseboat actually," Jack informed. He pulled out a small notepad from his back pocket and looked around the room, all business. "Took me a few years to get the renovations just right, but it's home." He jotted down a few notes as he scanned the space. "Beautiful place you've got here," he added sincerely.

Abandoning the fantasies of what Jack's houseboat might look like, Jocelyn's attention turned to the disheveled state of the room that they currently occupied. Lady sniffed at a stack of boxes that partially blocked the entryway into the dining room. Owner's manuals and overstuffed file folders littered the coffee table in the living room and the kitchen counter was cluttered with pots and pans that had been evacuated upon her discovery of the rodent problem. The space, Jocelyn considered with a cringe, was dangerously close to channeling an episode of *Hoarders*.

"Please excuse the mess," she offered apologetically. "I don't even know where to start." Restraining the urge to begin tidying up, she forced herself to move into the kitchen. "Can I get you something to drink?"

"Water would be great."

Captivated by the lines of her slender frame, Jack watched Jocelyn as she fixed them each a glass. She had developed into a woman who wore her soft curves like a dancer. Her hair was long, and her face was free of makeup. In all her natural splendor, she was the most attractive woman he'd ever seen, and by the way that she carried herself, he suspected that she underrated her own beauty. He could tell that she was a woman who led with her mind rather than her looks, though she could command a room with either, he had no doubt. Taking in a deep breath and letting it out slowly, he followed her into the kitchen.

"There's a lot of potential here," he remarked.

"It was my grandparents. I'm helping my parents get the house ready to put on the market in a few months," Jocelyn informed as she handed Jack his glass. "I'm pretty sure I bit off more than I can chew," she admitted for the first time out loud.

"Don't worry," Jack said, his smile casual and his stare piercing. "You're in good hands."

Jocelyn held his eyes for a moment, charged by the electricity that vibrated between them. She couldn't help but feel that he was looking into her soul. Flustered by his gaze, she shifted her eyes away.

"I certainly hope so," she countered.

"I've seen a lot of lost causes, don't get me wrong, but it's not in my best interest to fill your head with false promises. If the foundation's strong and the bones are good, then you're halfway there. You can make a few minor upgrades to polish it for resale, or we can design the home to your exact specifications, and I can give you plenty of reasons to want to stay rather than sell."

Jack hadn't been able to stop himself from offering such a bold statement. Nor had he taken care to leave the insinuation out of his voice when he spoke the last words. It was a remark he knew had little to do with the renovations and everything to do with the feelings that grew stronger as he remained in Jocelyn's presence.

Of all the women he had known, none had ever enticed him the way that she did now. He was a professional and he intended to maintain the proper boundaries while he was under her employment, but he would be lying to say that he didn't desire to get to know her intimately.

Jocelyn couldn't tell if it was the broken air conditioning or the subtle suggestion of his last words, but the air had quickly become thick with insinuation. She took a swig of her water to buy herself time and gather her composure.

"In the message you left with my secretary, you had mentioned four bathroom remodels and new flooring throughout the house." Jack gestured towards the walls. "What about the wallpaper and interior paint?"

Grateful for his professionalism, entirely unsure now if she had read too far into his words, Jocelyn relaxed. "Oh, I'll take care of removing the wallpaper myself," she said confidently. "I'm not sure yet how far I want to take the kitchen renovation. With the bathroom remodels, I'm left with a tighter budget. I could just paint the cabinets to freshen them up and save myself from having to buy new ones."

"I just finished a kitchen remodel. We keep anything usable from all our jobs in a storage unit back behind the office. The cabinets and countertops I removed from the job are beautiful. I'd even venture to say that I like them better than the stuff the owner had me install. Simple, clean, white cabinets with Carrara marble countertops." Jack studied the space. "With some rearranging, they'd fit perfectly in here."

"You would do that?" Jocelyn asked excitedly.

"I prefer it, if I'm being honest. I hate the idea of bringing perfectly salvageable materials to the landfill. I keep what I can in storage, and I've got a pretty good turn around going.

Everything I can keep for resale I install at a greatly reduced price. Just a small materials fee on top of labor and installation."

"Wow, I love that," Jocelyn mused. "I'll take you up on that offer."

"Recessed lighting is always a must," Jack went on.

"And some accent fixtures to add character," Jocelyn added.

Grabbing her own notepad, she began listing off the necessary repairs as well as the specifications she hoped Jack could find room for in the budget. A deep farmhouse sink, white subway tiles for the backsplash and all four showers, and gray faux wood tile floors throughout the main living space in addition to the bathrooms. Plush gray carpet upstairs as well as in the downstairs bedrooms. Jack agreed that screening in the back porch would be both a huge upgrade to the space and a small hit to the budget. The vision unfolded before them. Bright, airy, clean, but equally warm and welcoming. Nothing flashy or bold, but enough character to give the house a soul.

Jack had succeeded in taking Jocelyn's list and expanding upon it while also managing to simplify it. He had a keen eye for the finite details and a professional understanding of the repairs and upgrades Jocelyn hadn't even considered. He also provided her with the names and numbers for a good roofer as well as a guy he assured her could work wonders on the green bog that had once been a pool.

"I could take this wall out," Jack noted during their second pass through of the first floor. He wrapped his knuckles on the wall that divided the living and dining space. "Provided it's not load-bearing, of course."

"I attended Fixer Upper University," Jocelyn joked with a smile. "I know a thing or two about an open concept. What about exposed beams?" she ventured.

"I've got a ton of scrap wood back at the store unit we could use to add accent beams. I wouldn't even charge you for the materials. I'm looking to thin the pile out a bit as it is. You'd be doing me a favor."

"Don't tease me," she said excitedly.

"It's never been my style," Jack said plainly, raising a cunning brow.

There was that air again, the kind that made it hard to breath. Jocelyn fought against it, stubbornly steering herself away from the source of her breathlessness. Everything about Jack was alluring, it was a wasted effort to deny it. The way he carried himself, his expressive eyes, and his sturdy build. But his job wasn't to seduce her, it was to help her meet a deadline. A goal she was determined to focus all her energy on. She'd been distracted by far too many things in recent years. Career advancement and the wrong men came to mind. She couldn't sort out where she stood in regard to either subject until she knew not only *where* she was in life but more importantly *who* she was. If her instincts were worth anything, she suspected this remodel would allow her to discover both. And for that anyway, she had Jack to thank, but it was all she would look to him for.

Seated at the dining room table a while later, Jack and Jocelyn were wrapping up their meeting as Lady rested happily on the back porch. Jocelyn studied her list again, pleased with the plan they had set in place and eager to get started.

"Do you think you can get it all done by the deadline?" she inquired, not for the first time.

"Three months is a tight window," Jack admitted, mirroring concerns he had previously voiced.

Jocelyn's expression failed to hide her concern. With a strict schedule and her promotion already under a very real threat, she couldn't help but let her worries overshadow her need for a mental resct. It was her life, after all, she would eventually have to return to it.

"Listen," Jack said, sensing Jocelyn's mounting apprehension. "This house is officially priority number one," he offered. "In fact, if you're comfortable with the idea, I can dock my boat at your place so that I can get an early start every day and go as late as I need to every night."

Jocelyn met Jack's eyes. They were kind, understanding. Gazing into them centered her in a way she hadn't expected. There was no ulterior motive lying in wait behind his invitation. Just a generous offer made by a man who wanted to help.

"You would do that?"

"It's no problem," he insisted.

Jack had been little more than a nomad since moving out of his parents' place at eighteen. Shortly after starting his business, he had purchased his houseboat. He had made the repairs and renovations while he lived on it, accustomed to functioning without certain essential amenities and at times without a proper roof and walls. He traveled up and down the river as it suited him and docked at the various marinas depending on where his biggest jobs were. Of course, he had never docked at a client's place before. While he intended to keep the line of professionalism clear and firm, with Jocelyn, he had no desire to maintain the same boundaries he usually upheld.

He took a moment to study her. She had always been so determined. Even as a child, she would settle for no less than what she wanted. He was pleased to see that, despite her maturity and whatever challenges life might have thrown her way over the years, she still had that unwavering grit about her. When she looked up to meet his eyes, Jack couldn't help but smirk.

Intrigued by his boyish grin, Jocelyn smiled back.

"What's so funny?" she asked.

"It's nothing," he said evasively, snuffing out his playful smile.

Unconvinced, she crossed her arms, her own smile growing with amusement at his sudden discomfort. "What is it?"

He'd been careful not to jog her memory of their previous relationship in the hour they'd spent touring the house, but Jack figured it was as good a time as any to walk her back down memory lane. Afterall, he imagined that putting off the inevitable much longer would likely result in a feeling of betrayal on Jocelyn's part, and he didn't think that would foster a desirable outcome.

"You made my job easy today," he offered casually. "As far back as I can remember, you always knew exactly what you wanted." He felt both relief as well as nerves flood his senses as her eyes fluttered with realization. He went on. "I'm not sure what I expected from The Girl with the Green Shovel."

The alarms sounded so frantically in her mind that Jocelyn wondered briefly if Jack could hear them. Her posture stiffened, her eyes scanning for answers. Squinting reflexively, she studied the man before her and watched as past and present collided to create a mix of childish and primal responses that threatened to unravel her. The room spun around her, the air once again too thick to breath and her heart raced as if she'd dropped on a rollercoaster she hadn't realized she had boarded.

She fought to keep the anger and shock that rushed over her from poisoning her words. "*Jack? Jack Evans?*"

Every memory she had preserved of the boy who made up this man had been distasteful. A harsh contrast with the charming, easy-going, and humbly confident creature who sat before her. A man she had thought, more than once, was a refreshing change of pace, not to mention alarmingly attractive. But *Jack Evans*? How on earth could these two humans exist inside a singular body?

"By the look on your face, I take it your memories play against me."

Blinking hard, Jocelyn realized that his revealing comment hadn't been one of equal shock and realization, rather it had been calculated and measured. "You knew it was me *this whole time*?" She felt another wave crash over her, this time it was that of white-hot humiliation.

In hindsight, Jack realized that it might have been in his best interest if he had gotten the reunion portion of their meeting out of the way right at the start. He'd never claimed to have a knack for perfect timing. "I mean…" he evaded briefly, "…yes." Apologetic in his delivery, he was unsure of what feelings simmered just below the surface of her steel gray eyes.

"*Wow.*"

Jocelyn pushed herself away from the table and sprang out of her chair as if it had shocked her. She paced briefly in front of the window, running her hands through her hair before resting them on the tight muscles of her neck.

She played back the events that had taken place since Jack had arrived at the house. The remarks he had made that evoked her easy laughter. The moments she caught him drinking her in with his eyes when he thought she wasn't paying attention. How she didn't mind and discretely enjoyed it. The sexual tension had been palpable at times, though she felt safer with him than she had any other man she'd only just met. Now she knew why.

The feelings that raced through her mind in a matter of seconds were enough to make her sick. Embarrassment, anger, annoyance, and, though she wouldn't admit it, arousal, and he had recognized her *all along*. She couldn't decide how that made her feel. In many ways it felt as if the little boy who thrilled at tormenting her as a child had gotten one over on her yet again. But the fact of the matter was, Jack had treated her with such genuine respect, she couldn't rest her emotions in a place of indignation entirely.

Jocelyn hadn't noticed that Jack had risen from the table as well and was alarmed to see him walking towards her.

"I'm sorry," he offered sincerely, stopping in his tracks as he felt the wall snap up between them. "I should have said something earlier."

Shaking her head, Jocelyn collected herself. She recognized that it had been a chosen oversight on her part rather than a manipulation on Jack's part. She would never have intentionally connected the boy she had known growing up with the man she had just met.

"No, no. It's fine. I just…I didn't expect to see you that's all."

"I'm starting to think I owe you a much bigger apology."

"Don't be silly," Jocelyn insisted, still grasping at composure.

"I'm not convinced," he pressed.

"I'm just surprised that's all. You were always such a…" Jocelyn paused, hesitant to fill in the blank.

"A dick?" Jack offered.

Jocelyn didn't rush to correct him.

"Yeah, well, I'm not going to pretend that I could have been described otherwise as far as you were concerned."

"*Hmm.*" Jocelyn felt herself newly flushed with annoyance despite her greatest efforts to feel otherwise. "So, you're saying I hadn't just been imagining things all those years. You really did save all your *charm* for me?"

Jack rubbed his neck nervously, breaking his casual confidence with a fleeting glimpse of vulnerability. With a raised brow, he made an effort to explain. "Misguided as I was, I was convinced that was how to get a beautiful girl's attention. I'm not proud of how long it took me to learn otherwise."

She didn't even try to mask her disbelief. "Are you trying to tell me that you…" she trailed off, unable to put words to his insinuation.

"Had a crush on you?" Jack said with a shrug of confirmation.

Jocelyn studied him for what felt like the first time and the startling truth began to surface. His crisp blue eyes, thick brown hair, slender lips, and the subtle cleft of his chin were reminders of a face she still struggled to recognize. He'd grown muscular and lean where stubborn weight had once been and the boyish gap in his teeth had been corrected with braces, no doubt some time during those awkward pubescent years plagued by acne and greasy hair. He'd come out the other side of the years they'd spent apart an entirely new, nearly unrecognizable, version of himself. While she could see the similarities, Jocelyn still struggled to believe that these two people were one in the same.

"You grew up," she mused candidly.

Laughing easily, visibly relieved, Jack replied, "It happens." Shifting uncomfortably, he dug his hands deep into his pockets. "So...do you forgive me?" he presented again.

After a long beat, Jocelyn offered, "The past is in the past. Besides, I always just assumed you were under socialized."

Jack shook his head and smiled easily. "I guess I deserve that. If only homeschooling could take the blame for all my faults."

She could tell by his posture that he was used to carrying the weight of defending his upbringing and instantly regretted the comment. She backpedaled quickly in an effort to take back the remark. "That's not what I meant."

Jack shot her a friendly glare. "Of course, it's not."

Disarmed by his good humor, Jocelyn didn't enjoy being on the other end of their past relationship dynamics. The last thing she wanted was to fall into the role of being a bully out of subconscious spite. Fumbling to redirect their conversation, she blurted out, "So, how long have you worked for River View Construction?"

Jack shrugged, relieved that he had made it to the other side of their confrontation. "I started doing odd jobs for a few neighbors when I was about fourteen. By the time I was twenty-one, I had apprenticed with Robert Jeffries and was a certified electrician and plumber. To answer your question, this September marks twenty-three years of working in the field and nineteen years of owning my own company."

She couldn't conceal the surprise from her face. "This is *your* company?"

"It sure is."

Jocelyn's memories of who Jack had been as a child made it difficult at first to believe that he had started his own business. She could still feel herself fighting to acknowledge that he had grown up to be the man that stood before her. A man who produced and ran a successful company built on the ambitions and skills of the child she had once loathed beyond reason. As he spoke, however, the authenticity of his character came clearly into view.

While Jack remained vague as he answered Jocelyn's follow up questions, she felt her guard begin to lift once again, unpacking the disdain for a boy she hadn't even realized she still carried all these years later. It was a relief, she realized, to feel the weight of lingering resentment dissolve. Where anger and annoyance had once tarnished his name and the memories Jack occupied, she now felt admiration and an unexpected fondness for the man before her.

When he received a call from one of his contractors in need of assistance, Jack left after reassuring Jocelyn once more that he would get back to her soon with an estimate. In his wake, she was left to mull over the mixed emotions that continued to churn within her heart.

As she did her best to stay busy with what remained of her day and her to-do list, her thoughts continued to return to the man she hardly knew yet had known forever. She couldn't discern the array of mixed emotions he left her carrying, but she was willing to admit that she looked forward to getting to know Jack Evans all over again.

Chapter Four

From one of the rocking chairs on the back porch, Jocelyn gazed out over the river just beyond the property's edge. The water was calm and still, disturbed only by the osprey's talons breaking the surface as they retrieved breakfast for their young. The sun had crested the horizon, washing the sky in a crisp blue. Sipping her coffee and rocking gently back and forth, she could picture starting every morning like this. There was no hum from the highway or sirens and honking horns from the street. No buildings to obstruct her view. It was the kind of peace that felt unobtainable in the city. But even now, knowing how much work awaited her, Jocelyn felt as if she was the one being restored.

Her dance card for the day was full. The pool guy, the roof guy, the HVAC guy, and the water heater guy. One of their names was Thomas, but, for the life of her, she couldn't remember which. She and Jack had agreed that it would be a good day to get the porch screened in. While it wasn't their top priority in the remodel, it was a task that could be completed while the other crews worked inside. The following day the real work would begin.

As happy as she was to finally be getting the work underway, Jocelyn suspected she might have gone overboard. Then again, with just one week of vacation left, an aggressive schedule was necessary.

She let her eyes close and took a deep breath, exhaling slowly. After a long night of tossing and turning, she welcomed the solace the river provided. One day at a time, she reminded herself. Jack was there to keep the work on schedule. As much as she could manage it, her focus needed to remain on her work and gaining a renewed sense of vigor for her life back in Austin. If a promotion was in her future, she needed to have a clear head upon her return.

When she opened her eyes, Jocelyn noticed a lone watercraft rounding the corner into the inlet unlike any she had ever seen before. Intrigued, she pushed herself out of the chair and watched from the railing as it drew closer. To her amazement, she noticed that the front of the vessel was constructed mostly out of large windows and a glass door, pieced together by white wood framing. Light from the other side shone clear through, revealing that the back wall was also built entirely of framed windows. The bow of the boat had a large deck with narrow walkways that lead to a smaller deck in back. Attached to the main enclosure, was an addition covered in oak paneling. A set of stairs lead to an upper deck that provided access to a small captain's cabin.

Jocelyn walked in a trance down the steps of the porch, her eyes glued to the houseboat that seemed to grow in grandeur as it drew closer. Making her way across the property, she marveled at the structure and its industrial beauty.

Approaching the dock with expert precision, the vessel stopped, almost taking up the entire stretch of pier.

"*Damn*," she whispered to herself as she arrived at the dock.

The door to the cabin opened and Jack made his way down the steps to the front deck.

Jocelyn struggled to reconcile the modest and unpolished image she had quickly formed of Jack, with the reality that he lived on, as well as had designed, such an enchanting dwelling. His rugged appearance contrasted so drastically with the elegance of the structure, that she began to suspect that his deepest truths were hidden far beneath his rugged surface.

"Good morning," Jack called over. He got to work expertly tying off and anchoring his home, his movements instinctual and effortless.

"Morning," Jocelyn managed to reply breathlessly.

"Big day," he announced in reply. "One of my guys is on his way over now to pick me up. Once we grab the materials, we'll get to work on the porch."

He joined Jocelyn on the pier and started making his way up to the house.

"Woah, woah, woah," she interrupted, putting her hand up to stop him from taking another step. "There's no way you're showing up in *that* and I'm not getting a tour," she protested.

"Oh. I, uh," Jack rubbed his neck, instinctively hesitant. Jocelyn was unlike any client he had worked for in the past, he reminded himself. There was room for pleasantries, he allowed. "Yes. Of course."

Jack hopped back over the side of the boat and extended a hand to Jocelyn. She took a sip of her coffee, wondering off-handedly if she might be dreaming this, then took his hand.

"It's a pretty quick tour," he said, leading her past a procession of houseplants that framed the entryway and opened the large glass door before ushering her inside.

Jocelyn took in the visual buffet of texture, detail, and warm aesthetics. Minimalistic and industrial in style, she got the impression that Jack had no more and no less than what he needed. Despite its simplicity, the space was unmistakably home.

"I don't know what to look at first," she marveled. "My eyes are drawn to everything all at once."

While the front and back of the boat were made almost entirely out of framed windows, the adjacent walls were accented in distressed brick. At the top of each wall was a row of windows spanning across the entire length, letting in even more natural light. In the front corner, Lady was curled up on a rug beside a trusty leather armchair and ottoman. Simple shelves, mounted to the wall with black steel pipes and wood planks, were littered with books, an old globe, and some potted plants.

"Don't get up, Lady," Jack said sarcastically.

Lady looked up for only a moment before plopping her head back down, lazily licking her lips before closing her eyes again.

"See what I mean?" he said gesturing towards his companion. "She's taking this retirement thing a little too seriously if you want my opinion."

Jocelyn knelt and scratched Lady's head generously as she scanned the space, taking the time to study the sophisticated details Jack had included in his design. Occupying a large portion of the floorplan was an old farmhouse table with enough chairs to seat ten. Mounted above the table was a light fixture made of Edison bulbs wrapped around a wood beam hanging at various lengths from thick black cords.

When she spotted the long wooden box of well-used crayons in the center of the table, she scanned the room again and noticed a basket of colorful wooden toys she hadn't before. Unexpectedly, her pulse quickened, and she instantly felt foolish for it. Whether it was fear, jealousy, or something else entirely, she couldn't be sure.

Glancing back as inconspicuously as she could to Jack's ring finger, she convinced herself it was no more than a natural curiosity. It was bare, but for a man who worked with his hands, that wasn't always definitive.

"How does your wife like living on a boat?" she ventured.

"My wife?" Jack replied, his face awash with confusion.

"Oh, I'm sorry," she replied, keeping the unexpected relief out of her voice. "I figured since you have kids—"

"Kids?" he broke in, his curiosity mounting

"The toy box and crayons," Jocelyn responded.

"Oh. No, no. Nieces and a nephew," Jack corrected. "Uncle Jack," he exclaimed, his arms extended as if to present himself to her anew.

The relief the clarification evoked was nearly as unsettling as the jealousy her initial misunderstanding had made her feel. Filing the mixed feelings away, Jocelyn forced her attention elsewhere.

"Sarah and Will," she beamed. "How are they? How is Sarah? Gosh, I never stopped missing her."

"They're both great. Both married. Three kids and one on the way between them. Will has two girls. They do no wrong and have him right where they want him. Sarah has a little boy and is expecting a girl in a few months. She's a natural of course."

"How about you? Not a family man?" she asked.

Mentally calculating that Jack would be thirty-seven now, she couldn't help but want to know more. It was none of her business as to why he was unmarried. She knew it wasn't her place to pry, but her curiosity had gotten the better of her.

"Will always says that I'm married to my work," he replied with a shrug.

"Are you?" She couldn't help but wonder if the same was true for herself.

"I work as much as I do because I've got nothing better to do," he answered as a matter of fact. "I'd slow down in a second, but only for the right reasons."

"What would you consider to be the right reasons?" Jocelyn probed.

"A woman who keeps me in bed," he offered unapologetically. "Children who wake up before the sun and want to go fishing off the pier before the coffee's done its job. To name a few."

"How's the search going?" Jocelyn asked boldly. She didn't want to seem too interested, but she found it hard to believe that a man like Jack was still single.

"Not searching," he said easily. "Just taking life as it comes."

She could tell that, while the answer was simple, the reason behind it was complicated. No more interested in delving into her own turbulent love life, she offered him a change in topic.

"Where do you sleep?"

Jack led her through the space, motioning towards a platform that had been built into the other end of the room. The neatly made bed was tucked into a deep-set window, sheer curtains drawn to reveal a panoramic view of the river.

"This is where the magic happens," he said with a smirk.

Jocelyn appreciated Jack's playful flirtation. He made no effort to hide how comfortable he was around her even all these years later, and she was pleasantly surprised by it. When meeting most men for the first time, an air of formality and stiff trepidation lingered before they could get to know one another. Even if romance wasn't in the cards, she often found that breaking the ice with the opposite sex took more work than necessary. With Jack, the introductions had been made long ago, leaving only comfortable banter and a surprising air of instant friendship in place of reservation.

It was still difficult for her to believe that Jack had once been the same boy she had loathed so deeply as a child. He was handsome in a way that made her uneasy and feel dreadfully plain in comparison. Though she didn't dare to imagine anything but friendship existing between them, she wasn't oblivious.

She rolled her eyes playfully at his remark. While she wouldn't permit herself to picture the space igniting a more intimate relationship with Jack, she could easily imagine herself curled up in the bed reading a book in the soft light of morning. It was the kind of nook built for lazy weekends spent in bed.

Continuing around the room, Jocelyn marveled at the small kitchen. The cabinets were painted white with black hardware and antique glass inlays in the doors. The countertop was butcher block and cradled a small white farmhouse sink. On the counter, two full bottles and one nearly empty bottle of whiskey were accompanied by a single shot glass.

"Looks like you're ready for a party," Jocelyn said playfully.

Jack's ease broke and a hollow expression flashed across his eyes before his lips formed an agreeable smile. He moved through the space, leading her to a frosted glass door past the kitchen and pushed it open.

Crossing over the threshold into the bathroom, Jocelyn's eyes grew wide. "This is beautiful," she exclaimed.

The bathroom was floor to ceiling subway tile with black grout and a slate floor. The shower, not surprisingly, was glass with black trim, taking up the whole back wall. The toilet was set back in a small alcove and the square porcelain sink basin sat atop a floating wood countertop. The accents, she noticed, were minimalist and industrial as with the rest of the house.

"It's so open," she added.

"I did my best to work with the space I had and give the illusion of more space where I could," Jack explained.

"Mission accomplished. It's all just...perfect."

They exited the bathroom and she stood in the main entryway again, taking the space in. She glanced around, noticing for the first time that the room was filled to the brim with every size and variety of plant life imaginable. A detail that felt as random as it appeared to be deliberate. Various planters found homes on bookshelves, the kitchen counter, floor, and a few were even suspended from the ceiling in hanging pots.

"What's with the plants?"

"Sarah," Jack replied, shaking his head with a smile. "She thinks I'm crazy for living on a boat. But that's coming from someone who gets seasick in the bathtub. When I first moved in, she gave me that." He pointed to a hearty snake plant alongside the armchair. "She said it was to remind me of land."

Jocelyn chuckled.

"She has yet to visit me without bringing something leafy and green that I'm forced to try and keep alive," he added.

"Gosh, she sounds amazing," Jocelyn gushed.

"I've already told her you're here," he informed. "I'll get you her number, I know she's only awaiting a proper invitation out of obligatory politeness."

"Oh, I wish she wouldn't! I would love to catch up."

Lady lumbered over then, licking Jocelyn's fingers in greeting. She sat beside her new friend, a careless leg jutting out to the side lazily.

"Your majesty is in search of second breakfast," Jack said knowingly. "Not until you've had your walk," he added firmly.

At that, Lady dropped slowly to her belly, looking pathetically dejected.

"You're lucky I love you," he said sweetly.

Jack retrieved a small biscuit from a glass jar on the counter and tossed it to Lady. She quickly lurched up into a seated position and caught the treat expertly.

"I'm starting to think that privacy isn't a big concern of yours," Jocelyn said, noting the general lack of concealment Jack afforded himself.

"The limited privacy took some getting used to," he admitted. "I fell for the openness of the design before I considered the potential for unwanted audiences. In a space this small, you work with what achieves the desired effect, then you live with the rest. I don't even think about it anymore."

"How long have you lived here?"

"Here?" He studied his watch. "Oh, about fifteen minutes."

"Ha. Ha," she retorted.

"I bought the boat as an eighteenth birthday present to myself. It needed a lot of work, so I lived on it while I gutted it and finished about a year later. So, as long as I've had the business." He gestured around the room with pride. "What do you think?"

"I'm honestly not sure what I expected, but this wasn't it."

"I don't know how to take that," Jack said with an easy smile.

"As a compliment," Jocelyn insisted.

If Jack could make a boat look this beautiful, she couldn't wait to see what he would do with her family's home.

"What I wouldn't give to spend a night on this architectural wonder," she heard herself say, still mesmerized by the splendor of the space.

"I could arrange that," Jack offered. "I know a guy," he added coyly.

The current of excitement that his words and his piercing stare evoked robbed Jocelyn of a quick reply. Buying time as she collected herself, she moved towards the exit in retreat.

"Tempting," she replied casually, grateful that she'd managed to sound indifferent. "We'd better focus our attention back on the house for now, don't you think?"

Jack enjoyed the dance of emotions that played across Jocelyn's face. Though she tried to conceal it, she hadn't managed to keep the intrigue out of her expression entirely, and it aroused him. He had once believed his feelings for her to be all but abandoned. A childhood crush, after all, wasn't meant to be lifelong. Now, he wondered, as she awakened in him an affection much more potent than that of a boy's childish crush, if he'd succeeded as completely as he'd once believed in severing his feelings for her. The suggestion that she might be fighting the same pull towards him only made the prospect of spending the next few months together more electrifying.

"You're the boss," he allowed.

As he watched Jocelyn walk away, Jack amended his strict stance of keeping his distance in the name of professionalism to allow the possibility for something more.

For the remainder of the day, more workers and heavy appliances came in and out of the house than Jocelyn could keep track of. One motley crew carried out the old water heater and the HVAC unit, and another delivered new ones. The roofers had torn off the old roof and were already laying the new copper panels where the shingles had been by lunch. The pool had been drained and power washed, a few cracks were filled, and a handful of broken border tiles had been replaced. The chlorine filtration system had been converted over to a saltwater system as well. Jocelyn only hoped that the murky green water wouldn't return if she failed to keep up on the maintenance while the property remained in her custody.

Jack and his crew had framed out the porch by noon and had screened it in and added a door by three o'clock. Once the project was done, they left for the day to wrap up work on another job. By five o'clock, all the workers had finished, leaving Jocelyn in her own company once again.

She considered Jack's comment about slowing down for the right reasons and wondered if it was something she was capable of doing herself. She wasn't even certain she would recognize a good reason to modify her work-life balance if one came along. Even on a construction site, she found herself unable to sit on the sidelines and spent a few hours removing wallpaper in the master bedroom to stay busy. Was she so far removed from her ability to relax that she'd managed to misplace the desire to completely? This, she reminded herself, was one of the many things she hoped to unpack during her stay in Virginia. While she fully intended to help where she could, she would take care to find room for herself again as well.

Settling into a rocking chair with her book a while later, Jocelyn took a moment to marvel at the newly screened-in porch, pleased at how the simple change enhanced the space. Jack's work, she noticed, unsurprisingly, was seamless. The addition, apart from its new and polished finish, looked as if the porch had been screened-in by design rather than added on as an afterthought.

She leaned back in her chair, embracing the welcomed rest that the rocker offered. Throughout the day, she had worked hard to keep her focus on the renovation. Though it was difficult for her to admit, it had been a labored effort not to let her thoughts drift to Jack. As he worked, she caught his eyes on more than one occasion, startled by the current that jumped between them.

She would be lying to herself to insist that she looked at him as her contractor and nothing more. Jack and his childhood were a heady mix of contradiction and she struggled to resist the allure of everything his presence promised to offer her. He was both familiar and mysterious. His gaze a dangerous sanctuary. There was little in life that Jocelyn couldn't manage with some careful planning. That was except, of course, for her heart. Jack, she imagined, possessed the power to unravel everything she'd come to know and believe. As ready as she had been to run into the arms of uncertainty, the thought of running into Jack's arms in search of what was missing in her life back in Austin scared her more than the idea of standing still.

Jocelyn stepped out onto the second-floor balcony off the back bedroom. The sun had long since dipped below the horizon, leaving the landscape awash in soft moonlight. A few lights twinkled in the distance marking other homes, restaurants, and marinas.

In the water, she noticed the lights were on in Jack's houseboat. She had busied herself by removing more wallpaper in the master bedroom after dinner and had enjoyed a long hot shower to celebrate completing the strenuous undertaking. During which time she had managed to forget that he made a temporary home for himself off the pier. Taking in the sight of the charming watercraft again, she wondered what it must be like to live on the river.

Through the windows and glass door, the space was illuminated by a few dim lights. She felt intrusive as she marveled at the beauty of the interior again, but she imagined Jack functioned fully aware of how exposed his living quarters were. Just then, he moved into view, his bare chest wet, a Turkish towel wrapped tightly around his waist. Jocelyn jumped, startled, and shifted her eyes quickly away.

Her heart was pounding, her pulse racing. She hadn't expected to see him so exposed, nor had she anticipated how much of a strain it would be to look away.

Shifting her eyes back cautiously, hating herself for knowingly encroaching upon Jack's privacy, she looked on as if in a trance. His muscles were well-earned and sturdy, his chest covered in a rugged dusting of dark hair. He was, she mused again, the embodiment of masculinity.

He grabbed a few treats and tossed them to Lady then offered her a generous scratch behind the ears. As he moved around the home, the thin material of his towel hugged his frame, she felt her chest constrict uncomfortably and she fought against the feelings that bloomed in the cage of her chest. A warm heat of attraction raced through her veins she knew she'd have to be dead not to feel.

Jack was far from the boy with the gap-toothed smile who had once snuck grass into her salad. A different creature entirely from the boy who had put a pile of worms in her shoe. The man before her sparked feelings she'd resolved to consider might never exist for her.

She had formed the belief that she had chosen the right path in life. Rather than chasing romance and a love story, she had decided to focus her attention and her sights on something she had control over. Building a successful career. Now she found herself struggling to think of much else than a man she hadn't expected to reunite with, let alone catch feelings for.

Jocelyn closed her eyes and steeled herself against an attraction that threatened to unravel everything she had worked so hard for and retreated into the house. It was a dangerous temptation, given her impending return to Austin, to play with the kind of fire a man like Jack could ignite. Summer flings had never been her style, but even if she was willing to make an exception, he was hardly the ideal suitor for such an exploit. Grown up or not, she wasn't sure she would survive any more heartbreak delivered by Jack Evans.

Chapter Five

As Jack and his team filed into the house, ready for the first day of demolition, Jocelyn couldn't reconcile the idea of spending another day trying to stay out of everyone's way.

"How can I help?" she asked, throwing her hair up into a bun.

He studied her for a moment. She was serious. Of that, he was certain. He might not know her well as an adult, but as a child, Jack recalled that Jocelyn didn't enjoy being a spectator. She needed to be a part of the action.

He had checked the previous day for plumbing and to determine whether the dividing wall between the living room and dining room was load bearing or not and had confirmed that it was all clear to be removed. There were plenty of jobs to tackle for the day, and he was sure Jocelyn would be eager to take part in any one of them, but nothing was more ceremonious on demo day than tearing down a wall.

With a casual shrug, he reached into the toolbox on the floor and pulled out a sledgehammer. "Got any pent-up aggression you want to take out on that wall?"

"I think I can muster up some."

Jocelyn took hold of the tool as he extended it, surprised by the weight of it in her hands.

While Jack delivered final instructions to the young men and the only woman on his team, she approached her target. She squared off with the center of the wall, heaved the sledgehammer up and took a broad swing at the drywall with little hesitation.

The head of the hammer crashed through the partition with a satisfying crack as the sheetrock fractured. She dislodged the tool from the wall and swung again, widening the hole.

Jack watched Jocelyn for a moment, appreciating how focused and determined she was. The muscles in her arms relaxed and tightened as she moved, her body easily taking command over the task. After a few swings, he could see that she had found her rhythm.

"Now don't get any closer to that outlet," he warned, moving over to join her. "We'll need to use a crowbar to remove that section of wall."

He walked up beside her, placing a hand on her back, careful to position it high. She was hot to the touch, her body firm and damp already from perspiration. His instinct was to pull away at the sensation that her connection sent through him, but he resisted in the hopes that she wouldn't notice the effect she had on him.

"I've already shut off the power to this room," he assured her "but we don't want to damage the wires."

Jocelyn set the hammer down and watched Jack. He retrieved a screwdriver from his tool belt and got to work removing the outlet. Though they weren't keeping the wall, he extracted the wire box without damaging the sheetrock surrounding it. Once he had capped off the wires, he retrieved a crowbar and handed it to Jocelyn.

"Trade?"

"What do I do now?" she inquired, switching tools at his request.

"Now that you've got a good-sized hole to work with, you can use this to remove the rest of the sheetrock. It'll be quicker and less mess to clean up. Sledgehammers are mostly just used for removing walls on home renovation shows for added theatrics. Most contractors would rather not deal with the mess they make.

"So, why'd you give it to me to use then?" Jocelyn asked with a laugh.

"Tell me you wouldn't have been disappointed with anything less and I owe you a Coke," Jack challenged.

A playful smile danced across her lips.

"Exactly," he confirmed. "I usually use the reciprocating saw," he admitted. When her eyes lit up, he added, "You can use that to remove the studs."

Together they continued to go about dismantling the wall. As they worked, Jack explained the process and why he operated the way he did. Tying up the wires to the ceiling to remove later, piling up the boards neatly to avoid stepping on the nails, and how to carefully remove the top plate and bottom plate of the wall without damaging the floor and ceiling. When the job was complete, he ushered her over to the kitchen where a few of the crew members were in the process of taking out the old cabinets. He explained to her how they were able to remove them without damaging them, then demonstrated how to do the same with the Formica countertops.

Jocelyn appreciated how effortlessly Jack worked while offering insight and information along the way. Though she wasn't sure she would be able to remember everything he explained to her, working through each task and learning why he did it helped her gain a better understanding of what was being done. He was a natural instructor, she noticed as well. He used gentle corrections and was even open to considering alternate approaches if one of his workers made another suggestion. He would praise them often and provided guidance only when it was necessary, not leaving the overbearing impression of an arrogant perfectionist. While Jocelyn imagined he was very sure of how he wanted things to be done and had a high standard for the final product, it never reflected in how he treated his employees.

By two o'clock, the kitchen had been fully gutted save for the appliances, which were pulled out from the wall but remained in working order. A stack of pizza boxes sat in a pile on the stove and Jack's crew were littered around the space, scarfing down pizza and catching up on text messages or social media on their phones. Becky, the lone girl of the group, balanced the attention of a few of the boys, and it was apparent that she didn't mind.

As hard working as they had all been that morning, Jocelyn smiled at their evident youth. She was used to seeing big burley men in the field and enjoyed how much Jack's crew contrasted with societal norms, finding the oddity quite intriguing.

"You earned your lunch today," Jack said, handing her a paper plate with two slices of pizza on it.

Taking the plate in both hands, Jocelyn's mouth began to water. After the long morning of demo and hauling all the material out to Jack's truck, she was ravenous.

"Would you like to join me out by the pool?" she offered. "I think Thomas just finished filling it."

"Sounds great. I'm going to get Lady out of quarantine, let her stretch her legs a bit. I'll meet you there."

Jocelyn sat contently at the pool's edge, her feet dangling in the ice-cold water. She was already half-way through her second slice when Jack returned with Lady.

Lady meandered over and licked Jocelyn's face, stole a taste of pizza grease, then plopped down beside her.

"Woah, Killer," Jack exclaimed, sitting on the other side of his companion. "Want me to grab you another slice?"

Aware of how ravenous she must look, Jocelyn put a shielding hand to her mouth as she finished the bite she was chewing. "No, two is plenty, thanks." She placed the rest of her final slice on her plate, thinking it best to enjoy the remainder of her meal with a fraction more decorum.

"I should be embarrassed," she admitted "I don't usually eat like a slob. I've never been so hungry in my life."

"Demo day takes a lot out of you," Jack confirmed. "You did great. I think I owe you a paycheck after today."

Jocelyn laughed sweetly.

Jack took a bite of pizza and they sat in silence together for a while as they worked to refuel. Lady, the ever-subtle diplomat, rested her heavy head in Jocelyn's lap, eventually charming her way to a few scraps of crust.

Feeling less ravenous, Jocelyn leaned back, angling her face to receive the full heat of the sun. Swirling her feet in the cool clear water, she enjoyed the harsh contrast of temperatures as they played over the surface of her skin.

Turning to Jack, she remarked, "You've got a great group of guys...and girl, working for you." She paused to enjoy another bite of pizza. "They're younger than what I had expected from a contracting crew," she added.

"Most of them are college age," Jack explained. "But a few are still in high school."

"I suspect there's an interesting explanation somewhere in there," Jocelyn probed.

Jack shrugged casually. "Like I said, I had an interest in building early on. Unfortunately, there were not that many contractors willing to hire me when I was young. Not until I met Robert Jeffries, and even he was hesitant at first. Luckily for me, he was as desperate for the help as I was to learn the trade. When a back injury pushed him into early retirement, he turned over all his clients to me.

"As I grew my company, I decided I wanted to offer jobs to high school and college kids who might be coming up against the same snags I had trying to find a job in the industry."

"Wow, what a great idea. How many employees do you have?"

"About two dozen," Jack replied.

"And they're all students?"

"Most of them started out while they were still attending school, yes. I've got a bit of a mixed bag though. Some are just working to make extra cash over the summer. Others are homeschoolers who apprentice with me year-round with the hopes of pursuing contracting as a career. A handful have worked with me from the beginning and are seasoned professionals in their own right. My most seasoned guy is Jonas. He's my head contractor and works independently with his own team."

"I hate to sound ignorant, but I was surprised at first to see a woman working in construction," Jocelyn admitted. "But...Becky, is it?" Jack nodded. "She was keeping up with the guys."

"Most days she runs circles around them," Jack boasted. "If she wants it, she's well on her way to earning a head contractor position once she's completed all her certifications."

"Growing up I wouldn't have considered pursuing a job in construction. It just wasn't on my radar as a woman. It's nice to see that the industry is diversifying."

"Oh, absolutely. You can probably thank HGTV for that. I think this generation has a lot more female representation out there for trade jobs, especially in construction."

"I bet it helps to have a boss that believes in them as much as you do. You're a great teacher," Jocelyn commented.

"I don't know about that."

"You don't give yourself enough credit," she insisted. "I can tell they really look up to you."

"What about you," he asked, drawing attention away from himself. "What do you do back in..."

"Austin," Jocelyn said, filling in the blank. "I'm a National Sales Manager at a recruiting firm," she informed.

"What exactly does a National Sales Manager do?"

"Mostly, I maintain relationships with the accounts we handle. I also test resume algorithms on occasion and manage the conception of new interview structuring techniques. Recently, my team has been working on coming up with a new collection of interview questions to present to one of the company's largest accounts. Another team is designing a new resume algorithm for the same company. The team manager who delivers the strongest presentation, provided the pitch goes well, will be promoted to National Sales Account Executive."

"Do you think you'll get it?"

"I like my chances," she replied confidently.

Jack squinted curiously, trying to imagine Jocelyn working in a white-collar world. After watching her in action, wielding tools and throwing her weight around on the job, he couldn't picture her stuck behind a desk all day.

"Do you enjoy what you do?" he asked.

Jocelyn paused longer than she had intended. "It's challenging," she said at last. "I make great money," she added.

"That doesn't sound like a yes," he disputed.

"It's a job," she reasoned. "I don't enjoy everything about it of course, but I like the comradery of the team I manage. I like knowing that what I do makes a real difference in people's lives.

"I'm helping to provide companies with the best applicants for the positions they need filled. I'm sure you know how vital that can be. It can mean the difference between your business being successful or falling apart.

"We work with a lot of small businesses as well, and it's been amazing to watch some of them expand with the right connection of employees. Not forgetting the fact that I'm helping to link people with their next career advancement opportunity. Someone who was once jobless or stuck in the wrong profession is able to completely transform their life when they're hired by the right company."

Jack looked on with amazement. He had greatly underestimated the pride that Jocelyn took in her work. By the expression on her face, he could tell that she had needed the reminder herself.

"Did you always want to work in recruiting?" Jack felt inclined to unearth the nature of why Jocelyn was so far out of reach.

"When I was five, I wanted to be *Barbie*. I wanted to be a marine biologist when I was ten," she retorted gently. "Not everyone knows what they'll do right out of high school. Most of us don't even know what we'll do right out of college."

"True enough," he allowed.

Silence fell between them again. It was an easy and relaxed break in conversation. The kind that illustrated that their relationship didn't require meaningless banter or overtures in order to be comfortable around one another.

Jocelyn didn't feel the need to excuse herself when Jack informed her that he needed to take care of some work correspondences. Instead, she was content to remain in his and Lady's easy company, drinking in the beautiful spring weather, and enjoying the feel of the refreshing water at her feet. He skimmed emails and text messages, coordinating meetings, orders, and scheduling, all the while, she observed him candidly.

As easygoing and casual as Jack appeared to be on the outside, she sensed a heaviness that lingered just beyond the dark circles that rimmed his eyes and the neglected stubble that obscured his face. She suspected it was due to the physical demands of his job, but she couldn't be sure. From time to time, she felt that it was more difficult than he wanted it to be to engage in conversation. Though she didn't mind the silence between them, she couldn't help but wonder if he was suffering within it.

After some time, Jack tucked his phone back into his pocket and met Jocelyn's eyes, flashing an apologetic smile that caught her off guard.

It had been easy as they worked in a crowded and noise-filled construction site to put the image of him wrapped in nothing but a towel out of her mind. Now, Jocelyn felt her face flush hot recalling it. It was dangerous to admit, but she couldn't remember ever having been more physically attracted to another man in her life. Everything about him was pure masculinity. He was the kind of man that reminded a woman how perfectly she might pair with him. Like a rare steak and a full-bodied cabernet.

The thought played at the corners of her mind of indulging in a racy fling with Jack and worrying about the consequences later, if at all. One full of unapologetic rapture and reckless abandon. Blinking hard, she scolded herself for entertaining the idea for even a second. Jack was flirty, yes, but he was far from sweeping her up in a sizzling whirlwind romance. Not that she would know how to behave in such an encounter if he tried. Besides, she reminded herself, that was the last thing she wanted.

Jack glanced past her, and a smile warmed his face.

"Hey, you," he said in greeting.

Jocelyn, relieved for the interruption, turned to see a very familiar and very pregnant stranger standing at the base of the steps.

"Sarah?!" she exclaimed.

Sarah reached out her arms, holding a small potted succulent plant in one hand and beckoning her long-lost friend in for a hug with the other. She wore her dark brunette hair down her back in long natural waves. If Jocelyn's memory served her right, she was a spitting image of her mother. Her soft flowing dress couldn't hide that she was far along in her pregnancy, but from what Jocelyn could tell, she was all belly.

Jocelyn squealed like a schoolgirl, unable to contain her elation, and rose to meet her.

"I hope you don't mind my showing up unannounced. You said to drop by whenever, and I was in the neighborhood."

"Of course not!" Jocelyn exclaimed. "It's so great to see you after all this time!"

Jack collected their plates and joined the two women at the base of the steps, ready to get back to work.

"It's been so long," Sarah declared. "You're so beautiful! Jack, why didn't you tell me how *beautiful* she was?"

Jack pressed his lips together, certain there was no right answer. Deciding the question was rhetorical, he opted to change the subject instead. "I'll leave you ladies to catch up," he offered. "There's plenty of work to be done and I've relaxed for long enough. Thanks again for the help today, Jocelyn."

"It was a lot of fun," she replied, still buzzed from the excitement of reuniting with her childhood best friend.

Jack tried to edge past them, but Sarah intercepting him before he could make his way up the stairs.

"Wait, take your plant," she demanded, shoving the small pot into his hand. "Oh, hi, by the way." She pulled him in for a quick hug. "Gross," she protested. "Is that sweat?"

Jack raised his eyebrows playfully. "You did it to yourself."

When Lady lumbered over to follow him back to work, he put out a hand to halt her. "You know the rules, Lady. No demo days for you."

Noticeably disappointed by the rejection, Lady obeyed grumpily, plopping down at Sarah's feet.

Jack turned to Sarah and added, "Oh, and you're hereby banned from giving me any more plants while Jocelyn is in town. You'll sink my damn boat."

Sarah and Jocelyn burst into laughter, imagining the sight. Once they managed to collect themselves—well after Jack had entered the house—Jocelyn turned to Sarah and examined her more closely.

"I still can't believe you're a mom…and *pregnant*! You look *amazing*."

"Oh gosh," Sarah said on an exhale. "I feel like a beach ball with legs. They never tell you how much more tired you'll be the second time around, or how low the baby sits. I swear I didn't waddle the first time around."

"Well, it doesn't show," Jocelyn gushed. "Join me on the beach? We have so much to catch up on."

"Tell me everything," Sarah insisted, following Jocelyn across the lawn. "How old were we when I last saw you anyway?"

"Ten I think?"

"Wow. Yeah, you're probably right. That was a lifetime ago."

They walked down the sandy path between the tall grass of the dunes, with Lady trailing closely behind.

"I'm sorry to hear about your grandmother, she was such a sweet woman," Sarah offered.

"Thank you." Jocelyn didn't know how to explain that she had been mourning the loss of her grandmother for years. By the time she passed, her dementia had already taken everything else from her. Losing her felt more like finding peace after a long-drawn-out goodbye than anything else. "It's been so hard on my mom. I just want to do what I can to make things easier for her."

"That's why you're here right? Are you really going to sell the place?"

"It's for the best," Jocelyn said, only half believing it. "I just hope it goes to a good family who can appreciate all the work Jack's going to be putting into it."

"Yeah…" Sarah mused, interested in the way that her friend, who had once loathed her brother, now said his name. "I hope he's been on his best behavior."

"Of course," Jocelyn replied matter-of-factly.

She picked up a scrap of driftwood to examine it more closely, but Sarah suspected she was less interested in the small token than she was in drawing attention away from her blushing.

"He's been great, nothing like how I remember him."

"You always did get the worst of him," Sarah agreed. "I gave him so much shit about that when we were kids. I was so worried you wouldn't want to hang out with us anymore."

"Never!" Jocelyn insisted. "You were my *best* friend." She shook her head. "I still find his reasoning hard to believe though."

"He told you about the crush to end all crushes?"

"Get out of here. I'm sure it wasn't all that," Jocelyn said, downplaying her disbelief. Jack certainly hadn't made it seem like *that* big of a deal.

"Oh, it absolutely was," Sarah insisted. "I once found a scrap of paper under his bed with your name on it, surrounded by hearts."

Jocelyn rolled her eyes.

"The scrap of paper," Sarah went on, pausing for affect, "was in his 'Jocelyn box.'"

Jocelyn blinked hard in disbelief.

"Oh yeah," Sarah confirmed. "He had it *bad*."

Embarrassed, Jocelyn tucked a stray strand of hair behind her ear.

"Speaking of crushes," Sarah ventured. "You must have a special guy in your life."

Jocelyn couldn't decide which man made her more uncomfortable to talk about, Jack or Michael. "No, not really."

"Not really?"

"We broke up."

"I'm sorry to hear that. I'm sure he doesn't deserve you," Sarah proposed.

"I wouldn't say that," Jocelyn disputed. "He's a great guy. I just don't think he's the right guy for me."

"How so?" Sarah caught herself and quickly added, "I'm sorry, it's none of my business."

"No, don't be silly. It wasn't a messy breakup or anything like that. Michael is…" Jocelyn searched for the best words to describe her ex. "He's a great businessman," she offered at last. "Very practical. Smart. Witty. He's the kind of guy you want in your corner."

"He doesn't sound so bad to me," Sarah allowed.

"Like I said, he's a great guy," Jocelyn reiterated. "Working with him even after we broke up has been easy and completely professional. He just…" And that was precisely where her ability to explain her failed relationship with Michael fell short. Why everything he was still wasn't enough to make her happy.

"I think I understand," Sarah said knowingly.

"You do?"

"There has to be a magnetism between you," she offered.

"Yes," Jocelyn agreed, though she knew that it was far more complicated than just that.

"When you know, you know," Sarah confirmed.

"Do you?" Jocelyn still wasn't sure. "Is that what it was like when you met your husband?"

"I actually met Jonas through Jack."

Lady nudged Sarah's leg with her nose, presenting a stick she had found along the shoreline. Sarah took it in her hand and tossed it a few feet out into the water for the dog to retrieve.

"When Jack was getting started with River View Construction, he didn't always have a steady stream of workers, so he would ask Will or I to help out from time to time. I guess he knew that Jonas had a thing for me, so he started '*needing my help*' more often." She made air quotes with her fingers. "He's charming as hell and even more handsome," she allowed. "It didn't take much persuading. Before long, we were inseparable, and Jack was wondering whether or not my being on the job was actually helpful or just an unwanted distraction."

"Jack never mentioned that Jonas was your husband."

"Oh, I'm not surprised," Sarah replied easily. "He viewed Jonas as a brother well before we even got together. I suspect I was just a means to making the title official."

The way she said it, Jocelyn could tell that Sarah loved how much her brother revered her husband.

"Luckily for both of them, he wasn't a hard sell."

"How long have you been married?"

"Seven years in September."

"That's so great." Jocelyn could tell by the way Sarah spoke of her husband that she adored him. "I can't believe you're married and a mom. Whenever I see women our age starting families, I can't help but wonder if I'm doing something wrong."

"Why?"

"I don't know," Jocelyn said dismissively. "I guess it just looks so easy for some people. Like I'm going about it all wrong."

"You can't rush love," Sarah insisted.

"I'm starting to wonder if I will ever find it."

"If you want my opinion, I think that the people who struggle to find love are the ones who think they know what they're looking for," Sarah declared. "My advice to you is, stop looking for it. Love is something that finds you, not the other way around."

Jocelyn considered this for a moment. She didn't believe that she had any unrealistic prerequisites for the kind of man she wanted to settle down with, but she knew that she applied the pressure to find the elusive love of her life all the same, subconsciously or otherwise. Maybe Sarah was right, perhaps it was finally time for her to release the pressure and let nature take its course. Afterall, the worst that could happen would be to find herself right where she already was.

***

In the days that followed, Jocelyn embraced the chaos that came with the renovation, but she knew that working in the environment would yield a very different level of tolerance. When she had expressed her concerns about how the noise and dust might affect her work the following week, Jack had graciously proposed that use of his houseboat as a temporary office space. While she had hesitated to accept the offer at first, a valid argument against it couldn't be made.

Chapter Six

"*Ahem*," Jack cleared his throat, announcing his approach from the base of the steps to where Jocelyn reclined beside the pool.

Lying on her stomach, her nose buried in a book, she was draped over one of the lounge chairs that had been delivered the previous day, her curves amplified and unapologetically female in her black bikini.

It had been easy to put her beauty out of his mind while they had worked together on the remodel that week, but now, taking in her glistening sun-kissed skin, Jack felt fire in his veins. An inferno that threatened to consume his soul.

"I hate to interrupt," he offered, working desperately to remember why he'd approached her if not to act impulsively on the passion that burned within him.

Jocelyn swept her hair over one shoulder, tucked a scrap of paper between the pages of her book, and faced him. Using her hand to shield the sun from her eyes she said, "It's no problem. What's up?"

She was casual and relaxed as she reached for her water jug, shifting sensually to flip onto her back. The way she moved her body, he wondered if she knew what she was doing to him. Taking a sip of water, she seemed unaware of the affect she had over him, and for that Jack was grateful.

"The uh…the sink's been delivered, and the guys I have on schedule won't be by for another hour," he informed. "I wanted to make sure that the dimensions line up with the countertop.

Mind giving me a hand dropping it into place? Once it's in, I can take it from there."

"Sure thing," she replied easily.

"I hate to put you to work on your last day of vacation," he said apologetically. "Though, I will say, your idea of vacation includes a lot more manual labor than mine does."

Jocelyn laughed easily and pulled a knitted cover-up over her bathing suit. "Maybe if it was a real vacation, I would carve out more time for pleasure, but I'm here to work. I want to be a part of it," she asserted.

"Well, I'm grateful for the help," Jack said as they made their way up the steps. He stayed a few paces ahead of her, certain he wouldn't be able to restrain himself any longer if she took the lead.

Jack pushed open the sliding glass door that led into the kitchen and ushered Jocelyn inside. He and his crew had installed the repurposed cabinets and Carrera countertops earlier on in the week, arranging them in a layout that further opened up and enhanced the efficiency of the room. Though the install wasn't entirely finished, the pieces had been anchored in place and it was only a few finishing touches away from being complete.

"Here she is," Jack announced, gesturing towards the box on a dolly in the middle of the open floorplan. Inside, was a deep porcelain farmhouse sink.

"Wow, it's massive," Jocelyn exclaimed. "I love it!" She ran her hands along the base of the sink, imagining that it could probably fit all the dishes in the house at once. Never in her life had she thought of a sink full of dishes and been happy about it. "This is what adulthood looks like, isn't it?" she considered. "Fantasizing about a sink."

"At least it's not a toilet," Jack offered. "That fantasy comes with the senior discount at The Waffle House."

Jocelyn laughed easily at the quip.

"Let's see how she looks," he said.

Kneeling beside the basin, Jack took hold of the sink. Following his lead, Jocelyn squatted down and gripped the other side. On his command, they lifted together, balancing the cumbersome sink between them.

As Jack directed, Jocelyn followed, shuffling her feet, wishing desperately that she had thought to put on shoes. If the basin dropped, she knew she would have no toes to speak of in the aftermath.

Together, they carefully lowered the sink into place. When it sat snuggly below the window, Jocelyn marveled at it again. "It's a thing of beauty."

"If I had to pick one farmhouse style feature and leave the rest, it would definitely be the sink," Jack remarked in agreement.

Just then, there was a knock at the door. Jocelyn excused herself and was joined by Lady, who was already making her way over from her spot on the floor.

On the other side of the door stood Sarah holding the hand of a little boy, no more than three with light brown skin and curly black hair. Beside her was a tall Haitian man with warm chocolate skin. He was handsome with his short fade, neat beard, and an electric smile. His Henley T-shirt suggested that his build was strong, though his muscles were leaner than Jack's.

The small family, Jocelyn mused, was more stunning than she had pictured. Their son, Brian, was a beautiful mix of his mother and father with his warm skin and hazel eyes, and the way that Sarah looked up at her husband told Jocelyn that she was as infatuated with him now as she had been when they had first gotten together.

"Sarah," she exclaimed, bringing her friend in for a hug. It's so good to see you!" She turned to Jonas. "And you must be Jonas," she said, wrapping him in a friendly embrace.

"I've heard a lot about you," Jonas offered with a smile.

"All good things I hope." Jocelyn stepped aside as Lady greeted her family. "Come on in."

When they entered the living space, Jack was already getting to work hooking up the sink. Brian played happily with Lady while Jonas and Sarah joined them in the kitchen.

"Hey, Jonas," Jack said in greeting. "What brings you guys by?"

"I've got the tile for the master bath in my truck," he informed. "They were delivered to the office this morning." He hooked a finger in Sarah's direction. "She just needed an excuse to get over here again."

"Guilty," Sarah said with a shrug. "We figured we'd make it a family affair."

"No excuse or guilt required," Jocelyn insisted.

Jack stopped his work and brushed his hands off on his jeans. "Here, let me help you unload those tiles," he offered to Jonas.

"While the men work, why don't we head down to the beach," Jocelyn suggested.

"Sounds good to me," Sarah replied agreeably.

They watched Brian splash at the water's edge with Lady for a few moments in silence, enjoying the contrast of the dog's strong build and her sweet nature. She frolicked and jumped in the water like a rabbit as Brian was overtaken by fits of laughter.

"So," Sarah said at last. "Are you trying to kill my brother?"

Caught off guard by the remark, Jocelyn considered the busy schedule that Jack kept and was stricken instantly with guilt. Despite his insistence to maintain long hours, she couldn't help but notice that he seemed tired, even distant on the job. Perhaps she had gone too far in prioritizing an unreasonable timeline at the cost of his wellbeing.

"No, of course not," she said quickly. "But you're probably right. He can't go on working such long hours. I hadn't expected him to work through the weekend like this."

"Not the job," Sarah said, waving her hand dismissively. "Jack's a workhorse. Trust me when I say, no one works Jack harder than he works himself."

"Oh. I'm sorry," Jocelyn said with some relief. "Then I don't know what you mean."

Sarah gestured to her minimally shielded bikini. "You're sexy as hell in that swimsuit."

Jocelyn's face flushed. Somehow, she had managed to forget how little she was wearing. Considering it now, she wished desperately for an oversized sweatshirt and some shorts. "He's so busy with the renovation," she insisted. "I'm sure he hardly noticed." It was an easy thing to believe, given Jack's unyielding work ethic.

"He's a contractor, not a corpse," Sarah said with a laugh.

"I don't think he thinks of me that way," Jocelyn insisted.

"He's a straight man," Sarah insisted. "He thinks of you that way. Listen, I'm up for whatever it takes to keep you around. You have my full support."

If her face looked as hot as it felt, Jocelyn now had more than one reason to be mortified. She didn't make a habit of being brazen with her sexuality, but that didn't mean she hadn't known what she was doing, even if only on a subliminal level. Where Jack was concerned, her head and her heart continued to play a dangerous game of tug of war, and she still had no idea which side she stood on. All she knew was that where tensions built, sparks were sure to fly.

***

It was mid-morning when Jocelyn settled into Jack's houseboat for her first day back to work the following day. She meandered around the space, taking in his residence again as if for the first time.

Absently scanning the countertop, she noted that the two and a half bottles of whiskey she'd noticed earlier when he'd given her the tour had been reduced to a single open bottle. She couldn't help but wonder when Jack had found the time to consume the missing contents.

Though she knew it was none of her business how Jack loosened up at the end of a long day, she couldn't help but worry about the man she was beginning to view as a friend. She put the concern out of her mind for the moment, knowing full well that he was a capable adult and could take care of himself. Not forgetting the fact that, despite their past history, she still didn't know him well enough to pry.

After helping herself to a cup of coffee, Jocelyn set up her MacBook at the head of the table, affording herself the best view of the home's interior for when her eyes needed to wander. She had a virtual meeting with the department at noon to discuss plans on how to maintain and expand relations with the company she and her team were constructing their pitch for. Until then, she planned to refamiliarize herself with the company's long-term goals as well as brush up on the panel's proposal.

Many of the companies Bradford and Bend worked with were looking to hire future employees not based on education alone, but rather focusing heavily on their ability to problem solve, think outside of the box, and to come equipped with the hands-on experience to back up the words they put on paper. Sifting through applicants was hard enough when resume building had become a career field unto itself. The best way to determine if an applicant was a good fit for a client was during the interview.

Perhaps the most important part of the interview, besides going over the resume more thoroughly and evaluating communication skills, was the hard-hitting questions presented by the future employer to determine if an applicant knew what they had to offer as well as what they hoped to get out of being hired. It was Jocelyn's job on the project to ensure that the proposal honored the firm's mission statement, "A superior pairing of candidates and associates through innovation and intuitive connectivity."

While traditional interview questions remained beneficial in matching applicants with a hopeful employer, Bradford and Bend aimed to expand their approach with more comprehensive ones. What Jocelyn's team had set out to do was to determine which questions might pair their clients with candidates capable of rising above their resume and even the formal requirements of the position they were applying for. Seeking out the visionaries, forward thinkers, and problem solvers.

In the weeks since she had last worked on the project, Jocelyn had some new insight to consider. Did someone have to come from a certain career background to be an asset to a company? In some cases, she considered, a once seemingly unqualified applicant might be a better fit for a position than someone who had worked in the field previously or someone who had obtained a degree in it. The question was, how did one go about unearthing such applicants?

Jocelyn was still jotting down a few notes when she logged into her meeting.

"Hey, stranger," Bridget said in greeting. "How is life in Virginia treating you?"

"It's beautiful here," Jocelyn replied. "It's impossible not to feel rejuvenated even with everything that needs to get done around here."

"Looks like you're getting plenty of sun," she noted. "I hope you're still fired up to meet this deadline after some much-deserved rest and relaxation."

"I sure am," Jocelyn confirmed. "Hey, Chad," she said in greeting. "Hi, Melissa. Greg, how are you?" Her team returned pleasantries and a few friendly remarks.

When the remainder of the department joined in, Jocelyn intentionally neglected to address Michael directly. Though she had no ill-willed feelings towards him, it was easier if she drew a firm line between them. In the past, he had had a hard time understanding the nature of their relationship otherwise. While he was a sweet guy, he got his hopes up quickly and the last thing she wanted was for him to see an opening to jump through.

"Where are you, Jocelyn?" Melissa inquired. "From what I can see it's beautiful. Are you overlooking the water?"

"Oh…yeah." Despite herself, Jocelyn became tense. "It's my contractor's houseboat actually. While he's working on the house, he offered to let me work from here."

"*Wow*," Melissa replied in awe. "That's a *boat*?"

"And a house apparently," Chad chimed in.

"Can you give us a quick tour?" Greg requested.

"I…" Jocelyn glanced at Bridget for approval.

"Go ahead, my interest is equally piqued," she said approvingly.

Jocelyn took the laptop and slowly angled it around the room. The collection of coworkers along with her boss gazed excitedly past her to take in the home. Some even leaned into their computer screens, attempting to get a better look.

"That's legit," Greg declared. "I'm coming to Virginia."

"I hope that houseboat has provided you with enough peace and quiet to reflect on the proposal," Bridget said, ever the focused businesswoman.

"I've actually come up with a few new interview questions," Jocelyn replied excitedly, settling back into her seat.

With a few prompts from her notes, they were quickly engaged in a dialogue about how employers might benefit from looking outside of the typical parameters of their hiring guidelines, and which interview questions might serve that goal best. Michael even agreed that she had raised a few good points and added the argument that people use all kinds of experiences to boost their resumes whether it was directly related to the job they were applying for or not. Why not explore that element of resume building with more intention?

Bridget was just wrapping up the meeting when Jack burst through the front door of the boat, positioned directly behind Jocelyn. His white undershirt was blood stained and he was elevating his hand as it dripped blood onto the floor. Without pause, he ripped off his bloodied shirt and used it to wrap his hand. All in plain view of a now captivated audience.

"Are you okay?!" Jocelyn exclaimed, pushing herself away from the table.

"*That's* your contractor?" she heard Melissa say.

"Yeah, I'm fine," Jack said through gritted teeth. The steady trickle of blood running down his arm had her convinced otherwise.

"I...I've gotta go," she directed to her team distractedly. "Sorry, guys." She reached for her laptop. The dejected and sour expression on Michael's face was the last thing she saw before closing out the window.

Jack stood at the sink, holding his hand under a stream of warm water, watching as his blood circled the drain.

"Cut myself on a piece of backsplash tile," he explained. "It's not as bad as it looks."

"What can I do?"

"There's a med kit in the pantry."

Jocelyn moved quickly and after a frenzied search, retrieved the first-aid kit. With frantic movements, she worked to treat his wound. While he was right to say that it wasn't as bad as it looked, the cut was still deep into the meat of his finger.

She winced as she blotted the gash with a paper towel and then she applied an antibiotic ointment.

"*Shit*," Jack grumbled against the pain.

"Sorry."

"I'm the idiot who sliced my finger open."

"True enough."

"Sorry about that," Jack offered apologetically.

Jocelyn shook her head dismissively as she wrapped a bandage around his finger. "Don't worry about it. We were just finishing up."

"Not exactly the first day back you'd hoped for though," he presumed.

"Not what I expected anyway," she allowed. "How's that?"

"Better, thank you."

Jocelyn noticed Jack's bare chest. He was just inches from her, the scent of his masculine pheromones penetrating her senses. His scruffy jawline was so close she could feel the heat of his breath on her cheek. When she noticed the scent of stale alcohol, her heart twisted. Since their reunion, she had easily accepted that Jack had developed into a mature, responsible, and a surprisingly desirable man. She felt the pang of curiosity as she considered, not for the first time, that maybe that wasn't all there was to him.

He was practiced at keeping himself together, that much she could tell. But it was also clear that the boy from her past had become a man who was not quite perfect, and she figured it was just as well. Nothing would happen between them after all, and the last thing she needed while she searched for clarity in her life was to get caught up with a man who had conflicts of his own to sort out.

Returning her focus to the injury, she retrieved a few sheets of paper towels, wet them, and retraced Jack's steps, wiping the blood droplets off the floor as she went.

Jack stood poised at the sink for a moment, tested the mobility of his bandaged injury, then made his way to the back of the home. He bent down and pulled out a built-in drawer from under his bed and retrieved a new shirt then quickly stretched it over his head.

"Sorry again for the interruption," he said, his voice soft yet guarded.

Jocelyn looked on thoughtfully as Jack exited the houseboat a few minutes later. His posture told her that he was angry with himself for the mistake, or more accurately, for the cause of it. His eyes had been heavy, dark circles settled beneath them. It was obvious that he had hardly slept and that he'd been drinking well into the early hours of morning. As a picture of who he had become came into view, she wondered if he was truly rehabilitated from his former immaturities as she had so easily assumed him to be.

That evening, after running what little information she had about Jack through her mind over a dozen times, Jocelyn had finally broken down and called her sister-in-law. She needed to sort through the list of unanswered questions that had been troubling her since Jack's accident and gain some unbiased insight. While she didn't want to pick him apart, she desired to establish a bit more clarity about what had transpired earlier that day.

"I don't know," Jocelyn was saying into the phone. She sat propped up in bed with a cup of tea, tracing the rim of her mug absently. "Whatever it is, it certainly explains why he's still single."

"That's possible," Claire agreed.

Always willing to play devil's advocate, Claire had offered a few theories as to why Jack might be struggling with a drinking problem. Perhaps he was just immature for his age.

Maybe he was an avid sports fan or gamer and got carried away when he indulged in his recreational exploits. Quite possibly, he was an alcoholic, plain and simple. Perhaps he started drinking early in life and never quite got a hold of the habit. It certainly didn't make him a villain. Though Claire confirmed that it likely took him out of the running as a prospective love interest. A point Jocelyn had quickly dismissed as irrelevant and entirely beside the point.

"It's not like I was interested in him or anything anyway," Jocelyn affirmed again, though she knew deep down that the claim wasn't entirely true. "I'm trying to figure him out, that's all," she added.

It was true enough, she thought. By nature, she found people interesting, and Jack was no different. She was even willing to admit that she found him more intriguing than most due to their tumultuous history.

"Sarah just seems so grounded," she went on. "From what I remember, the whole family was straight out of a storybook. No trauma, no abuse, no financial strain, just your all-American family. Sure, Jack was a bit of a menace as a kid, but now that I've spent some time getting to know him better, I struggle to believe that he's deeply troubled in any way."

"We all grow up eventually," Claire offered. "Maybe you could blame immaturity if he was in his twenties, going out and partying every night, but he sounds pretty mature otherwise."

"He is," Jocelyn confirmed.

"Then I suspect that there's a deeper story behind what's going on. He just might not be willing to open up about it," Claire speculated further.

"You're probably right." Jocelyn couldn't keep the sadness from staining her words.

"Can I ask why this is bothering you so much?" Claire inquired delicately. "Are you afraid he won't be able to do a good job with the renovation because of it?"

"No, no, that's not it."

Claire waited patiently while Jocelyn searched for the words and the reason for her confliction. No matter how hard she tried, she couldn't untangle the complicated emotions that Jack evoked from her reply. Even if she could no longer deny them herself, she wasn't ready to voice them aloud.

Instead, she offered, "I view him as a friend, that's all. I hate to think that he could be struggling with something, and I've just elected to overlook it."

"Well, from what you've said, he sounds like a great guy with a strong family unit. I'm sure whatever it is will pass and he'll be stronger for it on the other side," Claire stated confidently.

"Yeah, you're probably right."

Jocelyn considered the palpable bond between Jack and Sarah. As a child, it was natural for a younger sister to look up to an older brother, but in adulthood, for such an admiration to continue, it had to be earned. Based on how Sarah seemed to view her brother, the way they spoke to one another and after watching their bond unfold in person, Jocelyn was willing to allow that it probably wasn't fair to dismiss Jack's other qualities because of one misgiving.

"Well, enough about that," she said flatly. "Is there any chance you and Andrew can make it back up here before I wrap things up? I would love the company."

"I think he does have a four-day weekend coming up, actually," Claire considered. "I would love to see the renovations in person. It already looks so different from the pictures you've sent. Jack sure does have an eye for design, I'll give him that."

Jocelyn tried to ignore the flutter at the mention of his name. No matter how hard she tried, no matter the questions that surrounded him, Jack triggered a response in her subconscious that left her feeling uneasily childish all over again.

Chapter Seven

Jack paced restlessly from one side of the houseboat to the other, concentrating an uncomfortable amount of his focus on ignoring the bottles of whiskey he kept on hand. He had never shown up to a job hungover. Though, a hangover was hardly the condition he would use to describe the state he had been in the other day. While Jocelyn had been understanding as well as gracious in the week that followed and hadn't pried, he found himself face to face with self-loathing.

She had insisted on giving him the weekend off despite his plans to work straight through to the end of the week again, and he couldn't help but feel ashamed. He had scared her, or perhaps he'd given her cause to question whether or not he was still the right man for the job.

Jack reminded himself that Jocelyn probably wanted to have the house to herself for a change as much as she was inclined to offer him a break, but that didn't stop him from wanting to clear the air. Since he had burst through the door of his houseboat, still intoxicated from the night before, she'd offered him more mercy than he deserved.

Before Jocelyn's return to his life, Jack had been satisfied with the solace he had found inside a bottle, dragged down by guilt. Now, he realized that he wanted the opposite, and, more importantly, he wanted her to know it.

Jocelyn slowly moved from downward-facing dog to upward-facing dog on her yoga mat. It had been so long since she had done yoga, or any workout for that matter, that the calculated stretching and strength exercises seemed to carry with them a more painful result. She moved from one pose to the next, focusing on her breathing, feeling her belly move in and out, contracting and relaxing each muscle as she called upon them. She closed her eyes, breathing in the scent of the eucalyptus and mint candle burning in the kitchen, and felt a welcome peace wash over her.

After a busy work week and the late nights she had spent painting, this was exactly what she had needed to start her day off on the right foot. Uncharacteristically, she had laid in bed that morning, ignoring her phone and her computer with calculated indifference. Disregarding the outside world and curling back into her pillow to drift off to sleep again was not her natural response to a new day, but today Jocelyn had basked in it.

The past week had been a hurricane of playing catch up. As her work at the firm threatened to consume her again, dredging up the nagging feeling that she wasn't entirely happy there, she worked to tamper her doubts.

Balance, she reminded herself. Balance was what she had been determined to find during her stay in the river house. Any job would be intolerable if she let it consume her as she had. While it took a great deal of effort to facilitate a healthy equilibrium now, she hoped that it wouldn't be long before it became second nature.

Alternating between cat and cow pose, Jocelyn breathed in and out rhythmically, feeling the coil of mixed emotions over her life move another step closer to untangling.

Jack paused as he reached the back door to the house. Through the window of the sliding glass door, he could see Jocelyn, her back arched in a yoga pose he couldn't name. Her lean body was intimately concealed in skin-tight leggings and a sports bra. As she relaxed her core, dipping her stomach and rolling her shoulders back, her muscles danced.

At the sight of her, Jack's pulse quickened, and he momentarily misplaced his reason for his approach. Blinking a few times to break his trance, he knocked on the door, hoping not to startle her. When she jumped, he cringed, albeit enjoying the clumsy way in which she collected herself. From her collapsed position on the yoga mat, she waved him inside. After a brief hesitation, he pushed the door open and slipped inside.

"Sorry about that," Jack offered apologetically.

"Don't worry about it," Jocelyn managed breathlessly, her hand still placed protectively over her racing heart.

"I was wondering if you wanted to check out the storage barn I've got out back at the office and pick out your beams for the remodel today. There's plenty else to rummage through as well. Maybe you can find some other features to use as design inspiration."

With no better excuse to seek Jocelyn out on a day they had both agreed they would take a break from their otherwise frequently shared company, he figured a bit of shopping could offer them a professional, as well as a casual, opportunity to discuss what he was anxious to say. Now that she had gotten a taste of the demons he wrestled with, he wanted, at the very least, to explain where they had come from.

The last thing he wanted was to hand her some hollow excuse for his behavior. In fact, he wasn't even certain he was prepared to open up to her at all. He had become so practiced in his denial, so determined to bury his feelings, that he wondered if he'd ever be able to open up, even if the intention to do so was beginning to surface. What he did know was that he desired to draw closer to Jocelyn, for he sensed that she was the only one who might unlock the chains that held him in his chosen solitude.

"You finally accept a day off and this is how you want to spend it?" Jocelyn said lightheartedly, rising from the ground. She moved past Jack as if he were a fixture in the house and retrieved her water bottle from the counter. She was already so used to having him around that, despite being startled at his unexpected approach, Jack's presence was as natural and as normal as the sunrise. "Is Lady sleeping in?"

With a smirk, Jack replied, "As always." His easy smile faded, and Jocelyn could tell that he was measuring his next words carefully. "I needed to get out of the house."

Jack was direct by nature. On occasion, he revealed a more playful side of himself, but, by and large, he remained measured in all things. Since the incident earlier in the week, he had been deliberate in restoring his professionalism and Jocelyn had managed to neatly stow away any concerns she'd developed about him. Now, she suspected it was time to finally address what had been swept under the rug.

"You probably have plans for the day," he inserted quickly. "I'm sorry." He edged towards the door, shaking his head in obvious regret.

"No, no," Jocelyn called out quickly. "Don't go. I would love that. Just give me a few minutes to change, will you?"

Jack sat in his idling truck with Lady resting her head on his shoulder from the backseat. She remained convinced that the biscuit he had given her earlier hadn't been the only one he had brought from home.

Scratching his companion's chin absently, Jack feared that he had made a fool of himself in front of Jocelyn. Again. The last thing he wanted was pity, but he knew that his alternate plans for the day weren't ideal either. The current of grief he continued to fight against was becoming too strong. While it threatened to carry him away, Jocelyn anchored him, giving him strength enough to escape the false cure that was slowly killing him.

Jocelyn jogged out to the truck a few minutes later and hopped in the passenger seat. Jack put the truck in gear and started down the driveway, pulling onto the road in silence.

The air around Jack was unusually constricting and Jocelyn could nearly feel the vibration of tension as she waited for him to speak. As the minutes ticked by, pressure growing and her discomfort increasing right along with it, she finally cleared her throat and asked, "Is everything okay?"

Jack let out a long sigh, releasing some of the tightness that had settled in his shoulders. After a pause, he turned to her and replied, "Do you remember when you would give me the silent treatment?"

Jocelyn smirked. "Absolutely."

"I think the longest you had gone was an entire day. We were all together and you had been especially stubborn. You wouldn't speak to anyone."

Jocelyn squinted at him, recalling the incident well but uncertain as to why he might be bringing it up.

"I remember how scared you got by the end of the day," he went on. "Part of me felt guilty, the other part of me enjoyed seeing you tortured by something you were doing to torture me." He shrugged apologetically. "Finally, you ran to your mom and started to cry. I overheard you say that you were afraid you'd scared your voice away."

Jocelyn revisited the memory easily. It was true, she had been absolutely frantic. She'd been trying so hard not to speak that she couldn't make herself talk when she'd finally decided she wanted to again. It wasn't until she had broken down and cried to her mother that she'd found her voice again.

"I remember," she said solemnly.

Turning to look at Jack, she studied him. "Are you playing the silent game?" she asked gently.

Jack pulled off to the side of the road and put the truck in park. He closed his eyes and massaged the bridge of his nose. He sat for a moment lost in deliberation. Uncertain if he would ever be able to utter a reality he still denied fiercely with every fiber of his being. Though he couldn't explain why, the comfort that Jocelyn delivered made him think that it was no longer a burden he had to carry behind a hardened exterior. Finally, he let out a long breath, releasing the pressure that had filled the car.

"My mom passed away last year," he said somberly.

Jocelyn's heart ached with his admission. "I'm so sorry," she said softly.

"Sarah says I'm not dealing with it," he went on. "Of course, she's probably right."

"She never said anything about it." Jocelyn looked back on her conversations with Sarah since she'd arrived and realized that she had never once brought up her mother's passing. Though she referred to her mother often, she'd never done so in the past tense.

"Sarah doesn't like to dwell on the loss," Jack said plainly. "She's not in denial or anything like that. She would just rather focus on what Mom left behind and who she was."

"That sounds like a good way to look at it." It was a reality Jocelyn couldn't wrap her mind around. Losing a parent, especially a mother.

"I don't know." Jack shook his head. "I'm just mad, you know?"

"I can't even imagine."

"The doctors said that the cancer was treatable." Jack's jaw tightened and he remained silent for a moment. "I took them at their word," he added soberly.

Jocelyn had no words. She knew that whatever she might say wouldn't be enough and that more than comforting affirmation, what Jack needed was to speak his truth. She wasn't sure why he'd decided to open up to her, but she suspected it wasn't something he did lightly.

"I had intended to cancel my trip to the Florida Keys," he continued, determined to unpack the heavy burden he carried. "But the woman I was seeing at the time insisted that we still go." His eyes were glassy with the threat of tears he wanted desperately to keep inside. "We were only there two days when I got the call."

Jocelyn placed a hand on Jack's shoulder. A knot formed in her throat, preventing her from speaking her condolences. She hoped, as she rubbed his shoulder, that her touch was enough to tell him how sorry she was.

Jack shook his head and wiped his eyes roughly. "Anyway," he said dismissively. "Monday it will have been a year since she passed. I've been dreading it. Running away from finally admitting that I've lived a whole year of my life without her. Maybe if I'd been there, I could view her death the way Sarah and Will do. Like she's not really gone, simply that her role in our lives has changed. But the guilt of abandoning her when she needed me most prevents me from dealing with it. I just want to have it to do all over again."

Silence hung in the air between them for a moment, though the weight of it had lessened. It all made sense now, Jocelyn thought. Loss was hard enough to cope with, but when guilt was attached it could feel nearly impossible to heal completely.

"She would be proud of you," she finally said.

Jack huffed. "For what?" he challenged. "Being a drunk?"

"Everyone deals with tragedy differently," she said firmly.

Jack shook his head. "I'm pretty sure I'm not dealing with it at all," he disputed.

"Why are you telling me this?" she asked softly.

"I'm tired," he said with a sigh. "I'm tired of being alone with it."

Jocelyn moved her hand to place it over Jack's. "I'm here," she said, wanting nothing more in that moment than to be the rock that he needed.

"Will has Ava and the girls, Sarah has Jonas and Brian. We take turns checking in on Dad, making sure he's getting by all right."

"But there's no one there to make sure you're all right," Jocelyn said knowingly.

"I don't want to burden any of them simply because I have no one," Jack reasoned. He gazed down the long stretch of backroad, experiencing a mix of peace and unaddressed grief as he opened up. Despite the discomfort it brought him, he knew that he was making the first real step in the right direction since his mother's passing. He turned back to Jocelyn and went on.

"Will and I had talked for a long time on the phone the night before I left," he explained. "He and Ava had just visited my parents and he said that Mom hadn't been doing well. She'd spent most of the visit in bed. In the end, I convinced myself that it would be okay. That nothing would happen while I was gone."

Jocelyn's heart broke for him, seeing so clearly the guilt that he still carried. "You couldn't have known," she asserted.

Jack shook his head, visibly in disagreement.

"Would she have wanted you to cancel?" Jocelyn asked boldly.

"No," he said easily. "She would have been pissed," he added with a surprisingly airy laugh.

"What happened to your girlfriend," Jocelyn asked, pushing down the unexpected feeling of jealousy that threatened to surface.

"I left her in Florida," Jack said unapologetically.

"You *left* her there?"

"As I was packing my bags, after getting the call that Mom was gone, she tried to make a case for staying another night since we'd already paid for the sunset cruise."

Jocelyn cringed.

Jack took in a slow and deliberate breath. It was the most he had talked about his mother's passing in months, and he instantly felt ashamed for it. Since her death, he had only addressed the reality of her passing when it was necessary. He had certainly never opened up about the guilt he wrestled with to anyone. Not even to his siblings. He had learned that most people weren't comfortable talking about death and often avoided the topic entirely. It had been an easy thing to embrace. When his feelings would resurface, he'd drown them out and join in with the mass majority and act as if he hadn't experienced a loss at all.

"Maybe Sarah and Will are right," he conceded. "I need to stop trying to suffocate it. I'm clearly not getting any closer to getting over it."

"I don't know a lot about loss," Jocelyn admitted. "Not the loss of a parent anyway, but I don't think the point is to get over it at all. As long as we have love for someone, our feelings towards them good, bad, or otherwise don't just go away. Love, guilt, sadness, anger. It's all still there. We just need to figure out how to manage those feelings and to let go of the ones that don't make sense to carry anymore."

She squeezed his hand.

"There's no reason to keep holding onto the guilt and the anger," she asserted. "Your mother wouldn't want that. She would want to know that her death hadn't resulted in you losing yourself. Sadness is inevitable. As long as you love someone, you'll ache when they're gone. But I think that's kind of beautiful."

Jack considered Jocelyn's words. He turned his hand over to lace his fingers with hers. His guilt had always felt warranted.

But he realized now that he had held onto both long enough. Continuing to do so would change nothing.

"You're right," he said, feeling an unexpected weight lift from his chest. He pulled Jocelyn's hand up to his lips and brushed a soft kiss across her skin. "Thank you, Jocelyn. Thank you for listening."

The rest of the drive into town had been quiet, though the silence no longer carried the weight of despair as it had before. Jack had spent the past year of his life trying to reconcile a reality he wasn't ready to face. He wouldn't do it anymore. Going forward, he was determined to focus on honoring his mother's legacy instead.

"Here we are," Jack announced as he parked in the lot in front of a small brick building off the main road.

Jocelyn's phone chimed. Instinctively, she cringed. Since Jack's revealing cameo during her meeting, Michael had taken to checking in on her regularly. It was safe to say that Jack's proximity to her life was unsettling to her ex. Whatever reservation he'd had about her going to Virginia before were now doubled, and he needed her to know it. In his own very subtle, seemingly supportive, and manipulative kind of way.

Her phone went off again. She confirmed that the text was from Michael on her lock screen then switched the ringer to silent.

"Do you need to get that?" Jack asked coolly.

"Nope. I would much rather ignore it, actually."

Indifferent, Jack shrugged and cut the engine.

Looking up, Jocelyn took in the modest building that acted as home base for River View Construction. Two black repurposed shipping containers bookending a modestly sized brick building. The face of the office had been affixed with large windows as well as a glass door. Jack clearly had a consistent design style for his brand. In front, wide cement planters ran the length of the structure, interrupted only by the walkway that led to the front door. A trellis covered in wisteria had been built over the flower beds and entryway.

"You keep wowing me," Jocelyn said breathlessly. "What made you think to use shipping containers in your design?"

"I've seen people do a lot of really cool stuff with them," Jack began. "When the business outgrew my dining room table, I knew I wanted to create an office space that married industrial and repurposed design elements. Recycled charm has sort of become an underlined theme for what my company is all about."

Jocelyn got out of the truck and peered through the glass. A few simple antique desks and a small meeting table were visible from the large window front. In the far corner of the office space was an elderly woman taking a phone call, jotting something down on a notepad. When Jack exited the vehicle, they exchanged a friendly wave. He gestured towards the back of the lot and she nodded before returning her attention to her work.

Jocelyn followed Jack and Lady around the side of the building. A few yards from the office stood a nondescript red barn. She was surprised at how ordinary and plain it was, given Jack's inclination to give everything a finished look. It appeared as though he hadn't quite figured out what to do with the structure yet. It was temporary at best, a space of means rather than one with a true purpose.

Jack removed the padlock on the door and pushed it open. Without any windows, the barn was pitch dark inside apart from the faint sunlight that shone through the doors and the cracks that littered the walls of the structure. Jack reached for a switch and turned on a set of wagon wheel chandeliers he had affixed to the rafters.

The space was filled with everything from furniture to boxes of left-over tiles, doors, molding, pavers, cabinets, collectables, and a few pre-cut marble countertops. Despite the potential for chaos, Jocelyn could see that there was a great deal of order in place. Designated sections, organized pallets and wide aisles separating them. In the corner, various light fixtures hung from the beam of the barn's loft. In another corner cans of paint were stacked in rows.

"You've got your own little store back here," Jocelyn mused.

"Every few months I open it up to the public," Jack confirmed. "There's a woman in town who repurposes furniture. She's one of my regulars. You should check out her place one of these days. She's got great stuff."

"Does all this come from your jobs?"

"Word travels fast around here," Jack said. He retrieved a biscuit from a small tin on a podium near the entrance and handed it to Lady, who had been waiting eagerly at his side.

"My clients know that they receive a discount for any salvageable material I take on the job, but after a few years people started calling up wanting to unload unwanted furniture or household items directly. As long as it's something I think I can sell, I take it off their hands for a fair price. Something they might have otherwise donated or thrown out earns them a few extra bucks."

"People buy used paint cans?" Jocelyn asked skeptically.

"I mix my own here," Jack explained. "Combining left-over paint from various jobs or partially used cans that customers drop off. I mix them up out back, paint a swatch and re-can them. They're great for small projects."

"I love that."

"My mom raised us with an intolerance for waste. As a kid, of course, it was a pain in the ass. I remember spending many a long night having a staring contest with my broccoli, just hoping I'd finally win a match." Jack smiled at the memory.

"I remember she used to bring a garbage bag whenever we went to the beach," Jocelyn recalled. "Sarah and I loved helping her clean up all the litter."

"I would have denied it at the time, but you were a big part of why I started listening to what she had to say." Jack picked up an old mason jar and rotated it in his hand. "You'd come back with a bag full of trash, smiling like you'd just saved the world."

"But you never joined in," Jocelyn pointed out. "In fact, I recall you took great pleasure in teasing me about it," she added with a playful raise of her brow.

"When you were there? Gosh, I was *way* too cool to pick up garbage on the beach," he sighed, rolling his eyes. "But when you *weren't* around, I started doing more and more to try and live greener, to repurpose, and to create using salvaged parts.

"When I started up River View Construction, I knew I wanted to be a better steward to the earth. It wasn't just about making something new but giving new life to something old. I wanted to repurpose where I could, purchase local, and choose greener materials and construction techniques." He nodded towards the expansive room. "This is only a part of that vision. One I hope to expand upon."

Jocelyn studied Jack, straining to remember the boy whom she had once loathed so intensely as a child. Everything that made up the man he'd become surprised and excited her, and she couldn't decide which version of him unsettled her more.

"It's really hard to believe that you're the same person," she confessed.

"I hate that that's who you thought I was," Jack admitted, averting his eyes. "I can't say that I'm surprised."

"Sarah always tried to convince me that you were a good brother. I remember one night, after a particularly unpleasant encounter, I prayed that God would make you my other brother. That way you'd be nice to me, too."

Jack closed the space between them, causing Jocelyn's heart to race. "Thank God for unanswered prayers," he said, brushing her hair back from her face with his fingers.

Jocelyn's pulse quickened. Dizzy from Jack's words and his gentle touch, she found herself lost for what to say in response. His piercing stare and the intimacy of the space he'd created between them came as such a shock, and she struggled to make heads or tails of the advance.

She scanned the barn, desperate for a distraction, unable to compartmentalize the electricity that had cropped up between them. Finally, she moved towards the furniture section.

"Oh, I love this," she declared nonchalantly, gesturing towards a large live-edge wood coffee table.

"I'll add it to your tab," Jack replied, seemingly unfazed by her deflection. He went back over to the small podium and retrieved a pile of red SOLD tags and secured one to a leg of the table.

"I could get in some serious trouble here," Jocelyn said, her eyes lighting up. "I've been thinking that the house might sell faster if it comes fully furnished."

"That's a great idea," Jack agreed. "Most people who look to buy in this area are purchasing vacation homes or rental properties and don't have an extra set of furniture lying around."

"I'm not sure if you're being helpful or just a really good salesman."

"Why not both?" he offered with a playful grin and a raise of his brow.

They spent the next hour hunting for pieces that would work well together for the house. In addition, they picked out the beams for the main living space along with a few light fixtures to, as Jocelyn had requested, give the home a soul. For the screened-in porch, they found accent tray tables to put between the rocking chairs and a few strings of Christmas lights and rolls of grapevines to affix to the ceiling for a bit of whimsey. They collected stacks of old books in complimentary colors to display around the house along with the coffee table and two out of the four bed frames they would need to furnish the bedrooms.

Having the collection of misfit donations all to herself, as well as Jack's trained eye to help create a cohesive design for the home, was a dream. Everything he touched, everything he created, was unrefined and organic. Every piece, every detail, worked collectively to tell a unique story. As they married their ideas together, she enjoyed the fact that the story the river house would tell was one they had written together.

Jack drove the truck down the long gravel driveway that led to the river house and parked. Jocelyn studied his posture, wondering if he was as hesitant to end their day together as she was. The way that he gripped the steering wheel, pausing absently before opening the door, she suspected he was.

Exhilarated by the inspiration she had gained from sifting through the barn, her thoughts lingered on the unfinished projects that remained in the house. It had been nearly a week since she had helped Jack on the job and she wanted to do something, anything, to feed her appetite for demolition and interior design. While she hadn't expected to enjoy the added satisfaction that partaking in the renovation offered, she found herself eager to get her hands dirty again.

"I know I sort of *demanded* that we take the day off," Jocelyn ventured. "But I'd be lying if I said I wasn't itching to get back to work."

Jack's shoulders relaxed, visibly relieved by the invitation of her words. He reached for the handle and propped the door open. "I'll meet you at the house in twenty minutes," he said easily. "We'll order some Chinese and you can help me tile the shower."

Jocelyn's eyes lit up, happy that she and Jack were both fueled by the same inclination to stay busy. As much as she had every intention to reintroduce rest into her routine, she was coming to find that keeping busy was sometimes more relaxing than staying still. Besides, working with Jack felt different somehow. Like it wasn't work at all.

"It's a date," she exclaimed.

Jocelyn ducked out of the truck and made her way up to the house, leaving Jack hanging on her words. She had made the remark casually, but after the day they had spent together, their relationship steadily growing in depth, he became increasingly more interested in exploring more intimate possibilities.

Opening up to Jocelyn that morning hadn't just relieved the pressure of his grief, it had liberated him from the bondage of solitude. Initially, it had been easy to enjoy her beauty and think that his longing for her didn't go further than the flesh. It wasn't until he had revealed more of himself to her than he had with any other woman, that he realized that what he wanted was far more than just to satisfy his carnal desires.

He had been testing the line between them all day, flirting with the hope that they might surpass the restrictive boundaries of client and hired hand, though he still couldn't gauge where Jocelyn stood. She was friendly and easy going, not flirtatious by nature, but he had glimpsed a touch of returned intrigue as he worked to determine her feelings toward him.

Jack had started his day as one man and found himself looking out from eyes that saw the world more clearly than he had in months. Perhaps for the first time in years even. Catching his reflection in the rearview mirror, he stroked his overgrown facial hair and decided that he wanted to give Jocelyn a chance to see him more clearly too. Feeling trapped beneath a façade, he suddenly craved complete transparency and a fresh start. He was done hiding from his feelings and most of all, he was done hiding from her.

When Jack entered the kitchen through the sliding glass door, Jocelyn was taken aback. He was not the same man who had come through the same entrance earlier that day. His once lightly bearded face was now clean shaven. His chiseled features were strong and handsome, amplified by his shy and playful smile. His piercing blue eyes reflected far less burden than they had only hours earlier and she wondered how she had failed to notice how much pain he had been in.

"*Damn*," she declared.

"I was overdue for a shave," he replied, matter of fact, passing a hand over his bare chin and raising a charming eyebrow.

"You're very handsome," she responded impulsively.

Without his beard, his appearance was striking. Jack wasn't just modestly good looking, he was gorgeous, and she found herself openly attracted to him.

With his head slightly bowed, Jack's eyes met Jocelyn's, it was a look that made her breath catch, wondering what words might be waiting on the other side of his stare. Words of invitation and seduction she doubted any woman could resist.

She broke her gaze, startled by the feelings that rose to the surface of her conscience. "Chinese is on the way," she informed. "My treat."

Before Jack could approach her, Jocelyn busied herself by getting a couple of glasses of water. Reading her body language, he allowed her to lead despite a mounting desire to take her into his arms. He was quickly discovering that since offering one piece of himself, he was struggling to withhold from her what remained of him, body and soul.

Jack could sense, as they enjoyed a casual lunch at the dining room table, that Jocelyn was as curious about the changing air between them as he was. Though she was visibly more apprehensive to act on her feelings, she seemed to like and easily indulged in a friendly exchange that tested the boundaries of flirtation. Where he had once carelessly relished playing with her emotions as a boy, he now used every opportunity presented to him to flatter her with compliments and admiration, but this time it wasn't a game. Jocelyn was deserving of all of it. She was, he mused, everything he might want in a woman and more. It wasn't just who she was as an individual, it was how she continued to make him feel about himself.

In addition, he was pleased to find that it was quickly becoming more natural for him to talk about his mother. Where he had once shied away from the stories she had been a part of, he now found himself gravitating towards them. As he worked to embrace acceptance over what had happened, he drew closer to the woman who had led him away from the darkness. He found himself both extremely grateful to Jocelyn as well as deeply attracted. It was a fatal combination, he knew, given how fleeting her stay in Virginia was, and he reminded himself that there was no promise in it. She could save him without owing him her heart.

After lunch, they retreated to the bathroom to begin work on the shower. Jack had—with his impressive ability to create space where none had previously existed—managed to double its original size by removing the tub inlay and replacing it with a custom-built shower pan. They could stand comfortably together in the space as he gave Jocelyn lessons on how to spread the mortar evenly and place the tiles.

She was quickly reminded of how relaxed and patient he was as an instructor. He explained the process a few times, demonstrating the right and the wrong way to place the tiles in order to achieve an even surface and neat grout lines.

While Jack had been boldly flirtatious throughout the day, in the intimate space, he remained strictly professional, being careful not to take advantage of any vulnerabilities that the tight fit could impose.

"Your mom must have been a great educator," Jocelyn offered. "I know that I've already said this, but you really do have a natural ability to teach."

"My mom hadn't originally planned to homeschool us," Jack began, smoothing a new section of cement on the bare drywall. "The first few years were hard for both of us. We were learning together, and, for all intents and purposes, I was the guinea pig.

"I was learning how to sit still and manage my time, while she was learning to grow her patience and figure out what approaches worked best for each of us as we all reached school age. We took turns apologizing to each other for years. I would waste an entire afternoon on one section of math, and she would scream after she had exhausted all other pleasantries.

"So many moms came up to her and said things like, 'I could never do it. I'm not patient enough to teach my kids.' I could see how guilty she felt as she assured them that she was far from a saint and that she had yet to master the art of patience.

"The truth is, we learned what patience was, what grace was, and how to forgive each other as well as ourselves at the same time. I don't know many parents who actually took the time to apologize to their kids, but my mom would always seek us out to deliver her sincerest apologies on the hard days when we all tested each other. She wouldn't just say that she was sorry. She made sure to explain that it wasn't something we had done or hadn't done; it was something she was struggling with herself.

"I'm pretty sure the most important lessons she taught me had nothing to do with academics, but with humanity. She was human and she made no excuses for it, but she never stopped striving to grow. By the time Sarah graduated, my mom had earned those diplomas as much as we had."

"Wow," Jocelyn marveled. "That's incredible."

"To this day I really don't know how she did it. I know it wasn't an easy decision for either of my parents to make. There are ups and downs to every choice concerning a child's formative education," Jack considered. "I'm sure my behavior didn't add any points to the pros column," he added with a chuckle.

"Now that you mention it..." Jocelyn laughed easily. "Really though, it sounds like a great experience for the whole family. Hard as hell I'm sure, but it sounds like your mother grew a lot from teaching you guys, and you obviously got some great lessons along the way in how to teach others, whether that was the intention or not.

"I don't know many people who would hire young adults. And you have such a way with them. It would be easy to assume that high school and college students aren't ready to take on the responsibilities and work ethic that construction demands, but you clearly don't see it that way."

"I never really related what I do with teaching before, but I guess you're right," Jack said contemplatively.

"Do you think you'll homeschool your kids someday?"

"If my wife is on board with it, yeah," Jack allowed. "I'd like to play an active role in my children's education, like my dad did, but I know a lot of the responsibility would fall on her. Also, everyone has different views. I feel strongly about homeschooling, but I don't intend to assert my preference over hers."

"Yeah, that makes sense," Jocelyn replied, considering it herself.

She couldn't help but try to imagine herself in such a role. It was a sacrifice that she had never thought of making herself. Her mother had stayed home with her and Andrew until they were both school aged, but then she'd returned to work. While the idea of stepping away from the corporate world for a few years was difficult to imagine, it was a decision she had already made peace with. Afterall, she didn't have so much as a prospective husband at the moment. She didn't exclude the possibility that he might choose to stay home either. If she was the breadwinner, it made sense. But to put her career on hold indefinitely? Was that what being a homeschool parent would look like? Was there any way to balance two full-time positions? She imagined it would feel like an impossible task.

Despite the discomfort the idea delivered, Jocelyn spent the next few minutes contemplating it. What she wanted in the end, after all, was a family of her own. She knew that status and money alone were hollow ambitions without a family to share it with, and she certainly wasn't willing to strive for either at too high a cost. She eventually wanted to settle down, but if one choice made more sense than the other, would she choose to deny it to her children for selfish reasons? Was it fair to say that a career was selfish? In the end, she found herself more conflicted then when she'd begun the line of questioning.

Jocelyn quickly reminded herself that Jack's plans were not hers. Why then, she struggled to reconcile, did his dreams weigh so heavily on her heart?

Work was a welcome distraction as Jack's feelings for Jocelyn grew stronger. He genuinely enjoyed the chance to work with her again and allowed his attention to remain on the task at hand. She was eager to learn and a quick study at that.

Even some of his own crew still struggled to achieve the steady hand that was required to evenly lay tile that she possessed. He couldn't tell what he found more attractive, her beauty or her work ethic. As he stole a glance at her, her golden hair loose around her shoulders, and her eyes fixed on the job, he decided he didn't have to choose.

They each worked at opposite corners, building their respective walls up towards the ceiling. Two hours came and went easily and neither seemed to notice the time lapse.

Nearly finished with the job, Jack asked, "How is your side coming along?"

In unison, they turned toward one another. Their bodies, mere inches apart, both stiffened. Jack's lips were close enough to brush the bridge of Jocelyn's nose. A space they had worked in with room to spare only moments before now felt impossibly intimate.

Jack's heart pounded in the confines of his chest, and he felt the mounting attraction that had been building between him and Jocelyn reach its summit. Her skin was soft, her lips full and inviting. Taking her lack of retreat as a tentative invitation, he slowly raised his free hand to her face and cupped it gently. She let her eyes flutter closed and lifted her chin slightly to receive his advance. He secured the gap between their lips and pressed his fiercely to hers.

Though he had meant to taste her gently, Jack no longer possessed the ability to restrain himself. He pulled her in closer and she dropped her trowel, taking hold of his shirt in both hands, clutching it in the hopes of grounding herself. He savored her as a man who had forgotten what intense desire could feel like. What it could taste like. In that moment, he knew that before Jocelyn he had been starving, mistaking sheer survival for nourishment. He kissed her greedily, hungrily, unable to restrain himself as he moved his free hand down her body to grip her waist.

When she pulled away slightly, he had to force himself to stop, holding onto her hips to regain his center. Breathless, he pressed his lips to her forehead.

"I'm sorry," he murmured.

"No, no," Jocelyn whispered. "It's okay, I just..." she trailed off, backing away.

She exited the shower, working feverishly to compose herself. It was all she could do to stop herself from doing something she might regret. "I'm sorry, I…I need to go wash up. You…um, you can let yourself out."

Jack rubbed his jaw, still tense from their kiss, and let out a groan. "*Shit.*"

Chapter Eight

Jocelyn had tossed and turned all that night and had spent her Sunday immersed in small projects around the house, actively averting her eyes from the houseboat that housed the source of her confliction. Her feelings about the kiss she and Jack had shared were mixed. She was drawn to him. It was no secret that he felt the same attraction towards her. But that didn't mean she was willing to enter into a relationship with him. Just the sheer thought of it terrified her. Falling for Jack felt like a deliberate choice to drop everything else in her life that she had a hold of, and it just wasn't something she was prepared or willing to do.

When Monday morning arrived, only hours after she had finally drifted off to sleep after another restless night, she wasn't ready for the ring of the doorbell that woke her. It wasn't like Jack to use the bell, she thought drowsily, pushing through a haze of sleep. He always let himself in and got straight to work. Checking her phone for the time, she noticed that it was eight o'clock on the dot. It wasn't lost on her that she also had three new text messages from Michael. Rolling her eyes, she abandoned her phone on the nightstand and pried herself out of bed.

Michael had a way of coming on strong in a subtle way. He never texted her with professions of love or attempts to reminisce about old times. He mostly just discussed work, provided office gossip (which she normally couldn't get enough of,) and asked her how things were going with the house. There was no heavy-handed probing or flirtation, but she knew his tactics well. If he was in her thoughts, if he was part of her day, then he had a chance. Or so he seemed to think.

No matter the attention Jocelyn was getting from the two men of close proximity in her life, she couldn't commit herself to firmly addressing either of their advances. Jack was raw male. He was sexy and hardworking and still very mysterious. His invitation had been hungry and alarmingly seductive. He was a man any woman would be happy to enter into a romance of any kind with. Michael, on the other hand, was like pulling on an old sweatshirt from high school that still fit the way it used to. He was reliable, familiar, and comfortable.

Michael was a part of the life that Jocelyn would eventually be returning to, and he was unwavering in his apparent efforts to remind her of it with his strategically placed friendship. Given the two very different men, and their contrasting approaches of pursuit, Jocelyn reflexively wanted nothing to do with either of them. If for no better reason than for fear of failing to make the right choice. Or for falling under the false impression that they were the only two she had.

After yanking on a pair of jeans and swapping out her t-shirt for a fresh one, Jocelyn hurried downstairs. When she answered the door, she was surprised to see Jonas where she had expected to see Jack.

"Sorry, did I wake you?" he offered in apology. "Jack said he usually starts at eight."

"Oh, no, it's fine," Jocelyn said reassuringly. She opened the door in invitation, unable to banish a yawn from escaping. "Will you be helping him today?"

"No, I, uh…" Jonas paused, choosing his words carefully. "Jack's mother passed away a year ago today," he informed. "He asked me to fill in at the last minute."

"Oh my gosh," Jocelyn exclaimed with remorse. "He only just told me the other day and I've already managed to forget."

Her heart twisted with guilt. "I wish I had thought to insist on giving him the day off. I feel so insensitive."

"Don't do that to yourself." Jonas put a reassuring hand on Jocelyn's shoulder. "You've got a lot on your plate and a limited amount of time to do it in. He understands that. That's what I'm here for."

"How is Sarah doing?" Jocelyn probed, making a mental note to reach out to her friend later.

"She's all right. She and Brian are with my parents right now. She will probably head over to her dad's later."

Jocelyn shook her head. "I can't imagine what they're all going through."

"I don't think Sarah expected it to be this tough," Jonas admitted. "As the new matriarch of sorts, she works really hard to be positive for her brothers and Peter, but I think some days the weight is more than she can carry alone."

"That's a lot of pressure," Jocelyn echoed, leading Jonas through the house towards the kitchen.

"I don't think the guys realize it," Jonas went on. "If they did, they wouldn't let her carry that kind of burden. But when a mother plays a role in the lives of her children like Margret did, it leaves a big void. I think Sarah's just trying to help fill it as best as she can."

Jocelyn searched for the right words and came up empty handed. She couldn't picture what it might be like to lose her mother. Her heart, her mind, or soul—whichever it was—wouldn't allow her thoughts to travel to such a place. While she had experienced loss, even recently with her grandmother, she had no idea what the loss of a parent might do to a person's world and way of life.

After making them both a cup of coffee, Jocelyn returned to her room with the intention of starting on her work for the day. Sitting cross-legged on the bed, staring blankly at her computer screen, her thoughts kept going back to Jack, alone with the heavy weight of his sorrow. The feelings she was developing for him and the conflict they stirred up in her heart were pushed to the back of her mind. Now, all she could think of was the man who had only just begun to scratch the surface of his grief. She suspected he wasn't prepared to endure the anniversary of his mother's passing on his own, no matter how much he wanted for it to appear otherwise.

After pacing around her room and peering out the window in the direction of the houseboat countless times—with no sign of Jack—she decided that doing nothing was far from enough.

When Jocelyn approached the houseboat, she noticed that Jack was seated at the table with a bottle of whiskey that was nearly empty. Lady rested her head at his feet as if to provide her master with what comfort she could.

His head was heavy in his hands when she boarded the boat. She edged the front door open, fighting the feeling that she was intruding, knowing that the last thing he needed was to be alone. Without words, she pulled up the seat across from him. His posture straightened and he let out a heavy sigh.

The silence that sat between them was weighted, but Jocelyn knew it was he who must end it.

After an immeasurable passage of time, Jack finally spoke. "I'm not sure why I thought it wouldn't be this hard," he said in a gruff voice. "After the other day…" He trailed off and shook his head. "I guess I just thought I had crawled out of this hole I've been living in."

Jack was willing to admit that he hadn't taken many steps in the grieving process. He had pushed his feelings down for so long, he had managed to convince himself that opening up once might be enough to ease the whole of his grief in one fell swoop. Then the guilt had washed it all away again. The guilt that only days before the anniversary of his mother's passing, he had pursued a woman who clearly didn't return his feelings. To do what exactly? Mask his sorrow with something sweet to make the bitter taste of reality more tolerable? Wasn't that how he had ended up in Florida when he should have been at his mother's side in her darkest hours?

Jocelyn could hear the whiskey in his voice. She wanted so badly to provide him with comfort, support, anything that might help him work through the pain.

"I'm so sorry," she said, wishing there was more she could offer him than a shallow apology.

Jack dropped his hands on the table, defeated.

Jocelyn moved the bottle aside then reached for his hands.

"Why don't you tell me more about her?" she offered.

Jack longed to feel the relief that he had the first time he'd opened up to Jocelyn again, but he was just as afraid to let himself believe that merely talking about it would make everything better. Still, he knew he couldn't continue to bottle up his anguish in the name of stubborn guilt. Jocelyn had been right. It was a pointless emotion to continue holding onto. He couldn't change the choices he had made a year ago, but he could control which ones he made going forward.

After a long pause, he finally said, "My mom was the most gracious and selfless woman I've ever known. I didn't see it until she died. Not really." He shook his head to sever the pain the admission delivered.

"She had played the role of my support system, my confidant, my cheer section so seamlessly that I'd managed to overlook the fact that she was the starring role in her own life. She had her own hopes and dreams. Her own past. Her own story." Jack fought against the lump in his throat as Jocelyn squeezed his hands tightly. "Once she was gone, I realized I'd missed out on the opportunity to learn her full story." A single tear escaped the corner of his eye and he wiped it away angrily. "I thought I had more time."

Jocelyn wrestled with her own emotions. "I can't imagine what that must be like," she offered. "Does your dad talk about her often?"

Jack shook his head. "When I visit, I usually just fix things up around the house. I don't bring her up because I don't want to make it harder for him. I'm pretty sure he does the same."

"It must be difficult at first," Jocelyn said with understanding "but I don't think I could lose someone I cared about that deeply then feel as if I couldn't talk about them anymore."

Jack's mind and body were heavy and uneasy with emotion and alcohol, but the weight of her words lifted a pressure from his heart he hadn't expected.

"I should talk to Dad more," he allowed.

"I know that it's not the same as sitting down with your mom, but you can ask him all the questions you might have liked to ask her. Get to know her in the ways you didn't have a chance to when she was alive.

"When my grandfather passed, and since my grandmother's passing, my family and I have made it a point to talk about them whenever we can. I learn something new about them every time I get together with my mom." She waited for Jack to meet her eyes before saying, "I bet your dad has got some great stories."

Jack offered her a glancing smile.

They sat like that for a long time without cause or reason to stir the air. As they remained in thoughtful silence, Jocelyn took Jack in another layer at a time. He was the kind of man anyone would easily dismiss as tough, sturdy, and unbreakable. She imagined it was easy for his friends and family to overlook the chinks in his armor. But as strong as Atlas was, the world was no lighter for it. The fact that most men believed they had to stifle their pain in the name of an unfair standard of masculinity was unreasonable. Even a man raised in what she could only imagine was a sensitive and nurturing environment had been hardened by a world that expected him to be carved from granite. As beautiful as Jack's virility was, she could see the weight of its required hardness slowly crushing him.

Finally, a smile tugged at the corner of Jack's lips. "She loved reading to us," he began. "She'd read everything from *The Lord of the Rings* to *Harry Potter*. The longer the series, the better. She wasn't the kind of mom that read the same book every night from memory. She wanted to read us stories that could stretch over a few months or even years. We would all get really invested in the characters and she gave them each their own voice. The way she read; it was like we were there. I remember being in high school and she still read to us after breakfast and before bed as if it were perfectly normal."

"I love that. That's really special."

"It was," he agreed somberly.

As Jack went on, Jocelyn continued to study him. A man defined by strength and his physical abilities was undeniably riddled with vulnerability brought on by the unexpected passing of his mother. As he spoke about her, she couldn't help but wonder how much her loss had shaped him. Had his edges smoothed or become more jagged? How different had the man before her been a year earlier? Had he been more carefree and careless or perhaps more rigid and mechanical? As much as Jack had changed since she'd last seen him, she knew that the past year of his life must have changed him dramatically.

It was the most Jack had talked about his mother since she had died, and he silently chided himself for it. He had worked so tediously to protect himself from feeling pain that he had unwittingly managed to deny himself the comfort that her memory brought him as a result.

Loss, Jack realized, painted loved ones in a beautiful portrait of their greatest qualities, most honorable triumphs, and fondest memories. As he reflected on his mother's life, he came to a much greater understanding of who she was, not just as a mother, but as a woman. He could see, as he told Jocelyn about the kind of person she was, and the moments he saw as definitive of her character, how influential she had truly been in every facet of his life.

Not only had the time together allowed Jack to reflect on his mother, but it had also given him the opportunity to get to know Jocelyn better. In many ways, and perhaps because it was what he was looking for, she reminded him of his mother. She listened. Really listened. Not to reply, but to allow him the space to say what he had been keeping in for far too long. Where others might offer insight or an opinion when a break in conversation allowed the opportunity to plant it, Jocelyn urged him instead to share more with gentle prompts. She was refreshing and easy to talk to and before he knew it an hour had come and gone.

"Thank you," Jack said sincerely. "Thank you for checking in on me."

"Of course," Jocelyn replied sweetly. "I couldn't let you go through today alone. I'm sorry I hadn't thought to reach out to you until Jonas showed up this morning and reminded me what today was."

"You have no reason to apologize," Jack insisted, piercing Jocelyn with a gaze so fierce she was unsettled by it. His words, though they said one thing, she could sense meant another. *You have given me more than anyone has in a very long time.*

Jack dropped his eyes and pushed his chair back, stumbling to stand. "I'm clearly not as sober as I thought I was," he said, balancing himself on the back of the chair.

"Why don't you hop in the shower," Jocelyn offered. "I'll make some coffee."

Jack staggered again. "Yeah," he agreed. "That's probably a good idea."

Jocelyn busied herself, tidying up after putting the kettle on. Listening to Jack speak so warmly of his mother left her with a growing urgency to call her own. Not only was she grateful for her mom's role in her life, but she also knew now on a much deeper level the loss that her mother was currently experiencing herself.

Though it was a poor substitute for a phone call, she sent a sympathetic text message to her mother and a similar one to Sarah as well. She intended to call them both as time allowed, but she didn't want any more time to pass before extending her love and condolences to them both.

Jocelyn had poured Jack and herself each a cup of coffee and was responding to a message from Sarah when he exited the bathroom with a towel fastened around his waist.

"I...I should go," she offered bashfully.

Jack ran a hand over his wet hair. "No, please stay. I'll just be a minute."

Unsure of how to afford him privacy in such a space, Jocelyn turned to face the front door, keeping her back to him.

"Thanks for the coffee," he said from the other side of the room. "I'm sorry you had to see me like this."

"Don't worry about it," Jocelyn called back over her shoulder. Lady joined her, licking her hand in invitation. She petted the dog's broad head, grateful for something to occupy her attention.

"You can turn around now," Jack said, a moment later, placing a hand on her shoulder.

She turned to face him. He was dressed in a navy t-shirt and a pair of black sweatpants. It was the most relaxed she had seen him. Despite his bloodshot eyes and dizzy stance, anchored by the kitchen counter, he appeared to be in a much healthier state than the one she had found him in.

"You look better."

"I feel better," he allowed.

His sobriety, Jack knew for now, was fleeting, but clarity washed over him like a tidal wave. No woman had ever sought him out in a storm as Jocelyn had and his gratitude for the gesture was impossible to measure.

After a brief and wordless hesitation, he brought her into his arms, and she tucked herself into the hug easily. He held her tightly, resting his head against hers. It was nothing like the hungry possession of the kiss they had shared, but an embrace between good friends. When they parted, he gazed into her eyes and took a deep breath.

"About what happened the other night."

Jocelyn felt her heartbeat quicken and, paranoid, feared that he could hear it.

"I'm really sorry."

In truth, he wasn't sorry for the kiss itself. More accurately, he was regretful that he had been brazen about it. If they were to kiss again, it would be under different circumstances and with more clarity. Until then, he would do his best to respect the fact that she so clearly desired to keep their relationship platonic.

"I want you to know that I respect you, Jocelyn. I'm sorry if I made you uncomfortable. It won't happen again. I promise." He took a few steps back, as if to emphasize his point.

"There's no need to apologize," Jocelyn said, hoping she was convincingly nonchalant in her delivery.

In that moment she wanted to flee. To put space between them so that she might be able to better construct the boundary she hoped to maintain. When she was around Jack it was much more difficult to convince herself that it was what she really wanted. Everything about him felt complicated. While his promise delivered peace of mind, she would be lying to say it hadn't also brought on an unexpected rush of disappointment. Jack, even in his most disorderly and helpless state, was the most attractive man she had ever met. And it wasn't just his looks. His beauty was soul deep. Even now, as he watched her with his romantic blue eyes, Jocelyn knew she would never be able to fully untangle her feelings for him.

When he reached for his cup of coffee and handed her the other mug, she accepted it and let out a breath she hadn't realized she'd been holding. She resolved herself to preserve the pretense that she was in control over and firm on her feelings for him.

"Tell me," Jack began, taking a seat at the head of the table. "How is Andrew doing?"

Relieved that her brother was the new topic of conversation, Jocelyn took the seat adjacent to him. "He's good," she said, then sipped her coffee. "He's in the Army. He works with computers, but don't ask me what his actual job is. I swear he tells me whenever I see him, and his heavy use of acronyms just leaves me more confused than I was before."

"Is he married?"

"Yes, married with three kids."

"Is he in Texas too?"

"He's stationed in Georgia now, actually. In a year they'll be moving again. I think he and Claire want to explore someplace new while the kids are still young. It's no secret my parents and I are hoping he'll be stationed in Texas though."

"That must be hard. Uprooting every few years."

"I don't even think about it honestly. Andrew and Claire make it look so easy. Exciting even. They have their system. But it must be harder at times than they let on. Especially when Andrew is away. Claire took on the mentality a long time ago to romanticize it all. If you think of it as an adventure, as a new opportunity, or as a chance to grow closer, that's exactly what it will be. It seems to work for them."

"How do you like her?"

"Oh, I love Claire like a sister," Jocelyn replied sincerely. "She keeps Andrew motivated. Not to say that I think he wouldn't be successful without her, but I see the fire she lights within him, and I appreciate how much she supports him."

"That's great," Jack replied.

They each nursed their coffee for a moment. Still fighting through the fog of his clouded mind, Jack knew that he wanted Jocelyn to stay. Though he sensed she was putting off responsibilities that needed her attention, her company brought him the kind of peace nothing else could. He had reestablished a boundary between them, not for his sake, but for hers. It was a lie to say that physical attraction was as far as his feelings for Jocelyn went. As the alcohol pulsed through him and his control waned, he knew it would be difficult to respect the intentions he had only just proclaimed.

"It appears our siblings have all found love," he offered, aware that his direction for their conversation was more careless than he might have ventured in a clearer state of mind. He leaned in. "There must be a special man in your life," he added.

Jocelyn blinked a few times, working to calm her nerves after the unexpected question. Her thoughts went to Michael, and she internally scolded herself for it. Damn him for planting himself so strategically into her life even now that they were thousands of miles apart and very much uncommitted to one another.

"It's complicated," she heard herself say.

No. I'm not seeing anyone. That was what she meant to say. So why hadn't she? Because Jack was the kind of man a woman would sacrifice everything for, she thought boldly. Sexy, smart, hardworking, funny, and a family man. She could tell that he had the potential to become all consuming. She had far too much to lose and no guarantee that he wouldn't break her heart.

Squinting at her, Jack wondered exactly what *complicated* meant, but he couldn't find the words to delve further into the inquiry. Without a solid *I'm single*, he'd lost his nerve to challenge her. Not to mention, he was trying to convince

Jocelyn, as well as himself, that he wasn't interested in entering into a romantic relationship with her.

Jocelyn wasn't the kind of woman he would have the intention to love and leave, and the truth of the matter was, he was hardly in a place to start a serious relationship either. That didn't change the fact, however, that he was drawn to her.

As the alcohol that ran through his veins licked at his thoughts, making it impossible to care and considerably more difficult to practice a respectable etiquette, he allowed her to center him once again, gazing unapologetically upon her beauty. She was, he considered, the calm in the storm.

Jocelyn noticed Jack's eyes growing heavy as they raked across her body and finally settled on her face. Clearly unable to command his stare to do otherwise, he drank her in. She imagined that, despite his efforts to flush the liquor from his system with a hot shower and caffeine, only time could deliver him true sobriety.

"Listen, I better get back up to the house," she said, rising from the table and depositing her cup in the sink. "I have a meeting at one o'clock and I need to get a few things done before then."

Jack moved from his seat, more calculated than before, but still unsteady. "I'll probably head up there to give Jonas a hand in a bit," he said moving to the carafe to pour himself another cup of coffee.

"With all due respect," Jocelyn offered. "You should get some sleep."

Jack rubbed the back of his neck. "Yeah. You're probably right," he agreed. "Thanks again," he said offering up a sweet smile. "I'm sorry you had to see me like this."

"There's no reason to apologize." Jocelyn made her way toward the door. "Now get some rest."

Jack grabbed the bottle of whiskey from the table and brought it over to the sink. Removing the cap, he poured the remaining contents down the drain. Change wouldn't happen with just a catalyst, he considered, it would also need a significant amount of grace and intention. Talking openly with Jocelyn about his mother had provided him with the much-needed reminder that she hadn't been strong and successful in life because it came easily to her, but because she was never too proud to forgive her own shortcomings and try again. Jack had spent the last year of his life suffocated by his pride, unwilling to admit that he'd made mistakes and that he wasn't broken, only bruised.

With the right care, he truly believed now that he could heal. It wouldn't happen overnight. In fact, it would likely take a lifetime, but the restored hope that he could overcome the loss of his mother was enough to keep him moving forward.

Chapter Nine

The next few weeks passed in a blur as Jack and his crew worked overtime to complete the remodel on the first floor. They were only half-way through the second month of Jocelyn's stay in Virginia when they began work on the second story renovations.

Well ahead of schedule, Jack began to daydream about what more free time with Jocelyn might allow. He didn't discount the possibility that wrapping up early could mean she may decide to leave before she had originally planned to.

While they remained friendly, even flirtatious on occasion, the electricity that had been sparked during the kiss they'd shared had since receded. Most days, he was so focused on other things, he didn't give it much thought. They were both so busy with work that neither seemed to have time to entertain the idea of something growing between them.

All the same, he couldn't ignore the reality that he wished that things could be different. Jocelyn was gracious and friendly, nearly flawless in her façade of disinterest, then he would catch her watching him with a quiet contemplation. As if she too was considering the pursuit of something more. At times, she seemed as torn as he still felt by the sensual energy that existed between them, but he had made too many missteps already. If they were going to move toward one another, he had decided, it was she who would have to take the first step.

As they had become accustomed to doing each evening, Jack and Jocelyn retired to a pair of rocking chairs on the screened-in porch. They rocked absently for an immeasurable amount of time, taking in the scenery and reflecting on the day's accomplishments.

Jack studied the woman beside him as she looked out over the sleepy landscape that stretched out before them. Her hair was wavy and uncontrolled, cascading down her shoulders with abandon. It was lighter than when she'd first arrived; sun-bleached and set free from office life. In contrast, her skin was tanned and glowing. Her gray blue eyes reflected the twinkle of the lights he had fastened to the ceiling, woven into the tangled branches of the twisted grapevines. Her lips were relaxed, a slight part suggesting she had something to say but was in no rush to say it. Enveloped in a light blanket, despite the warm night air, her posture beckoned to be held in a loving embrace. He wanted to wrap his arms around her and tuck her head against his chest. The effort that was required of him to resist the urge to do just that was close to faltering.

"It's so beautiful, isn't it?" Jocelyn remarked softly.

Unable to pull his eyes away from her, Jack replied, "Yes, very beautiful."

"I'm going to miss this place," she admitted.

The words sliced through him, an unwelcome reminder that this wasn't the beginning of a new life, simply a dream nestled inside the old one.

"Who says you have to leave?" he offered boldly.

"My life is back in Austin," she replied automatically.

While he knew that Jocelyn had never intended to stay, Jack wondered if it was so hard for her to picture a life in Virginia. A life with him. Was she as determined to return to Austin as she claimed? Without opening her eyes to other possibilities, he wasn't sure what he could really expect. He didn't want to keep pretending not to care for her. In fact, it was a physical strain to do so, but he respected her too much to push her. If she ever gave him so much as the slightest indication that she returned his feelings, he would do whatever he could to show her the dream that was clear in his own mind.

"Life is where you are," he couldn't help but say.

Jocelyn couldn't think of a rebuttal. It was an argument she already wrestled with herself. Austin was familiar. It was where she had spent the past twenty-four years of her life. Her parents were there. Her condo. Her career. But she wondered...did that all really mean that her life was there too?

In a few short weeks, Jocelyn would be headed back to Austin for her team's mock presentation. A month later, she would be gone for good. She wanted that promotion. To allow for all she had worked for fall by the wayside because she was enjoying her time in Virginia and Jack's company was careless in the least and insane at best. They weren't even together. She knew that it was mostly her doing, and she was inclined to keep it that way.

Jack allowed the space between them to fill with the comfortable silence they'd become accustomed to sharing. He didn't want to push her. A woman's will was her own and the last thing he wanted was to make an effort to bend Jocelyn's.

"I forgot to tell you," Jocelyn finally said, ending the stalemate. "Andrew and his family are visiting this weekend. I was thinking it might be fun, for old time's sake, if we get all the siblings together. What do you say?"

"That sounds great. I'll reach out to Sarah and Will tomorrow."

Jack couldn't change the circumstances that surrounded Jocelyn's inevitable departure, but he could appreciate that, if nothing else, they had been given the chance to rewrite their story.

***

"That's it, I'm getting a limousine next time," Andrew announced as he exited the rental. "I can just raise the window and forget that I've got three screaming kids in the back. I don't even *care* what they do back there. Insurance will cover it!"

Jocelyn could hear the feral screams of her nieces and nephew permeating from the backseat of the car parked in the driveway. She put a hand to her mouth to muffle her laughter as Andrew and Claire unbuckled their children, releasing them as one might unhook a shark from a fishing line.

"I have to pee!" Wyatt screamed.

"I pee! I pee!" Elizabeth exclaimed.

"*Oh geez*," Andrew reached for his daughter as if he were approaching an armed bomb. "Have kids, they said. It'll be fun, they said."

"Long drive?" Jocelyn asked with a forced smile.

Andrew just stared blankly, holding his daughter at arm's length.

"*Long drive* was thirty minutes in," Claire informed. "If nothing else, kids are consistently inconsistent. Last time they were angels, today they were out for blood."

Jocelyn approached her sister-in-law who was being tugged towards the beach by Vivian and wrapped her in a welcoming embrace. "I'm so glad you guys are here."

"Give me thirty minutes and a stiff drink and I'll be glad too," Claire said with a delirious chuckle.

Once inside, Jocelyn gave Andrew and Claire a tour of the main floor. The kids even settled down long enough for her to show off a few of her favorite details that Jack had been able to include. The coffered ceiling he had created using the salvaged beams, the frosted glass inlays he'd added last minute to the kitchen cabinets, and the fixtures he'd installed that they'd found in the barn.

"The pictures do it no justice," Claire said, astonished. "This is *amazing*. The paint job is phenomenal," she added with a wink.

Jocelyn feigned bashfulness.

"And you said *Jack Evans* is your contractor?" Andrew asked, running his hand over the kitchen counter.

"I still can't believe he's the same boy who tortured you throughout your entire childhood," Claire remarked. "Small world."

Jocelyn shrugged her confirmation. "He's upstairs actually." She gestured towards the muffled nondescript noises that came from the upstairs bathroom.

"Hey! Jack!" Andrew called up the stairs.

With a playful gallop, Lady rounded the bend appearing at the top of the steps. She bounded down the newly finished staircase with practiced paws.

"Woah," Andrew said with hesitation.

"Don't worry, Lady's a sweetheart," Jocelyn informed, kneeling to greet the friendly Rottweiler.

Before they could receive permission, all three children had the canine surrounded. Well versed in child wrangling, she distributed sloppy kisses amongst them evenly, then pounced at the ground, announcing her eagerness to play.

"Settle down, you big bowling ball," Jack called from the top of the steps. "I don't think Andrew wants you getting any strikes with his children."

Jack descended the steps and reached out his hand to his old friend. "Andrew, it's been a lifetime, hasn't it?"

Andrew returned the handshake. Together they seemed to decide the gesture was too formal and they entered into a friendly hug.

"Wow," Andrew said. "I'm not sure why I expected to see a chubby little kid come bounding down the stairs."

Jack laughed.

Jocelyn didn't miss Claire's effort to crane her neck and shoot her an accusatory glance, as if to say, "*This* is Jack?" She shot back a dismissive glare then turned her attention to her brother just as Claire mocked fanning herself.

"Jack has invited Sarah and Will over for the evening," Jocelyn informed. "It'll be just like old times."

"I'll do my best to resist pouring sand down your bathing suit," Jack joked.

Jocelyn laughed awkwardly. Somehow, at their current juncture, the act was akin to something more sensual in nature as she played the scene out in her mind. She quickly banished the unwanted fantasy and plastered on an easy smile on her face in an effort to feign nonchalance.

The banter between his sister and his old friend wasn't missed on Andrew. He could see the hesitation in Jocelyn's posture. The way that she stood so firmly in her effort to maintain space between them.

"So, you guys have had plenty of time to catch up," Andrew probed. "How's life, Jack? Will your family be joining us tonight?"

If subtlety had been his goal, Jocelyn could see that her brother had missed his mark by a mile. She groaned internally, knowing full well what he was aiming at.

Jack, ever the casual diplomat, shrugged. "It's just me and Lady."

"She's a beautiful dog," Claire offered, stepping in before her husband could steer the conversation back into dangerous waters. If Jocelyn's expression was any indication, that was the last thing she wanted. "What made you pick a Rottweiler? They don't have the best reputation."

"She picked me," Jack said simply. "But she's won me over. I don't see myself owning another breed now."

"She's winning the kids over too," Claire granted, watching her three children probe and crowd the large animal without so much as a tucked tail in response. Whenever their proximity became too much, Lady simply licked them to the ground, even if only long enough for them to wipe their slimy cheeks clean.

"I'm just about done for the day," Jack informed, digging a hand into the pocket of his jeans. "Why don't you guys get settled in and I'll let Sarah and Will know to head over. We can order a bunch of pizzas and party on the houseboat."

"*Party*?" Jocelyn said nervously.

Jack smirked.

"Houseboat?" Claire asked enthusiastically, peering through the window to catch a glimpse.

"*That's* where you live?" Andrew asked in amazement.

"Home sweet home," Jack confirmed.

"*Damn*. I want your life," Andrew replied dreamily.

"*Excuse me?*" Claire said with a sideways glance.

"Sorry," Andrew said cringing.

"Uh huh," Claire replied, feigning forgiveness.

"It was a *really* long drive," Andrew directed at Jack.

Jack laughed. "Solitude has its upsides," he confirmed.

After grabbing a quick shower, Jack invited Jocelyn and her family over to wait for the arrival of Sarah's and Will's families. He'd performed one-and-a-half detailed tours of the houseboat, including an inside look at the engine as well as the plumbing system. Elements Jocelyn hadn't cared to inquire about the first time and to which she maintained a disinterest in exploring this time. The kids had discovered the basket of toys early on and had raced to the bottom of the cache in record time, delighting in each toy they pulled out. By the time Sarah and Will arrived, only a few moments apart, the three children had taken over the dining room table and were scribbling energetically on printer paper.

Sarah's son Brian and Will's two young girls Diana who was three, and Mary, a wobbly one-year-old, quickly joined Andrew's children at the table in no need of formal introductions.

As Sarah and Jonas introduced themselves to Andrew and Claire, Jocelyn edged around the room to meet Will and his wife. While Will was a year older than her, at thirty-five, he appeared to be younger due to his youthful and boyish good looks. His hair was dark to match his brown eyes and a playful grin tugged at his lips. His eyes sparkled with a childlike glimmer and his dimples softened the hard lines of his face. He was more slender than Jack and a few inches shorter, but he was handsome in his own right, albeit his good looks being less forward than Jack's were. His wife was a mousy brunette, petite and elegant like a ballerina. Despite the evidence that proved otherwise, it was hard to believe that her body had carried and delivered two children.

"Will," Jocelyn exclaimed. "It's so great to see you again!" She threw her arms around him then held him at arm's length. "You've hardly changed," she exclaimed.

"Ever fighting the hands of time," he countered. "This is Ava, my wife. She gets all the credit."

"He's my most perpetual child," Ava said with a smirk. "It's great to meet you," she added politely, bringing Jocelyn in for a hug. "Will filled me in on the ride over. It sounds like the five of you were inseparable growing up."

"We had some great summers here," Jocelyn allowed. Though her relationship with Jack had certainly blossomed in the past month or so, she couldn't attach the word "inseparable" to the memories they'd shared as kids.

"Pizza's here," Jack called over, pointing to the confused delivery man standing poised on the dock.

"I'll get it," Jonas offered.

Everyone moved over to the dining room table and each respective parent took on the task of corralling their children along with their scattered art supplies. Together, the eight adults worked to set the kids up with food at the table then headed out onto the boat's deck to enjoy their pizza, opting for quiet over available seating.

Ava balanced Mary on her hip, a practiced hand as she fed small morsels of food to her daughter between taking bites of her own pizza. When he finished his first slice, Will scooped Mary up and allowed her to take greedy mouthfuls of his second helping, offering his wife a chance to enjoy her food in peace. Jocelyn looked on, marveling at how well the couple balanced responsibilities with one another as if it wasn't even a question. She couldn't help but think to herself, *that's the kind of relationship I want to have some day.*

While the men often gravitated towards one another, inclined to discuss politics, sports, and business, the women congregated by the windows to keep a close eye on the kids as they caught up on introductions and updates. Still, they managed to all flock together and maintain an open and fluid assembly of personalities.

The easy atmosphere and the way in which Jocelyn clicked so effortlessly with everyone pressed on her heart. Jack's family was wonderful. They were exactly the kind of people she wanted to be surrounded by in her daily life.

Each of his siblings had chosen a complimentary spouse that added to their collective dynamic and the magic of the mixture was tangible. Will's humor was dry and unforced. He managed to find the comedy in nearly everything without taking away from the underlying mood of the discussion. Ava, the flattering counterpart to her husband, was surprisingly funny despite a strong air of sophistication. Jonas, stoic in his physical presence, was in fact one of the warmest and friendliest people Jocelyn had ever met. In addition to supplying fun anecdotes from work, he captivated the group with stories of his upbringing in Haiti. Sarah, effervescent and sociable as always, added just the right element to every topic of conversation, never missing an opportunity to contribute but equally unimposing. It was clear that she was the thread that wove her family together. Andrew and Claire clicked easily with the siblings and their spouses, mingling over the trials and tribulations as well as the pleasantries of parenthood and marriage.

And then there was Jack. Surrounded by his people, he radiated contentment and a fulfillment that Jocelyn had yet to bear witness to. As he engaged in conversation, Jocelyn could see the love that he had for each of his siblings, including those who had married into the family. Despite not being a parent himself, he fell into the rotation of checking in on the kids. At one point, she had even caught him coaxing a few of the children into smuggling small potted plants into Sarah's purse.

He checked all the boxes for perfect marriage material, and yet he remained single. Jocelyn wondered offhandedly if he had planned on marrying the infamous woman he'd abandoned in Florida. Might he even have intended on proposing to her there? The thought of it was so unsettling that it unnerved her. What right did she have to be jealous over a man she had no intentions of pursuing herself?

Andrew caught Jocelyn staring at Jack, and it wasn't the first time that night. He wondered if she knew how obvious it was that she had feelings for him. More importantly, he wondered if Jack had any idea. It wasn't his place to pry, but he suspected by the way that the man glanced on occasion at his sister when she wasn't looking, that he returned her feelings.

Andrew knew that casual relationships weren't Jocelyn's thing. She had only ever dated two men seriously. He imagined a fling with a man like Jack wasn't on her radar, so he wondered then what might exist between them if not a transient affair.

Sometime after the sun went down, everyone filed in from the boat deck to find Jack getting himself a glass of water at the kitchen sink.

"Where are the kids?" Claire asked in alarm.

"Oh, don't worry," Jack said with a dismissive pass of his hand. "They're playing peek-a-boo-potty."

"I'm sorry…They're playing *what*?" Sarah asked with confusion.

"They're standing around the toilet covering their eyes and playing…" he illustrated with his hands, then opened them like doors to reveal his wide eyes "peek-a-boo-potty." At the sound of erupting giggles, he jerked his thumb in the direction of the bathroom. "See, it's hilarious."

"If they're touching the toilet," Sarah exclaimed "*I swear.*" She marched over to the bathroom door and swung it open.

"On that note," Jack announced, "I'm going to take Lady for her evening bathroom break. I'll be back in a few."

"Can I join?" Andrew asked.

"The more the merrier," Jack replied.

Alarm bells sounded as Jocelyn watched her brother follow Jack off the boat. Instead of letting her growing sense of dread overtake her, knowing full well it would be a wasted use of her headspace, she joined Sarah in the bathroom. Andrew was a lot of things, but suicidal wasn't one of them. When she entered, her friend was working strenuously to lift the kids up, one at a time, to the faucet to scrub their hands with soap and water. Plucking a child from the floor, Jocelyn joined her at the sink and got to sanitizing.

Jack and Andrew walked wordlessly up the dock, meandering past the house to the gravel driveway and through the front yard. Jack could feel the ulterior motive behind Andrew's inclination to join him but thought better of breaking the silence first. He knew that whatever Andrew had to say would be said soon enough and on his terms.

When Andrew finally spoke, he confirmed Jack's suspicions. "So, what's going on between you and Jocelyn?"

"Nothing's going on," Jack replied casually.

"I know what nothing looks like," Andrew challenged. "And the way you look at her suggests that there's at least the hope for *something*."

Jack shook his head, unable to deny the accusation with words. "I respect your sister," he said, hoping the truth of his sentiment was enough to pacify.

"I can see that too," Andrew offered. "But playing games borders on carelessness."

Jack turned to face him. "I'm not playing games," he insisted.

"Aren't you?" Andrew challenged. "Are you going to deny that you have feelings for her?"

Jack couldn't answer.

"Do you have feelings for Jocelyn?" Andrew repeated.

"It's not that simple," Jack insisted.

"Isn't it?" Andrew challenged again. "She clearly has feelings for you."

"Jocelyn is determined to return to her life in Austin," Jack professed. "Unless that changes, I don't see a reason to pursue a relationship if it won't last, and I don't think she does either."

Andrew considered his words carefully. Jack's unyielding respect for his sister only gave him more reason to support a relationship developing between them. After spending the evening catching up, Andrew saw in Jack a great many traits his sister could benefit from in a significant other. He was easy going, confident without being cocky, and he was a man with a vision and the skills to back it up. Maybe he wasn't the kind of guy she was used to dating, but perhaps that was the greatest reason for earning the high approval rating.

Jocelyn had spent too much time committing to the wrong men, and it wasn't easy to understand her hesitation when she finally found a good one. Still, he could see how complicated a relationship between Jack and his sister might be.

"Jocelyn's scared," Andrew said softly. "I know that she's not entirely happy at the firm. Not in the last year or so anyway. But for someone like her, that's not enough to walk away. She's worked so hard all her life to build up this dream for herself and I think she forgets that sometimes dreams change."

"It's hard to walk away from something you've built," Jack replied with understanding.

"I'm really proud of her," Andrew added. "She's paved the way for herself with no help from anyone. I just don't know if it's enough to make her happy."

"I'm not sure that I'm the right person to say this to."

"Maybe not," Andrew admitted. "But Jocelyn has never belonged anywhere as much as she so clearly belongs here. Honestly, I think that scares her the most. I can't tell if it's the fresh air or the way she looks at you, but I felt like it was worth mentioning either way."

For the remainder of the night, Jack couldn't get Andrew's words out of his head. It didn't help that his thoughts had been pulling to Jocelyn all evening, imagining that their life together might look just like this. Someday maybe they would even have a few screaming toddlers of their own to chase around.

He wasn't in the habit of daydreaming, but Jocelyn's unexpected return left Jack wondering if his life could be more than anything he'd ever imagined for himself. If only she was willing to take a chance on the unknown.

Chapter Ten

If he wasn't careful, Jack realized that he could let Jocelyn's entire stay come and go, consumed by work and the renovations, without even so much as trying to show her what a life with him in Virginia might look like. He struggled to find cause enough to pursue her under the pretense that she would leave in little over a month's time. Walking out of his life forever. But if he gave her a reason to stay… maybe, just maybe, there was hope of something more.

He found her on the porch, typing away on her computer, rocking absently in her chair.

"Do you know what we need?" he asked, striding over to lean casually against the post opposite where she sat.

Jocelyn looked up, half distracted by the facts and figures that littered her screen. The week that had followed Andrew's visit had been hectic at work to say the least. Her team was working to tie up any loose ends on their proposal before their mock presentation at the end of the month. On top of that, she had taken on a new client. In addition to assembling a compulsory list of necessary prerequisites for future candidates, she was pulling and reviewing a few resumes she already knew were a good match for the company. With limited resources and added pressure, even Saturday wasn't safe from the spill over created by the deadlines that continued to close in.

During any other season of life, being overwhelmed by her job might be suffocating, but, now more than ever, it felt like an anchor. A reminder that she did have something she'd been working towards. Since the idyllic evening spent with Jack's family, Jocelyn needed her career goals to use as a lifeline to keep her bound to the much different world she would return to in Texas. Her blinders were on, her focus was steady. She was once again excited about the promise of promotion and career advancement.

Once she moved up in the company, she could buy herself a house on the outskirts of the city. That would change everything. She could have the high-paying job and a place out in the suburbs away from the constant hustle and bustle of the city. She just needed to stay focused on her goals and take the proper steps to achieving them.

"What?" Jocelyn replied absently, straining to give Jack her full attention.

"A real day off," he offered, reaching over to close the computer in her lap.

"Oh, I—" she began to protest.

"When was the last time you really enjoyed this place?" Jack challenged, sliding the slim notebook off her lap. "It's the weekend. Work will be right where you left it," he asserted. "I promise."

"Jack," she objected.

"I guess I'll just have to try out Will's new jet ski without you then."

Jocelyn couldn't remember the last time she'd had an adrenaline rush of any kind. It was a stretch to remember when she'd had any intentional fun. Looking out over the water, she noticed, for possibly the first time that it was the perfect day. As much as she wanted to remain focused, she knew that her efforts could easily backfire if she pushed herself too hard.

"All right," she announced. "I'm in."

"Good answer."

Will and Ava's place was less than ten minutes down the road, tucked away along a bend in the river. It was a humble farmhouse, rustic, warm, and free of flashy adornments. The white tin roof matched the exterior, giving the home a clean appearance to contrast the wild foliage that surrounded the cleared plot of land. Neat landscaping adorned the perimeter of the porch, bridging the gaps between what man had created and God's work.

As they pulled up, Jocelyn noticed a trail, fashioned out of wide flat stones that wrapped around the house and she wondered where it might lead. Behind the home stood a thick wall of trees marking the edge of the forest, nearly blocking the river from view entirely.

By the time Jack and Jocelyn exited the truck, Will and Ava were outside to greet them, surprisingly overdressed for a day of water sports.

"That's what you're wearing?" Jack inquired.

"I, uh," Will began, clearly lost for the proper response.

"Will double booked us," Ava interrupted.

"Come on, man," Jack replied.

"I'm *so* sorry, but we made these plans with my parents a week ago," Ava informed apologetically.

When Ava met her husband's eyes and flashed a forced and firm smile, Jack suspected this wasn't entirely true.

Will turned to face his brother, certain of only one thing. There was a right response and a wrong one, and his wife had already made it very clear which was which.

"Next time," he offered regretfully. "I've done a few test laps. She's fast," he added. "I left a full tank of gas on the dock for you." He gazed back at Ava, as if to receive approval, and with a warm smile, she gave it.

"It's a beautiful day to be out on the water," Ava added cheerfully.

Will's disappointment was tangible.

"Are you sure?" Jocelyn questioned. "We can come back another time."

"Don't be silly," Ava insisted, cradling Mary on her hip while Diana circled at her feet. "Have a great time," she asserted, already moving toward the car. "Oh, and the Yamaha isn't running properly. I wouldn't use it," she added, poking her head out from the car as she buckled Mary into her seat.

Will's face was newly bewildered.

"Come on, honey, we're going to be late," Ava forced through her teeth.

"Yeah. Late," Will added automatically, unsure if he believed the words himself. He made his way around the other side of the truck and began buckling Diana into her seat.

"Have fun!" Ava called out her window a few minutes later as the vehicle tore out of the driveway.

Jack watched them fade from view, torn between disappointment and gratitude. He hadn't intended for the day to be intimate. All the same, time alone with Jocelyn wasn't likely to fall quite as effortlessly into his hands again. It wasn't hard to surmise that he had Ava to thank for the rare opportunity.

He turned to face Jocelyn, raising a single eyebrow as he studied her expression. When she met his eyes, a visible mixture of hesitation and delight flashed across her face. Decidedly, she lifted her chin with resolve.

"I'm taking it out first," she declared before heading down the path.

Pleased with her tenacity, Jack followed.

Jocelyn led the way over a raised boardwalk that snaked through the trees. Once on the other side, they approached a wide pier and a covered structure that housed a pontoon boat. At the end of the pier were two jet skis seated on a floating dock; one covered and the other ready to ride.

Two life vests hung from a hook on the pier. Jocelyn pulled off her tank top, revealing a sporty royal blue one-piece.

Leaving her jean shorts on, she shrugged on the smaller vest and secured it around her body. Following her lead, Jack shucked off his shirt and slung it over a nearby post.

"You sure you want to take her out first?" he asked, reading her apprehensive stance.

Bravery had been an easy thing to assert on the walk down to the dock, but Jocelyn struggled to hold onto her nerve as she studied the watercraft.

"Absolutely," she lied.

"Do you need help getting on?" Jack offered.

"Nope," she lied again.

"Ready when you are then," Jack said, wondering if Jocelyn's stubbornness was strong enough to overcome the fear in her eyes.

After another moment of deliberation, Jocelyn guided her body carefully off the pier onto the buoyant dock. Once she had established her footing on the uneasy surface, with little more than stubborn will alone to guide her, she mounted the jet ski with little physical effort, though mentally, her head was spinning.

As playful as she had been to insist that she get to ride the machine first, she was quickly reminded that she was far from an expert on such equipment. Once she was comfortably cradled on the seat, having eyed the various buttons and gauges, she was reminded that she didn't typically seek out adventure, because she was far from adventurous. Stubborn yes, but an adrenaline junky, not by a long shot.

Jack stood poised on the dock, arms laced over his bare chest, waiting for her to speed off across the surface of the water.

Swallowing the knot of nerves in her throat, Jocelyn attempted to sound casual. "Aren't you coming?"

The absolute last thing she wanted, more than embarrassment, was to fling herself into the jellyfish infested

Rappahannock with no one to fish her out, solely responsible for what she could only assume was a very expensive piece of equipment.

"I..." Jack unfolded his arms and glanced around. He could see that, despite Jocelyn's well practiced air of confidence, she was terrified below her calm exterior. As much as he didn't want to ride pillion on a jet ski, he wanted Jocelyn to enjoy herself more. "Yeah. Uh, I'll be right there."

He pulled on the other life vest and slid his phone into a water safe pouch which he stuffed into the pocket of his swim trunks. He boarded the floating dock and climbed onto the back of the jet ski, pushing his frame up against Jocelyn's. The feeling of her body pressed against his sent a shock wave through him. The softness of her warm skin was electrifying, and he hoped she didn't notice that their proximity had an effect on him.

"What do I press?" she finally asked.

Jack suppressed a chuckle. He leaned over and pushed the start button. "Easy on the throttle until you get a feel for it," he offered as the engine hummed to life. "Every machine is a bit different, just like a car. So, don't feel like you need to be polished right out of the gate."

"Yeah...okay," Jocelyn replied uneasily. She clutched the accelerator and they lurched forward. "Sorry," she called back over the engine apologetically. "It's been a hot minute since I've ridden one of these."

"I'll say," Jack said with a laugh, happy for the jostle that stole his attention from more intimate things. "When was the last time you took one for a spin?"

"Well—" They sputtered forward again, water kicking up around them. "Actually," she called over the noisy engine "...now that I think about it, it was only the one time!" she shouted. "And...technically, I've only been a passenger," she yelled over the escalating sound "It was maybe…eight years ago?"

Jack instinctively took hold of the loops of Jocelyn's life vest, his eyes wide with a sense of dread so sobering his body knew no other feeling but the tense grip of his legs anchoring him to the seat.

"And this is how I die," he muttered.

"What?!" Jocelyn called back as they jerked forward and abruptly lurched to a stop the moment her attention was drawn from steering the machine.

"You're doing great!" Jack called back. "Just keep your eyes forward!"

After a short and jarring trip down the coast of the river, Jocelyn confirmed her growing suspicion that driving a jet ski had little to no appeal to her. The amount of focus it took to keep the watercraft moving smoothly was enough to give her palpitations. Whenever a crabbing buoy crossed her path, which happened at an alarming rate, she had to force the full brunt of her focus on avoiding it. Just below the surface of the water, she could see the undulating tentacles and billowing forms of the thousands of jellyfish that awaited her if she were to fly over the handlebars. The images of the many ways in which she could be seriously injured were so vivid it was hard to see the landscape in front of her, let alone spark some joy from the experience. How anyone could find the sport fun or relaxing eluded her. The fact that Jack, despite his obvious tension, allowed her to navigate the waters without constant interjection helped her feel more in control and at ease, yet equally abandoned to learn the ways of the water on her own. By the time they approached the dock again, she was certain she could check "drive jet ski" off her bucket list for good.

"You did great," Jack said as they docked again.

"I can't feel my hands," Jocelyn retorted, unable to voice the words, *I hated every minute.*

The last thing she wanted was to admit that a well-intended day away from the office had resulted in a higher level of stress than if she single-handedly ran the firm.

"My turn," Jack announced. "Hop on."

Jocelyn had only just planted her feet on the very welcoming and very solid dock and wasn't quite ready to leave it again. "Oh no. I think I'll sit this one out."

"Come on," Jack called from the driver's seat, waving her over. "I think I dropped my man card. Let's see if we can't find it."

Despite herself, Jocelyn laughed, only now just picturing what Jack might have looked like riding on the back of the jet ski as they sputtered along. With no valid argument against granting him the small gift of his returned dignity, she slid in behind him wordlessly, tucking her arms tightly around his waist.

"Mmm," he cooed. "That's better."

Jocelyn felt her cheeks grow hot and was grateful that Jack couldn't see her blush.

When he started up the engine once more and eased the throttle, they left the dock for open water. The ride was smooth, fast, and calculated. Jack commanded the machine as if it were an extension of himself. Weaving easily between the obstacles in the water, gliding over its surface at speeds Jocelyn hadn't even attempted to reach, he was like a modern-day knight mounted upon an untamable beast. Contrasting with the swarm of hornets in her stomach during the first ride, she felt the gentle flutter of butterflies as she clung to him.

From the back seat, she looked out over the river, taking in the beautiful sights of the coastline on either side. Families spending the day out on their boat, other jet skiers as well as kayakers and teenagers being pulled behind boats on inflatable rafts and wakeboards. The sun beat down mercilessly, but the spray of the water and the wind kept them cool. It was the most fun Jocelyn had had in years, which she knew spoke volumes about her life. How had she so willingly forfeited fun for the hope of continued professional achievements? Without intending to, Jack had managed to unravel yet another tangled truth she hadn't recognized about her life in Austin. It, like the relationships she had tried to foster there, lacked a pulse.

They had spent the better part of the morning riding up and down the coastline, and despite herself, Jocelyn took another crack at driving. Though she mostly just reaffirmed that she preferred being a passenger, she was willing to admit that it got better as she became more comfortable at the helm. By noon, they were both ready for something greasy and satisfying to eat.

"This is my favorite place to get burgers," Jack informed, pulling the truck up to a nondescript building that looked more like a rundown pawn shop than it did a burger joint. "Don't let outward appearances fool you. They're the best."

"I'm so hungry I'll eat anything," Jocelyn declared.

"Perfect," Jack said with an easy laugh.

Once inside, Jocelyn was surprised to find that the overall appeal of the establishment was vastly downplayed by its deceptive and unflattering exterior. The floors were smooth concrete, the walls a distressed brick, with one wall almost entirely converted into a chalk board. Dividing the accent wall horizontally, a live edge wood bar top counter stretched nearly the entire length across. Every few feet metal stools provided seating for those who preferred a more casual dining experience. At one end of the chalkboard, the specials and drink menu had been penned in a neat curvy script, leaving plenty of room for guests to write their names or other remarks and doodles. At the ground level sat a big bucket of thick colorful chalk and under the bar top, scribbles drawn by children decorated the remaining surface of the wall.

The restaurant wasn't very big, but the intimate setting had about a dozen small tables paired with a colorful assortment of mismatched farmhouse chairs. The charm of the establishment was very distinctive, and Jocelyn suspected that Jack had a hand in the design.

As was becoming a regular occurrence, he had managed, yet again, to change Jocelyn's mind about something.

"Wow," she said, taking in the space. "Did you do this?"

Jack shrugged modestly. "Come on, let's get some burgers."

Jocelyn mostly observed as Jack exchanged greetings with the server at the counter. They were soon joined by the owner, Steve, who shook Jack's hand and brought him in for a friendly embrace. When Steve glanced over at Jocelyn and insisted that the meal was on the house, Jack failed at refusing the offer. They enjoyed a few more pleasantries while they waited, and when their order was up, they said their goodbyes and selected a table in the back of the room. It wasn't lost on Jocelyn that Jack had slipped two twenty-dollar bills into the tip jar on the way over.

"You're famous," Jocelyn said, before sinking a generous bite into her burger. Distracted momentarily by the flavors that delighted her taste buds, she wondered offhandedly if ecstasy could be achieved with food.

"It's a small town," Jack insisted, brushing off the remark. "Good, isn't it?"

"*Amazing*," she said approvingly, then added, "I really needed this. Thank you for dragging me out of the house today."

"The pleasure is all mine," Jack insisted.

"I think I finally got the hang of it," she declared. "I'm pretty sure my legs are going to be sore tomorrow though. I never clung so desperately to anything in my life."

Jack laughed. "I'll be right there with you."

"It's too bad Will and Ava weren't able to join."

"Yeah, too bad."

As much as he cherished his family's company, Jack was glad to have had the chance to spend some alone time with Jocelyn. Though they had enjoyed one another's company before, the air of unscripted spontaneity they'd experienced together on the jet ski had been refreshing and exactly what he'd been hoping for. He might have simply been imagining it, but Jocelyn seemed to be falling back in love with Farnham. And if her feelings could grow for a place, he held onto the hope that they could grow for him too.

"I never think to go jet skiing back in Austin," Jocelyn said, interrupting his thoughts. "Maybe I'll pick it up when I get back."

Jack's mood dropped slightly at the mention of Austin, and he was reminded why he had been so quick to draw a line in the sand between them despite his growing feelings for Jocelyn. He'd been burned before, and far too recently to be careless with a woman. She brought center back to his life and it worried him. What scared him most was how easily he was being drawn to a place from where he would never be able to return. The point of being lost to her completely.

Determined not to let midnight strike early, Jack refocused his attention on enjoying the time they did have and hoped it would be enough. At the very least, he could maintain a friendship with Jocelyn. One that might provide room for more in the future.

"Water sports in Texas? I can't picture it," he probed, hoping she hadn't noticed his lingering disappointment.

"Oh, Austin's got a little bit of everything," Jocelyn boasted.

"What do you usually do on your days off?" he asked.

"I'll admit, I've been so focused on work lately, I usually just stay home and decompress from the long work week. But there's a lot to do in Austin," she informed. "There are great boutiques, restaurants, live music, parks, natural pools and springs as well as the Colorado River. It really is such a beautiful city."

As she went on describing the place that she called home, revisiting old memories and sharing her favorite stories, Jocelyn was reminded of why it was so easy to picture herself returning. She had managed, in her desperate need for enlightenment, to forget how much she loved Austin.

Jack had reminded her with their spontaneous excursion that her inability to enjoy the world around her had far more to do with her drive to work harder than she played than it did a lack of opportunities. She'd hardly even tried to enjoy what Austin had to offer in the last few years as she had with Virginia in only a matter of a few hours.

Jack could hear the sentiment and longing in Jocelyn's voice when she spoke of her life in Texas. As she continued to describe her city, elaborating on the elements that she adored most, he wondered how he had managed to convince himself that she might ever consider leaving such a place.

Austin offered her something he couldn't. Endless possibilities. He could steal a few moments with the woman who had reentered his life just in time to save him, but he couldn't rightfully expect to take what he greedily wanted to claim, which was all of her.

Chapter Eleven

Jocelyn preferred working from the screened-in porch most days, but a heat wave had rolled in, and the thought of venturing outdoors to get the mail was unpleasant, let alone spending her workday without the comfort of central air. Even dressed in a pair of jean shorts and a t-shirt, her hair fastened into a single French braid, she knew she'd be soaked through in a matter of minutes.

Instead, she had pulled up one of the bar stools she'd ordered online and worked at the kitchen counter, enjoying the change of scenery. From there, she could manage her spreadsheets, reply to emails, jot down notes, and soak in the beautiful kitchen, living, and dining space Jack had designed. She wasn't sure she would ever grow tired of looking at it. Every detail had been perfectly placed and thoughtfully executed. She couldn't help but wonder if she would ever love a home as much as she loved this one.

Jack had been busy working outside all morning on various jobs around the property. Jocelyn hadn't seen him since he had stopped in with Lady for a quick cup of coffee before getting to work. By lunch time, she figured he was overdue for a break. Knowing that he would likely choose to work through lunch as he often did, she closed her laptop and started making him something to eat.

Along with a turkey sandwich and potato chips, she poured him a tall glass of lemonade. Balancing both in one hand, she slid the back door open and made her way through the porch.

Below, on the pool patio, she could hear the distant noise of the table saw at work, and she followed the sound.

When she descended the steps, Jocelyn noticed Lady first. She was stretched out over one of the lounge chairs on the patio. Jack had moved it into the shade, and there she lie, indifferent to a machine most dogs would cower from. She was always surprised at how comfortable the Rottweiler was on the job, content around any level of noise or chaos as long as she had Jack for company.

As her eyes moved to follow the sound, Jocelyn saw Jack at the table saw, guiding the wood expertly to deliver a measured cut. Though he faced her, he hadn't yet noticed her approach. While she had seen him with his shirt off a few times already, the sight of his bare chest always had the power to disarm her. Butterflies erupted inside of her stomach, and she suddenly felt ill equipped to appear uninterested. The sun danced across his muscles as he worked, and he glistened under a sheen of sweat that accentuated the definition of his physique.

As she approached, she flashed a friendly smile and a wave when he finally noticed her. Instinctively, she trained her eyes to look away from his bare chest as she always did whenever she found herself presented with his raw masculinity. Which, she was coming to find, was more often than she was comfortable with.

Jack flipped the switch on the machine and removed his safety glasses and ear plugs.

"You didn't have to do that," he called over the dying hum of the motor.

"Don't be silly," Jocelyn replied dismissively. "You can't work in this heat without a proper lunch."

She placed the plate on an open space at the end of the table saw and reached across with the lemonade where Jack graciously received the glass. He raised the cup to his lips and tipped it back, taking a long swig of the drink.

"That's the best lemonade I've ever had," he proclaimed before chugging the rest.

"You're just dehydrated," Jocelyn reasoned. "I could have brought you out a glass of ice-cold prune juice and you'd have said the same thing."

"You're probably right," he replied with a laugh.

Reaching for the shirt he'd draped over the edge of the table saw, Jack used it to dry his face and neck. Jocelyn, despite herself, used the opportunity to study the hard lines of his body. Dressed in jeans and work boots, he looked like he had walked out of a raunchy calendar where all the men were shirtless and jacked. Though he couldn't be oblivious to the fact that he looked great with his shirt off, he led with his personality, and that perhaps was the most attractive thing about him.

As Jack slung the shirt over his shoulder and Jocelyn went to shift her eyes away from his body once more, she noticed a scar on his abdomen she hadn't seen before. Perhaps, she realized, because she'd always been controlling herself to look away from his physique rather than examining it.

She moved closer to him, transfixed by the scar, drawn in by memories that began flooding her senses like a tidal wave. "Is that the scar from when they took out your appendix?" she asked, mesmerized.

Jack glanced down, reflexively touching the nearly invisible incision. "Yeah," he said, the memory clearly returning as he met her eyes. "I forgot you were there for that."

With alarming force, Jocelyn's heart pounded, pushing against the cage of her ribs. She blinked hard, overcome with the sensation of past meeting present as the boy she had once known and the man she had come to know suddenly became one person.

Jack had complained of a dull stomachache all morning at the beach. He had spent the last half-hour of their time there resting on the blanket beside his mother, Margaret. Finally, both families agreed that it was best to head back for the day.

Because Jack insisted that he was fine, The Larsens accepted the Evans's invitation to join them for an early dinner back at the house. There, Jack could rest upstairs and the other children could continue to spend the day socializing while the adults played board games downstairs.

Jocelyn, only eight at the time, wrestled with conflicting feelings over Jack's condition. Without him around, playing with Andrew, Sarah and Will was an entirely different experience. As the oldest, Jack always kept them busy with new ideas for games to play or planning wild adventures for them to go on. Even if he did manage to find a way to pick on her whatever they were doing. She couldn't believe she was thinking it, but she actually missed him. His siblings and Andrew seemed to agree without outright saying so. Though Will didn't seem too concerned about Jack's state—for the time being, he was far more disappointed about the boring afternoon than his brother's mundane stomachache—Sarah was visibly concerned and made no effort to hide it.

When Andrew and Will went down to the beach, Sarah insisted on staying in the house. Jocelyn didn't protest and sat quietly on the floor, absently rotating a Barbie with matted hair in her hands as Sarah's eyes remained fixed on the stairs.

"It's been a long time," Sarah finally said, worry woven through her words. "He still hasn't come down. Do you want to check on him?"

Jocelyn didn't understand her feelings when it came to Jack. Only the day before he had been calling her nicknames until she cried. Now, her stomach was twisted with feelings of remorse and concern she would never have imagined she'd feel for him. Why was his absence dominating her attention?

"Yeah, sure," she conceded, since neither of them could focus on their dolls anyway.

Together, they made their way up the stairs. They walked down the length of the hallway and finally reached the door at the end. Sarah pushed it open and they both laid eyes on Jack, crumpled up in bed, wincing in pain.

They moved quickly to the side of the bed and noticed that he was covered in a sheen of sweat. His hair was soaked at the roots, his pillow stained with the runoff from his fever induced perspiration.

He groaned in agony, clutching his stomach. "It hurts," he managed through clenched teeth.

Sarah bolted from the room and down the hall, leaving Jocelyn uncertain as to what to do. Whether she should stay or go. She turned to the door, panicked by the intensity of the fear that flashed across Jack's face and the panic that grew inside of her as she watched him.

"Please," he managed, reaching out to take hold of her hand. "Don't leave me."

Stunned by his vulnerability, drawn to the tenderness in his voice, Jocelyn didn't pull her hand away. "Okay," she said softly.

"I'm scared," he said, his body shaking uncontrollably. Tears began streaming down his face and she didn't know if it was from the pain, fear, or both.

"You're going to be okay," she assured him. Though she was just as worried as he was.

Jocelyn had never seen someone so sick, nor had she ever seen Jack so defenseless. He had always seemed so strong. So brave and fearless. She recalled the time he had jumped off the dock once only to land unknowingly into a swarm of jellyfish. He had waded through them, getting stung mercilessly the whole way back to shore, as he gritted his teeth through the encounter, not shedding a single tear. The Jack she knew *seemed to believe that being the big brother meant he didn't cry. Now, he looked completely helpless.*

Jack was still grasping Jocelyn's hand tightly when his parents came rushing into the room.

"Oh, Jack," Peter, said. "Why didn't you call us?!" The distress in his father's voice was tangible.

Margaret swept her son up into her arms. "Jack," she cooed. "You're burning up."

Though Jocelyn tried to move out of the way, Jack kept her hand firmly clasped in his as if she were keeping him tethered to life.

"What hurts?" Margaret asked softly.

"My stomach," Jack managed to say. "It feels like a knife is in my stomach."

"Where?" Peter asked, moving closer.

Jack lifted his shirt, indicating a spot just beside his navel.

"Peter, we need to take him to the hospital," Margaret urged.

"Could be appendicitis," Peter said, echoing his wife's concern.

Jocelyn looked on, absorbing the information in pieces, lost almost completely in the grip of Jack's hand. She felt solely responsible for making sure he was okay, but of course she knew that was not the case.

Peter scooped Jack up from the bed while Margaret swept the damp hair off his forehead. Jocelyn pulled away to give them room, though Jack had tried to keep her from letting go.

"Jocelyn," he said feebly as his father crossed the room with his son cradled in his arms. "Thank you for staying with me," he added before they disappeared into the hall.

The memory was so vivid, Jocelyn could still feel the pang of fear that she'd experienced waiting up that night to hear back about how Jack was doing after his emergency surgery. The doctor had said that if they'd waited much longer his appendix might very well have ruptured. She recalled the sheer terror that overcame her at the realization that he could have died.

Of course, by the time she saw him again, the old Jack had returned, and she had wondered if she had simply seen something that wasn't there. A kindness, a sweetness, that might allude to something softer below his hardened surface. After a while, she had stopped looking for it anymore. She wondered now, if perhaps she hadn't put her guard back up so quickly, if she might have gotten to know Jack's compassionate side earlier.

Jocelyn felt a flood of uncontrolled and conflicting emotions so intense she couldn't think straight, and she struggled to push past the weight of them. Jack had always been so practiced in his indifference towards her as a child that she had completely dismissed the one time that he'd allowed her to see a glimpse of the boy behind the façade. A front, she now understood, he had erected in an effort to protect himself from his true feelings for her. Seeing it now, making peace with a boy who hadn't known better was almost more than she could take.

"Is everything okay?" Jack asked, his concern mounting as she remained wordless.

He made his way over from the other side of the table saw that stood between them like a defensive barrier. He stopped just short, giving her space, standing between her and the edge of the pool.

Jocelyn felt panic set in as she forced the feelings down like a snake in a can. She couldn't let him know that she was wrestling with feelings she could hardly accept, let along consider acting upon them. She looked up, pressing her lips together, doing her best to snuff out the uncertainty from her expression. She could tell that she hadn't managed to dispel his worry and considered quickly what she might be able to do to break the tension that hung between them.

His brow was glossy with fresh sweat as they stood baking under the relentless heat of the midday sun. Behind him, the pool shimmered with the promise of cool relief.

Before she could talk herself out of it, and with no better idea of how she might draw Jack's attention away from her raw and unchecked emotions, Jocelyn said, "I'm really worried about you being out in this heat all day. I'm starting to think the lemonade just isn't going to cut it."

Jack's expression shifted quickly to confusion. He was still caught in a web of bewilderment when Jocelyn took a step toward him, reached out, and shoved him hard in the chest, launching him back into the pool.

When his body broke the surface of the water, Jocelyn took a deep breath. He went under and came quickly back up, shaking his head and letting out a sharp exhale. Running his hands over his cropped hair, he began to laugh good-naturedly. Jocelyn let out the breath she had been holding in her lungs as relief washed over her.

Excited by the commotion, Lady dismounted the lounge chair she'd been lying on and bounded towards the pool, jumping fearlessly to her master's side. When she splashed him, Jack laughed again, splashing her in return. Jocelyn, momentarily free of the emotions she wasn't ready to address, shucked off her sandals and took a running leap into the pool.

As they thrashed around playfully, Jocelyn allowed herself to indulge in the effortless friendship that had blossomed between she and Jack. Whatever the misplaced or unrequited feelings that might exist between them were, whatever their origin story, she wanted nothing more in that moment than to relish the fact that they had found one another again. She knew that what they had now more than made up for what they had lost in childhood.

Chapter Twelve

Jocelyn had completed her work early for the day, leaving the rest of the afternoon to do with as she pleased. Determined to enjoy her remaining time in Virginia, she looked forward to her girls' day with Sarah.

She had taken her time getting ready, happy for the excuse to wear her mauve sundress and rose gold sandals. She had even run some hair gel through her natural golden waves. While she didn't apply makeup often, she had curled her lashes and had put on some light mascara and eyeliner, along with her favorite shade of light pink lipstick.

In the recently mounted bathroom mirror, a nearly unrecognizable sun-kissed and vibrant young woman stared back at her. She was a far cry from the exhausted and uncertain girl who had run away from her life in search of clarity. Despite how busy she still was with work and coordinating the remaining renovations, her goals continued to come into focus.

While she knew that plenty remained unaddressed, namely the complicated feelings for Jack that she continued to push out of her mind, she couldn't discount the good that had come of her stay thus far. She had been reminded of why she loved her job. She had a better idea of what her life in Austin was missing. And she had a clear picture of how she might go about fixing it.

Jocelyn could never have known if her hopes of finding refuge by the river would be fruitful or not, but she felt grateful that she had taken the chance. Life had been too predictable, and she'd taken too easily to handing all her time over to her career goals. Though she knew her time in Farnham would never be enough to satisfy, she was content to have discovered a side of herself she forgot existed.

On her way out the door, Jack caught Jocelyn as he headed upstairs to the fourth and final bedroom remodel, Lady trotting loyally at his side.

"You look—" He stopped himself. The words beautiful, ravishing and seductive all felt like an overstep; though they were the most accurate words he could think to describe her. Her short purple dress scooped dangerously low. The delicate floral print fabric wrapped tightly around her waist, cinched at the back with a neat tie. And her makeup was refreshingly subtle, while still amplifying her naturally beautiful features.

"Nice," he finally said, settling miles below the homage Jocelyn's beauty deserved. "Hot date?" His fist clenched reflexively around the spool of wire he held at the mere thought of it.

"With your sister," Jocelyn replied with a friendly smirk.

"I should have known," he said with a smirk. "She settles for no less than the best."

Flattered and slightly unnerved by the compliment, Jocelyn combed a hand through her hair shyly.

"She just texted from the driveway," she informed casually. "I'm not sure when I'll be back. We'll probably grab an early dinner after we scope out the shops in town."

"What? She's too good to come in and see her own brother now?" Jack remarked with mocked offense. "I see how it is."

Jocelyn rolled her eyes playfully. "I'm sure you'll have plenty of time to lick all those wounds before I get back."

The store fronts that lined the main strip of downtown Farnham were an array of eclectic beauty with a mix of brick, stone, and German architecture. A local brewery, a few coffee shops, a collection of boutiques, and an assortment of eateries each displaying their own unique personality while all coming together to create a warm and rich atmosphere. Outdoor seating areas were occupied by patrons, filling the air with laughter and conversation as they enjoyed the reprieve from the summer's heat under the shade of umbrellas. The streets were alive with tourists and locals alike.

Jocelyn and Sarah stopped in at the local pastry shop, indulging in a variety of French macarons and freshly baked croissants. Strolling on, they grabbed coffee from the corner café, content to sip slowly on their drinks as they meandered around with no firm destination, all while catching up and exchanging stories of the years they had spent apart.

"Oh," Jocelyn exclaimed. "I think this is the place Jack was telling me about."

Written in a delicate white script, the quaint storefront sign read, "Lost Treasures: repurposed furniture and locally made goods." The brick building was adorned with old teal shutters and a pane glass door to match. A large wood planter was mounted under the window, filled with an assortment of colorful succulents that spilled out of the box with wild abandon.

A collection of small furniture pieces, planters, and knickknacks poured out onto the sidewalk in a carefully arranged display, giving a taste for the novelties that could be found inside. Through the window, Jocelyn could see colorful displays of candle holders, stemware, rare treasures, handcrafted merchandise, and more.

"Oh, I love this place!" Sarah squealed.

"Let's check it out," she said, following Sarah who was already headed inside.

It was safe to say that one pass through the store wasn't enough to soak in the entirety of what there to see. Managing to establish a delicate balance between wild and orderly, the shop was filled to the brim with items that exuded whimsey as well as sophistication. Prints and canvases painted by local artists, handcrafted soaps, baskets of every shape and size, and ceramics made on the potter's wheel in the back of the shop were only a few of the pieces that caught Jocelyn's eye.

All through the store, repurposed furniture, she could only assume had been acquired from Jack's barn sales, was displayed in carefully thought-out arrangements. She could see most of the pieces fitting in with nearly any design style. Some of the furniture was more modern or streamline while others were rustic or of a farmhouse style, but they all had a sense of family in the shop.

"I'll take one of everything," Jocelyn exclaimed. "How am I supposed to choose? More importantly, how do I get all this back to Austin."

"I keep forgetting that you're only here for a little while longer," Sarah said on the coattails of a disappointed groan.

"I can't decide if it feels like I only just got here or if it feels like I've been here forever," Jocelyn remarked.

"If you ask me, it hasn't been long enough," Sarah asserted. "I'm so jealous that Jack gets to see you *every day*. It seems like such a waste that he's the one who spends the most time with you."

Jocelyn chuckled. She hadn't ever thought about it like that. It was true, she spent at least part of every day with Jack. Even if only on the weekend as she watched him leave the property to take Lady for a walk and they exchanged a wave. The few times she had spent the day with him, whether they had been taking a much-needed break from work or they were making something work related more fun, she was willing to admit that it was effortless to be in his company. Mostly, he worked around her within the house so naturally that the river house and Jack felt tied together somehow. She quickly banished the idea that either of them gave her a sense of home in fear that the sentiment might make the departure she knew would be difficult, even harder.

"As sad as it makes me that you're leaving," Sarah went on "I'm happy for the excuse to see Texas." She shifted the weight of the items she balanced on her pregnant belly.

"You'll love it," Jocelyn confirmed, as the pang of homesickness tugged at her heart.

"Once I get this baby out of me and it's safe to travel again, you're going to have to bar the door to keep me away."

"I wouldn't dream of it!"

"Looks like my little warrior princess is on board too," Sarah said with a wince, moving her hand over her belly where subtle movement could be seen rolling across the surface of her stretched shirt. "Wanna feel?"

Hesitant, Jocelyn reached out to place a hand on her friend's swollen belly. Suddenly, she felt the distinct roll of an assertive limb as the baby fought for room inside the safety of her mother's womb. "*Wow*," she said in awe.

With her hand still in place, she felt a series of other movements, entranced by the beauty and wonder of it. She had never felt a baby move inside of its mother before and wondered what it must be like to carry a child. To be its first home.

"That's crazy," Jocelyn mused, finally withdrawing her hand. "What is it like being a mother?" she asked.

"It's wonderful," Sarah began. "And *hard*," she admitted. "Whatever you imagine motherhood to be before having kids, it's nothing like the real thing. I thought I knew everything. What love was. How much patience I needed to get through a day. I just *knew* I would stick to my guns on the important issues like nutrition and screen time. I wondered how moms could live with themselves feeding chicken nuggets to their toddler while they sat glued to an iPad. I had to eat all my words, all my judgments, and they tasted like self-loathing. Sometimes I still manage to think I know better now that I am a mom. It's never too long before I'm proven otherwise. Every day is like learning something I thought I understood all over again."

"It sounds difficult," Jocelyn replied.

"It is," Sarah admitted. "But my mom always said that anything worth having wouldn't come easily. It's beautiful, seeing the world through your child's eyes. Like experiencing everything again for the first time.

"Being a parent is like seeing the world more clearly than you ever did before. But it also means carrying the weight of that clarity. Everything just matters a little bit more once you bring a child into the world. You're not just worried about yourself anymore, you want them to have a beautiful life too. At the expense of your own if that's what it takes.

"You give up a lot. You have to make sacrifices to put your kids first, change your expectations, and wait to indulge in the selfish stuff until your kids are older. It wouldn't be a very good idea to prioritize crossing sky diving off my bucket list with two small children at home, you know? But I would never want to go back to who I was before having kids."

Jocelyn tried to picture herself in Sarah's position. Pregnant with a toddler running around and a husband of seven years. No matter how hard she pressed, she couldn't imagine it. Clint, the man she had dated before Michael, was an even less suitable match for her than she felt Michael was. Even if he had been, she couldn't see herself starting a family all those years ago. Unlike Sarah, she hadn't been ready. As she watched her friend, perusing the small assortment of plants, she felt peace wash over her in a way it never had before.

Sarah had been ready to be a wife and mother at a young age. Jocelyn, on the other hand, had been so career driven from the start, that the idea of slowing her momentum to add a husband and children to the mix would have felt like drowning. Now, she considered for the first time, she could see the space in her world for more than just a career, perhaps she was finally ready to share her life with a family of her own.

"I haven't been here in a long time," Sarah exclaimed as she held the door open to the small Mexican restaurant just on the outskirts of town. "They have *the best* street tacos."

"Oh, I love street tacos," Jocelyn said approvingly.

The establishment was small, as it seemed most places in town were, but it was quaint and welcoming with its ornate Mexican décor. The walls were a warm yellow, covered in artwork and memorabilia, and the red terracotta tiles added to the authentic feel. Strung from the ceiling were colorful paper flags with beautiful designs cut into them and mariachi music played softly in the background.

The hostess sat Jocelyn and Sarah at a small corner booth where they had a good view of the whole restaurant. They both opened their menus and began scanning the options.

"I'm starving," Sarah moaned. "I don't know if it's my stomach growling or the baby kicking, but I'm getting two orders of tacos."

Jocelyn skimmed over the menu. "Can friends have sympathy cravings? I don't think one order is enough for me either."

"*Oh*," Sarah exclaimed. "Get the watermelon margarita."

"That sounds good."

Jocelyn studied the drink menu. Though all the choices looked delicious, the watermelon margarita was definitely calling her name. After looking over the wide assortment of starters, traditional dishes, and street tacos, she made her selection, almost certain her appetite was too big for her stomach.

"Buenas noches, Sarah," a thickly accented woman's voice said in greeting.

Jocelyn lifted her eyes from her menu to see a Mexican woman who made more sense on a magazine cover than she did in a waitress apron. Her big brown eyes were as sultry as her voice. Her skin was a creamy brown, speckled with dainty freckles, perfectly placed on the bridge of her nose and across her cheeks. Her dark hair was thick and glossy, falling just past her shoulders. Her body was curvy and voluptuous, while her waist seemed impossibly slender. Her lips were full, coated in a bright pink lipstick, and her eyes were made up to accentuate her thick long lashes.

"Selena," Sarah replied awkwardly. "Hi….er, Hola."

Jocelyn couldn't place the tension that hung between the two women, but its presence wasn't lost on her. "Hi," she said, sweetly, relieving her friend of the beautiful woman's focus. "We're *starving*," she said, punctuating the statement with wide eyes. "I think we're actually ready to order if that's okay."

"Sí, of course," Selena replied easily. Void of a notepad and pen, she stood poised, ready to commit the order to memory.

"I'll have two orders of the carne asada street tacos and an iced tea," Sarah informed, passing over her menu.

"Okay," Selena said in confirmation.

"I'll take two orders of the al pastor street tacos and a watermelon margarita," Jocelyn relayed cheerfully.

"I'll put those right in for you," Selena replied. "I'll be back with complimentary chips and salsa as well," she added before turning on her heels and walking away.

Jocelyn watched as Selena glided away on pumps, she would never dream of wearing at a job that kept her on her feet, or at any job for the matter. The three-inch heels made her calves pop, her hips sway, and all the men in the establishment stare.

Sarah groaned and sank back into the booth, releasing some, but not all, of the tension that the attractive waitress had brought with her.

"What was that all about?" Jocelyn whispered, leaning over the table to close the distance between them.

"That's *Selena*," Sarah informed.

"I gathered that much," Jocelyn said, raising her eyebrows.

"*Selena*, as in. Jack's ex," she enunciated. "The one he left high and dry in the damn Florida Keys."

Jocelyn instantly felt sick. The pain in her chest was so unexpected, she wondered if she might pass out. Twisted in a tangled mess of feelings she couldn't explain, most of which she hadn't earned the right to feel, she sank back in her own booth. Her eyes shut slowly, and all she could see was the swaying hips and the flawless face of a woman she was willing to wager was the most beautiful she had ever seen. A woman who had likely set an impossibly high bar in Jack's mind for what a lover should be.

The assault of feelings was enough to throw her. The immediate urge to reject them came just as quickly. Why did she care who Jack's ex was? Why was the image of them together taunting her?

While her own mortification was heavy, it wasn't lost on Sarah how struck by the news Jocelyn appeared to be. Though her friend worked to compose herself, she had seen the glimpse of jealousy and sadness wash over her face that only a woman who had fallen for her brother might feel. The more she looked on, however, the more she suspected she'd been mistaken. Jocelyn was the picture of indifference as Selena approached the table again.

"Here you are," Selena said, delivering their chips and salsa as well as their drinks.

"Thank you," Jocelyn and Sarah echoed in reply, each hoping their tone wasn't telling.

"De nada."

Blinking hard, Jocelyn took a huge swig of her margarita. She noticed it took more effort than it should to enjoy how delicious it was.

Once Selena was out of earshot, Jocelyn leaned in and ventured, "What happened between them anyway?" She hoped that her tone sounded less desperate than she felt to receive answers.

"Selena suspected that Jack was going to propose to her during their trip," Sarah began.

"*Was he?*" Jocelyn felt her heart twist again and took another swig of her drink.

"Yes," Sarah whispered. "They had been together for a few years at that point. With my mom sick, I think he felt more inclined to rush into marriage than he would have otherwise. Selena was still pretty immature for her age. Jack was captivated by her, of course, but I think he knew she wasn't wife material. Not yet anyway. She still had a lot of growing up to do.

"But Mom had been there for both my and Will's weddings. She got to see us both become parents. Jack knew that she wanted him to be happy. She wanted to know that when she left this world, he would have someone to spend his life with. I always suspected that Selena wasn't the best fit for him, but with blinders on, I think he was ready to make the only choice he had at the time."

"Did he love her?" Jocelyn asked, ignoring the discomfort the question left in the pit of her stomach.

"Oh, yes," Sarah said quickly. "I think every man in town, in one way or another, is in love with Selena."

Jocelyn sipped her drink absently, glancing again at the woman who had enchanted the man she refused to admit mesmerized her. She imagined a woman that beautiful and confident always knew what she wanted and never wasted time talking herself out of it.

"How old is she?" she inquired further.

"I guess she'd be about twenty-nine now," Sarah speculated.

The pain of insecurity grew deeper and Jocelyn had no better chance of explaining it.

"Anyway, after receiving the news about Mom, she tried to insist that they stay a little longer. I think, in her mind, if they just went on that cruise together, he would propose, and they'd return to Virginia engaged to be married."

"Wow."

Putting her own erratic feelings aside, Jocelyn considered how much of an emotional devastation that must have been for them both. For Jack, losing his mother and his future bride on the same day. For Selena, believing she would return home engaged just to find herself returning alone after Jack had left without her.

"Do you think they would ever reconcile?" Jocelyn probed, reaching for her glass again.

"Oh, gosh no. That bridge was burned, packed up, and hurled into the Rappahannock a year ago," Sarah said brazenly.

"Do you think they would have gotten married if things had gone differently?" Jocelyn wasn't sure she wanted the answer.

"Yeah, I do," Sarah admitted. "But I think being hurt like that by someone you care so much about can turn love to hate pretty quickly. Jack was entirely unfair to Selena as well, if I'm being honest," she added. "He wasn't thinking clearly. He had been too upset about Mom to realize that he'd been cruel to her as a result."

"Yeah," Jocelyn replied somberly. "Do you think she hates him?"

"The first thing she did when she returned was lob half a dozen bricks through the houseboat," Sarah offered.

"Ouch." Jocelyn winced, picturing it.

"It was heartless to say the least. Jack wasn't in a place to deal with that on top of losing Mom. But once the dust settled, he later admitted he didn't blame her for it. He understood that they'd both been hurt by what happened and neither could see past their own pain long enough to empathize with the other."

Jocelyn fell silent as she digested the information Sarah had just divulged. While it didn't sit well with her to picture Jack's past love life, it did give her a better idea of who he had been before his mother's passing and the man he had become in the wake of it. He had been a devoted partner, ready to settle down with a woman who appeared to be perfect in every way. In the past year, he had suffered from so much separation, it was as if he had drifted out to sea. Though she couldn't be certain, she suspected he was beginning to find his way back again.

When Selena returned with their food, balanced perfectly on her practiced arms, Jocelyn felt her appetite shrink.

The remainder of their meal was spent discussing their purchases and the plans Jocelyn had for staging the house. She did her best to rid herself of the discomfort that Selena's presence and the potent thoughts of Jack's romantic past and its imminent demise gave her. Half-way through her third margarita, enjoying the warm feeling of indifference it delivered, she had finally convinced herself that she didn't care.

"*Woah*," Jack said, opening the front door to the house. He had finished for the day, ready to head back to his place, when he saw Sarah walking Jocelyn up the front steps.

"It's my fault," Sarah admitted sheepishly.

"*I'm fine*," Jocelyn slurred.

Jack glanced down at the to-go bag in her hand and the heat of anger flooded his veins.

"*Really?*" he hissed at Sarah through clenched teeth.

"What?" Sarah said innocently. "The tacos are really good," she justified.

"Mmm," Jocelyn cooed. "*Sooo good.*" She hiccupped. "You know what's even better?" she said, then gently poked Jack's nose. "*Watermelon margaritas.*"

Jack groaned and massaged his temple. "I'll take it from here," he said, pulling Jocelyn to his side.

"Are you sure?" Sarah asked apologetically. "She's going to be in for a rough night."

"Don't worry," he said, his tone softening. "I owe her one."

Jack guided Jocelyn upstairs and encouraged her to get dressed for bed. Affording her ample privacy and time to collect herself, he headed downstairs to close up the house and check in on Lady.

Peeling her sundress off felt like the most complicated and strenuous task Jocelyn had ever attempted. She was almost certain she had broken one of her sandals in her effort to unlace straps that apparently were meant to be decorative. As luck would have it, she was too drunk to care. She couldn't remember when she'd last had that much to drink, but she was happy she was intoxicated enough not to worry about the morning that inevitably awaited her on the other side of her buzz.

Sitting at the end of her bed in a bra, panties, and mismatched socks, she thought offhandedly that Jack might return. She couldn't decide, in her careless state, if she would throw herself at him or throw up. The idea of Jack wrapped around the sultry waitress made her desperate to stake claim on a man she wasn't willing to admit sober that she wanted.

In the end, she decided that she didn't trust herself around Jack with her guard down. Her head might be fuzzy, but she knew enough not to play with a flame that might very well burn her. Stretching the limits of her ability to function coherently, she yanked on an oversized T-shirt just in time for Jack to walk through the bedroom door.

Jocelyn was seated at the edge of her bed, minimally clothed, and Jack had to collect himself as he breached the doorway, though he guessed she hadn't noticed.

"Did you steal my socks?" she asked absently, studying her feet.

"What?" he asked, confused.

"My socks," she repeated. "I can't find the other one." She lifted her right foot, displaying a black sock with smiley faces on it. "They're my favorite," she added before dropping her foot back down.

"Why would I take your sock?" Jack challenged with a chuckle.

"I don't know," she responded, shrugging. "Maybe you really like feet."

"I have many flaws," Jack said coolly, "but a foot fetish isn't one of them."

"Are you *sure*?" she asked accusingly.

Jack held his hand up, tucked his pinky under his thumb and held his three remaining fingers together. "Scout's honor."

Jocelyn's face twisted, a brief glimpse of sobriety and regret flashed across her eyes. "Ugh," she groaned, her hands moving to her stomach. "I'm going to be sick."

She rushed from the room, making it to the toilet just in time.

Jack cringed and wondered if it was best to leave her alone but decided against it in case she needed his help in the aftermath. He moved over to the window as he waited and peered out, realizing offhandedly that the view offered a direct line of sight to the docked houseboat. Lady, he noticed, sat loyally at the door, back lit by the dim dining room light as the sun began its lazy descent in the sky.

It took a few spirited rounds of vomiting for Jocelyn to finally empty the full contents of her stomach. Perhaps the worst part, worse even than throwing up half dressed in earshot of Jack, was that she would never be able to look at a watermelon margarita the same way again.

When she finally emerged from the bathroom, Jack noticed how helpless and in need of protecting Jocelyn looked and he was decidedly glad that he had stayed.

"Why don't you lie down?" he offered. "I'll get you a glass of water."

When Jack returned, Jocelyn was curled up on her side, straddling her comforter with one long bare leg sticking out of the bedding. As fragile and helpless as she appeared, she was sweetly seductive and beautiful with her mismatched socks and striped underwear. Jack picked up the throw blanket at the end of the bed and draped it gently over her body, then placed the glass of water beside her on the nightstand.

"Don't go," she said, her voice soft as she fought back sleep.

"I…" Jack hesitated. He cleared his throat. "I should let you rest. You'll feel better in the morning," he promised, knowing it probably wouldn't be the case.

"*Mmm*," she cooed, patting the spot beside her. "Can you just rub my back a bit? Sometimes it helps."

Jack grew stiff, fighting the urge to join her on the bed. Knowing how vulnerable and persuadable she was, he was certain that a lesser man might try and take advantage. The idea of it filled him with a fierce desire to protect her.

"You shouldn't invite strange men into your bed when you've been drinking," he advised.

"You're not a strange man," she asserted. "Besides," she added "I trust you."

Jack let out a heavy sigh. Honorable or not, maintaining his composure in such close proximity to Jocelyn's scantily clad body was no small task. Without a good excuse, and if he was being honest, the will to leave, he rounded the bed and sat beside her. Placing his hand on her back, he began gently rubbing small circles into her shoulder.

"Mmm, that feels good," she murmured sleepily.

He traced the lines of her tense muscles, guiding his thumb with precision as he moved his hand over the surface of her shoulders. He moved his left hand up and worked in unison, tracing mirrored patterns into the muscles of her back. He drew his hands as low as he could bear, sweeping gentle strokes across her ribs, then the small of her back, and up to her shoulders again. She moaned blissfully as his mind and his body waged war over the proper response. It was a form of torture he had never thought could be so painful, yet the idea of leaving seemed a greater impossibility to endure.

"I hope this means we're even," he said sweetly, happy with the casual tone in which he'd managed to deliver the comment.

"*Mmm*," was all she said.

Silence filled the room as he continued to rub her back, and Jack closed his eyes, allowing himself to imagine a life in which this scene made sense. A life built together, full of ups and downs, weathering the impending storms and relishing in the peace they found on the other side of them.

"Do you speak Spanish?" Jocelyn asked absently.

Jack's eyes eased open at the soft sound of her voice.

"Hablo un poco," he replied, brushing a stray strand of hair from her face.

She whimpered into her pillow. "*She's beautiful*," she grumbled.

"Who's beautiful?" he asked, though he suspected he already knew the answer.

"*Selena*," Jocelyn said on the tail end of a sigh.

Jack winced as she confirmed his suspicions. When he had seen the to-go bag, he had wondered if they might have run into his ex, and now he felt inexplicably ashamed for it. As if he'd been caught in a scandal.

"You're beautiful," he whispered back boldly.

"Not like *Selena*," she replied grumpily. "*Her and her... perfect... everything*," she rambled on in a sleepy fog.

"Shhh," Jack cooed, unable to banish a chuckle upon the detection of her jealousy.

"*Don't you laugh at me*," she hissed in a harmless snappy tone. "I can't help that you only fall for perfect women. Selena...with her perfect hair. Her perfect body. The lips, and the eyes...and the *shoes*. She had *great shoes...Perfect...Perfect...Perfect*."

"She's far from perfect," Jack assured Jocelyn.

Her quick snort confirmed that she believed otherwise.

"Get some sleep," he tried coaxing again.

"I bet you put sand down her bathing suit once or twice," she drawled lazily.

Pressing his lips together to suffocate a smile, Jack was willing to admit that he was enjoying Jocelyn's tirade.

"No, *never*," he said firmly. "I save that for only the extra special girls."

"*Good*," she cooed.

Jocelyn smiled into her pillow, seemingly content with the results of her one-sided combat. It wasn't long before her expression relaxed as she gave in to the weight of exhaustion that washed over her, falling asleep at last.

Jack kept his eyes on his hands for a while as he continued to caress her back. They'd once shared a sensual kiss, but this somehow felt much more intimate. Comforting her, as she had comforted him once. They had spent far too little time getting to know one another again. Yet, within that small window, they had bonded in ways he never had with another woman.

With Selena, there had been lust and untamed passion. She was a firecracker of emotion and heat and energy that had instantly drawn him to her. From the moment he had first laid eyes on her in the restaurant, he had been captivated by her sensuality and her quick wit. She had been like a drug to him. Mood altering intensity, euphoric highs, and cavernous lows. She was a woman he thought himself a fool not to propose to, which was ultimately the reason he had been set to do just that. Though, he questioned now if he could really picture a life with her.

When the dust had settled from his brash emotional response to her selfishness surrounding his mother's death—not to mention her retaliation for his reaction—Jack had waited in anticipation for a withdrawal of regret and remorse that never came. While he couldn't deny that he'd loved her, he wondered now what kind of love it had truly been. The love of possession perhaps? The love of good fortune? She was a woman of more substance than just her sheer beauty, but was she the kind of woman who might make sense in his life? In the end, Jack had realized that the answer was no. For months he had even begun to question, if he couldn't love a woman like Selena enough to justify reconciliation, was he capable of feeling that way for anyone?

Loving again, in the very least, had felt like an impossibility. Until Jocelyn. Like a dream, she had walked back into his life just as he had been balancing on the cusp of giving up on it entirely. She reminded him that his heart still pumped warm blood through his veins and his body still craved the company of a good woman.

Jack swept the hair from Jocelyn's face, and felt his heart ache at the thought of her walking out of his life again. He was drawn to her as he'd never been to anyone else. A once boyish crush had grown into an undeniable need.

"I love you," he whispered softly, enjoying the peace professing the words aloud granted him. "I always have," he added.

He kissed her forehead then rose from the bed, forcing himself to walk away as Jocelyn slept, fully aware of how much of himself he had left with her.

Chapter Thirteen

Maybe it was because she hadn't experienced a hangover in years. Maybe it was the fact that seeing Selena that night had filled her veins with a jealousy she hadn't anticipated or been equipped to make sense of. Whatever the reason, it took several days for Jocelyn to clear the fog that interrupted her ability to focus on much else.

It hadn't helped that when she had woken up, suffering from a sizable headache and a dry mouth, her thoughts had been consumed by the most vivid dream she ever had. So real, in fact, that she had needed to walk herself back through the vision to determine from the inconsistencies that it had in fact been only a dream.

In the fantasy, she had been swaying gently in a hammock a few feet from the shore of a white sandy beach, suspended by two bare tree trunks that jutted out in the impossibly clear blue water. Cradled by the woven cords of the hammock, she was tucked neatly against a man's bare chest. When she looked up to see his face, she realized that it was Jack. Rather than responding with embarrassment or shock, she had smiled dreamily, nuzzling closer into his embrace. In response, he had kissed the top of her head and brushed his fingers absently through her hair.

She had realized at that moment of the dream that they were wrapped in soft white bed sheets, and she knew by the way they fit together in the intimate space that they had recently finished making love. The feelings the dream had provoked were both welcome and overwhelming, delivering a sense of peace and arousal all at once.

As the image began to fade, Jack had whispered softly, "I love you…I always have."

Jocelyn had fought to get back to the fantasy. Not only to escape the discomfort that came with consciousness, but to return to a scene that made sense only in her dreams. A scene that felt too good to be true, because, of course, it was.

She hadn't exactly avoided Jack in the days leading up to her brief return trip to Texas, but she was willing to admit that she'd managed to see far less of him than usual. When she wasn't wrestling with embarrassment brought on by what little she could remember having said to him that night, she was picturing them lying together as he whispered the words "I love you."

Whenever they met in passing, she could tell that unspoken words lingered just beyond the depth of his blue topaz eyes and his gently parted lips. She suspected they had more to do with the fool she'd made of herself after running into his ex, but deep down she wished that they reflected something more akin to the sentiment of her dream. She knew that what she was beginning to want with Jack was far more than she could ask of him, and worse still, more than she could ask of herself.

***

Suspended in the air as the lights of Austin greeted her from below, Jocelyn challenged herself to determine what she really wanted. Though she had assumed that arriving back in Texas would provide that answer, she was no more certain than when she had left. Instead, she fought to maintain that the city beneath her was home. Despite every expectation that this would be the sentiment, the city below felt foreign to her now.

How had a couple of months in rural Virginia corrupted her strong loyalties so completely? It wasn't as if Farnham offered much that Austin couldn't. Truthfully, it offered far less in many ways given all that awaited her back in Texas. Though, she considered candidly, it did offer one thing nowhere else in the world could. Jack. But to abandon everything she knew, everything she had built, for a man she wasn't willing to pursue? It felt childish. Foolish. Careless even.

But, she allowed herself to consider, what if she did pursue him? What if she permitted her feelings to take charge in the discovery of where a life with Jack might lead? Was he really such a risky gamble, or was she just too afraid to play the game? The thought of it still scared her beyond reason. The fact remained that Jack was in Virginia and her life was not.

Jocelyn took a deep breath, combed her fingers through her hair, let out a steady breath, and reminded herself that this trip was more important than some juvenile infatuation. It was more important than the feelings she wasn't willing to address and a dream that meant less than nothing. This was her life, her livelihood and more importantly, she reminded herself, a dream she had *actually* worked for. A goal she had spent years building from the ground up. This promotion was the most tangible representation of her efforts. And that was something she could confidently say she believed in.

***

When Jocelyn exited the team meeting the following day, she felt rejuvenated. For weeks she had separated herself from everything that kept her anchored to reality. She had wagered that the time away would bring her clarity, and she believed now with certainty that she had been right. Her team had put on a mock presentation that was worthy of a standing ovation. She was proud of everything Melissa, Chad, and Greg had put together in her absence. She was even happy to admit that the time away had offered her the opportunity to view the assignment from a different vantage point. With new insights and consideration, she had managed to use her absence as an advantage rather than a hindrance to the team's final production.

"Great work in there," Bridget beamed, placing a friendly hand on Jocelyn's shoulder. "I'll admit, leaving this close to the deadline was not a risk I was happy for you to take. But you really proved yourself in there. I can only imagine you've had to work twice as hard these past couple of months in order to tie up all the loose ends that I was worried might be our undoing. You know as well as anyone how stubborn companies can be to amend their approaches when what they're doing works. But you showed me today that you know how to take what works even better and make it work for you."

"Wow," Jocelyn said breathlessly. "Thank you, I really appreciate it."

"I'm only speaking the truth," Bridget insisted. "You know I'm not one for blowing smoke. It's a waste of time and energy. But praise where it's due, that I refuse to withhold."

Jocelyn smiled warmly and the heat of it filled her heart with affirmation. She really had managed to pull off what she had worried might be impossible given the circumstances.

"I can't wait to have you back for good," Bridget professed, squeezing Jocelyn's arms affectionately. "I hope you like the view from your new corner office."

A wave of excitement washed over her as Jocelyn absorbed the direct hint at her making the promotion. She never considered anything a sure thing until it came to fruition, but this was as close as she would get to confirmation that the position was hers until the news became official. Whatever she had felt since leaving Austin, the pride she clutched now was the most certain thing she had grasped in months.

"You deserve it," she heard a familiar voice call over from behind.

Startled, she turned around, already knowing whose lips the compliment had been delivered from.

Michael, dressed in a smart all black suit and tie, stood casually at the end of the hall. With perfectly coiffed dark hair, his expression was relaxed with a friendly smile. His cloudy blue eyes gazed at her as only a man who had seen past her clothes could. His face, Jocelyn thought, looked more chiseled, adding a rough edge to his handsome features. Had he lost weight? Put on muscle maybe? Perhaps he had finally started using the gym membership he'd once joked was a charity he made regular donations to? Whatever the case, Jocelyn found herself drawn to what was familiar about him as well as what appeared to be new.

"Don't speak too soon," she answered. "I don't want to jinx it."

"Even if I believed in superstitions," he said with a smirk, "which you know I do. I'd be willing to put money on it. In fact, I'm in for a hundred bucks."

Jocelyn rolled her eyes playfully.

"What do you say we play hooky for the rest of the day?" he asked, shifting his eyes across the room where Bridget stood with her back turned.

"I haven't been to the office in months," Jocelyn protested.

"Perfect," he said, closing the space between them easily, then ushered her towards the elevator. "Then they won't notice you're gone."

The sophisticated ambiance of the lavish hotel restaurant Michael had chosen for lunch was breathtaking. The room was airy and bright, creating a spacious yet warm and intimate atmosphere. The far wall had been fashioned into an accent feature with an assortment of mismatched tiles, creating an artfully constructed mosaic. The tables were natural wood, matching the light varnish on the floors. Different rugs ran the length of the spaces between tables; each one unique in pattern and color; combinations of maroon, cream, yellow, and blue. The chairs that surrounded each table were upholstered in various fabrics with patterns of blue, cream, and splashes of golden yellow.

"I've always wanted to eat here," Jocelyn beamed, her eyes dancing around the spacious room from her seat.

"I know," Michael said, pleased with himself.

Jocelyn began to question if being comfortable and familiar was such a bad thing. Since she and Michael had broken up, she had convinced herself that there must be more out there. That life wasn't just about finding pieces that fit neatly together. Perhaps, she had begun to consider, that life was about adventure, the unknown, and taking risks. But as she sat across from the man she'd spent the past two years of her life with, she felt the pang of uncertainty over their chapter's end begin to surface. Was it so terrible to have things figured out? Wasn't that everyone's goal? Why had she become so eager to overcomplicate her life with the ideas of breaking free from familiarity and running into a man's arms simply because he was nicer to her in adulthood than he had been as a child?

"You look great," Michael complimented, studying her before turning his attention to the menu. "I had my doubts, but this time away seems to be exactly what you needed."

"Told you," Jocelyn boasted, satisfied.

"When do you head back to Virginia?"

"Tomorrow," she replied, unexpectedly regretful.

"So soon?"

"I'm eager to finish getting the place ready to sell. There's still plenty left to be done before we can put it up on the market.

I'll be back before you know it." She felt her heart growing torn at the idea.

Taking a moment to make their selections, they both reviewed the menu in comfortable silence. Michael's company, though he didn't set her heart to racing in the way that Jack could, was like riding a bike. They picked right back up where they had left off with ease. Again, Jocelyn questioned why she had grown to view that as such a bad thing.

"So," Michael ventured. "Has your heart grown fonder?"

Jocelyn considered his question, deciding that Michael was referring to Austin rather than himself. While she had certainly gained a deeper connection to the river house and knew she would always consider it home on some level, she did feel herself pulling back towards Austin in a way she hadn't expected to.

"Yes," she confirmed. "Yes, it has."

"Good," Michael said contentedly.

It hadn't been easy for Michael to wait in the wings as Jocelyn jumped at the first opportunity to run from everything that had ever made sense between them. They had only ended their relationship a few months before her retreat to Virginia, and he was certain now that she regretted her brash decision to sever the ties between them.

Initially, he had afforded her the space to venture off without reaching out to her in fear that he might come off as being desperate. After all, what about a small Virginia town could possibly give her pause? But after hearing how close she had become with the man who worked on her family's home— a man who was perfectly comfortable ripping his shirt off in front of her—Michael knew he couldn't let their time apart grow too cold.

He'd sent her messages only when it seemed reasonable to do so to stay in her thoughts, as she always did in his. And in the meantime, he worked on himself knowing Jocelyn would eventually return. He had started a strict diet, a running regimen, and attended the gym five days a week. She was a beautiful woman, and he was willing to admit that he had let himself grow lazy in the years they'd been together. He'd become soft, careless, and passive, convinced that what they had didn't require maintenance.

It was obvious now that he needed to work harder at keeping her attention. Sometimes all a man needed was a little freshening up to remind a woman he was worth sticking around for.

Michael knew that Jocelyn liked the idea of adventure, but she enjoyed the comfort of familiarity more. If only he could remind her of the life they could have together, perhaps she would see what he had known all along. That they had invested so much into a perfect plan. A perfect life together.

"I've missed you terribly," he offered boldly.

Jocelyn's thoughts shifted briefly to Jack, before banishing them shamefully. She took a sip from her glass of water to buy time and smiled across the table at Michael, unsure of how to reply. Had she missed him? Not exactly. But here she was. She had been excited to see him, that much was true.

"It feels like it's been years," she offered, hoping that the evasive response gave him the assurance he needed without confirming something she didn't entirely reciprocate. "It's great to be back," she added honestly.

"In only a few more weeks, you'll be back for good," Michael proclaimed, victoriously. "How shall we celebrate?"

Jocelyn searched her mind. Not only for a reply but for a pulse that indicated how the idea made her feel. She felt both lost and found all at once. Equally torn and decidedly incomplete. The more Michael talked about her return, the more she believed she was ready to do it, and the more her stomach twisted at the idea. The rush of excitement she'd felt back at the office was fading and she grasped around anxiously to relocate it.

"I'd love to go jet skiing," she replied, scrambling for an answer to his question.

The response was ridiculous, she decided quickly. She still couldn't say she'd enjoyed the activity overall. Rather, she'd enjoyed experiencing it with Jack. Would she enjoy it as much with Michael? Was it fair to assume otherwise simply because he wasn't Jack?

Michael laughed easily. "Jet skiing. Okay."

The remainder of their meal together was a mix of feelings that made Jocelyn's head spin. At first, whatever Michael mentioned seemed to draw her thoughts to a memory she had made in recent weeks. The barrister bookcase he'd found for his apartment at a thrift store made her think of Jack's barn and all the antique furniture it housed. When Michael talked about his neighbor's yappy dog, her thoughts returned to Lady in all her regal beauty. The mention of downtown traffic had her dreaming of the beautiful winding backroads that wove through Farnham.

But not all her thoughts were drawn away, and it was those that she did her best to cling to. Michael, as she'd noticed back at the office, was leaner and decidedly more handsome than she had remembered. Complimented by his easy personality, it wasn't hard to get lost in his eyes or the conversation.

He was both intellectual as well as conversational. He could read the room as if he were reading minds. When Jocelyn's interest on a subject waned, he would shift easily to an amusing anecdote that freshened up the space between them. Then he would pose a question that made her think on her feet or challenged her with a full-bodied discussion about something he'd read in a news article that week.

By the time they'd finished their meal, she had herself convinced that her conflicting thoughts were only natural, but this was where she belonged.

"Anyway, enough about me," Michael declared after a compelling analysis of the algorithms he and his team had cultivated for their own upcoming presentation. "How is the house coming along?" He casually polished off what remained of his cabernet.

"Oh, it's beautiful," Jocelyn gushed. "It's hardly the same house. Jack has been working overtime to finish the project by the deadline. Today he and his crew are scheduled to start repainting the exterior."

"That's great," Michael said coolly. "I bet your parents will be able to sell it for a handsome profit."

"I'll be sad to see it go," Jocelyn admitted. "But I'm happy to know that we've given the house a second chance."

"I would love to see the place you've called home these last couple of months."

"You should come up," Jocelyn proposed without thinking.

Maybe it was the wine. Maybe it was the way Michael looked in his well fitted black suit. Perhaps it was the way her loyalties seemed to fight to find their rightful place. She couldn't be entirely certain. What Jocelyn wanted more than anything was for her head to stop spinning and for her heart to be firmly planted in one place. Maybe she ventured, in order to do so, first her two worlds must collide.

It had been difficult to read Jocelyn throughout their meal. Just as she would let her guard down, she seemed to become aware of her abandon and worked quickly to rein it back in. He could see that she still hesitated. That she wore the expression of a woman who feared she had left something behind. He didn't care what arrangements, groveling, or favors he would have to call in to make the trip happen. All he knew was that he had no choice but to go to Virginia and show Jocelyn once and for all that nothing remained there for her but a dusty old pile of memories, and that her future was and always had been with him.

Michael massaged his jawline thoughtfully. "I'm in," he said firmly. "I'll book a flight out with you tomorrow."

Chapter Fourteen

Not eager to see another employee whisked off to Virginia, Bridget had only permitted Michael an overnight leave of absence. Jocelyn decided that the brief stint had been a small miracle, just shy of refusing the request all together. She had spent the night questioning why she had extended the invitation in the first place. If he was there any longer, she imagined he might get the wrong idea.

It had been awkward telling Michael that she preferred that he stay in a hotel rather than at the river house with her. Luckily, he was too polite to try and insist otherwise. No matter what her indecision over returning to Austin meant, she was almost certain it had nothing to do with him, and she needed to set enough ground rules in place to make that point abundantly clear.

***

Seeing Jack's pick-up truck parked beside the raised bungalow as she rounded the bend of the driveway set Jocelyn's heart to racing. Michael followed closely behind in his own rental—of course he had selected a BMW—and a mix of emotions consumed her at the thought of the two men meeting. It felt as if she was ushering one alpha into another alpha's territory. Coaxing them both into a fight over what was rightfully theirs. Though, she reminded herself, neither of them had a claim over her, nor did they reserve the right to assume otherwise. Maybe, she was willing to admit, she wanted to see the men contrast against one another. Did she intend to make a decision? Or perhaps she merely wanted to make it clear that she wouldn't. Her thoughts were so clouded trying to decide what she wanted that she hardly had the time to determine what she had been thinking when she'd invited Michael to Virginia in the first place.

Her thoughts were quickly drawn from the two men as Jocelyn recognized the newly painted exterior. The sea foam green she had selected for the façade was stunning, more beautiful even than she had pictured it would be. As she approached the house, she noticed Jack and a few of his crew members applying what appeared to be a second coat of white to the trim. Now the outside of the home matched the beauty Jack had created within.

Jack had spent the days leading up to Jocelyn's departure trying to find the right words to express the depth of his feelings for her. When he had sensed that she was intentionally pulling away, he had hesitated to tell her what he'd been withholding for the last nine weeks. She seemed conflicted, protective, and unready to address the shared feelings she struggled to conceal. But during her short time away, not even a full seventy-two hours, he felt the weight of her absence. Guarding his heart from attachment no longer felt pertinent when he had fallen victim to pining over her all the same. He loved her, and there was no longer any sense in denying it.

Upon her highly anticipated return, his excitement was abruptly intercepted by the unexpected second vehicle that pulled up to the house. When the two cars parked, and Jack saw the man exit his expensive rental—his clothes finely pressed and of affluent taste—he immediately wondered if perhaps this man had been the reason for Jocelyn's hesitation all along.

Had Jack been too distracted by his rekindled boyhood crush to see that her heart was already taken? He had advanced on her, and while he'd felt her draw towards him, in the end, she had pulled away. Was this man—cut from a far different cloth than he was—the reason behind her withdrawal?

"Hi, Jack!" Jocelyn called as she approached the house. "It looks great!" she beamed. "What a difference!"

"I'm happy you like it. You picked a great color," Jack replied, his voice friendly but guarded.

"This is Michael," Jocelyn, said, introducing the man who now stood at her side.

Michael put up a hand in a friendly yet indifferent greeting.

Jack grew tense, the smile on his face forced and fake. He offered a raised hand in the man's direction, uninterested in being overly cordial but unwilling to be blatantly rude.

"He works with me at the firm," she added.

Jack didn't miss the ambitious look in Michael's eyes as he brazenly studied the curves of Jocelyn's body. Alluding to the fact that something more existed between them.

"He was dying to see all the work you've done."

And pictures wouldn't have sufficed, Jack wondered abrasively to himself. Had he fixed up the place only to have Jocelyn bring home a different man to bed there? Not that he had a say in the matter, but he certainly reserved the right to have feelings about it.

"Take a look around," he offered, doing his best to sound neutral. "She's just about finished." The effort to remain casual and seemingly unphased by another male's unwanted company was nearly an impossible burden to shoulder.

Jocelyn smiled sweetly, her eyes lost on Jack for a moment as he returned to his work, then escorted Michael inside.

"Eager to see the work I've done," Jack huffed. Bullshit he was. No man traveled half-way across the country to see a piece of property he clearly had little to no interest in without an ulterior motive. The way he had placed his hand on the small of Jocelyn's back as they entered the house was clearly meant for Jack to see. Not only was it obvious the man was in hot

184

pursuit of her, but Jack also recognized the comfortable proximity he maintained. The assertion of a man who had already enjoyed the pleasures of a woman's body.

Once inside the house, they were greeted by Lady who had been camped out by an air duct. Always eager to meet new humans, she gave Michael a generous sniff. Though he did his best to act casual, he had been momentarily alarmed by her presence.

"You never said you got a walking security system," Michael said, reluctantly petting Lady's massive head. "I thought you didn't like dogs. A Yorkie maybe, but a Rottweiler? I would have lost that bet."

Jocelyn knew that Michael didn't particularly care for animals, least of all dogs. She found his strained attempt to pretend otherwise entertaining.

"I never said I didn't like dogs," she clarified. "You did. But, no, Lady's not mine, she's Jack's," she informed. "Don't let the stereotype fool you either, she's a real sweetheart."

"He brings his dog to work?" Michael challenged. "Doesn't seem very professional."

"He doesn't always, but he likes to. I love it personally. She has taken to keeping me company while I work or lounge out by the pool or on the porch once I've finished for the day," Jocelyn informed, feeling slightly protective.

"There's a pool?"

Michael grew tense at the thought of the contractor laying eyes on Jocelyn in a bikini. He imagined the man was as unsophisticated as he looked and could easily picture him grunting at the sight of a beautiful woman dressed in little more than some swatches of fabric.

"Would you like to see it?" Jocelyn offered.

"Maybe later," Michael said agreeably.

The house was beautiful, there was no doubt that Jack possessed a skill for construction and an eye for design. But a house was just a house. And a house in Virginia was of little interest to him, no matter how much Jocelyn loved it. He could buy her a finer one in Austin.

He knew being interested in the renovation was the key to illustrate he cared. Even if he had no real interest in the project itself, it was an easy way to reconnected with Jocelyn on her terms. An opportunity to mend what had fallen to disrepair between them. Feigning interest in a handy-man's meal ticket was a small price to pay to build a bridge between himself and where he wanted to go.

"What's your favorite room?" Michael asked easily.

"I *love* the screened-in porch," Jocelyn gushed. "It was the first project Jack completed. I've spent every morning and every evening out there. The sound of the water is so peaceful and the lights on the ceiling make it so serene. If I lived here, I think I would install a hammock in the corner over there." She pointed through the window where she could picture it being suspended.

"I'd hang a bunch of sheer white curtains, bunched up in front of each of the posts. I don't even think I would close them. I just like the idea of how much softer it would make the space look. There's room at the end for a porch swing," she mused. "I'd want a white one with big fluffy pillows and chunky woven blankets."

Michael could see how invested Jocelyn had become in the small house and did his best not to make his concern known. "That sounds great," he offered. "A screened-in porch has endless possibilities," he allowed.

Jocelyn led Michael upstairs next and showed him the two bedroom suites. In the front bathroom, a large natural wood octagonal mirror was mounted above a porcelain bowl sink atop a long floating wood countertop with two deep drawers. The bedroom, with its white walls and thick gray carpet was dressed up with a round chandelier that had three tiers of wooden beads draped around it. Jocelyn had set up two queen bed frames and would add some accent furniture and mattresses in the coming weeks.

Through the wide hallway, they crossed over to the back bedroom where Jocelyn stayed. Her space, unlike the other bedrooms, looked lived in. A few photo boxes and scrapbooks remained at the foot of the bed, her laptop and notepad took up most of the nightstand. A similar chandelier as the front bedroom hung from the ceiling above the bed. A small decorative lamp added a pop of color with its antique glass base and a long dresser provided enough space to store her belongings. The few pieces of jewelry she had brought with her were kept on a small dish she'd purchased during her trip with Sarah. Her clothes hung in the closet with a small selection of shoes lined up below. The room looked dwelled in, and not in a temporary way. Jocelyn had made a home for herself in the space.

As she continued to gush over the house, Michael sensed the growing need to draw Jocelyn's thoughts back to Austin. He could see now why she had appeared so torn. Because, he realized, she *was* torn. As much as she loved Austin, it was apparent that she loved Farnham equally. What might tip the scales, he was certain, was an affection for something more than just a place. It would be who, not where, that claimed her heart that would ultimately sway her decision, and he was determined to try and regain that position in her life.

"When you return to Austin, you can buy a place outside of the city like you've always talked about," Michael offered smoothly. "It will be a whole new opportunity to have a home designed to your specifications. With the porch swing and the hammock."

"Yeah," Jocelyn said halfheartedly.

Michael could tell, perhaps more than she knew herself, how attached she was to the house. He hoped that attachment wouldn't shatter her focus on the possibilities of a life together in Austin.

"What are these?" he asked, grabbing one of the scrapbooks at the end of her bed, grasping at something to steer their conversation in a safer direction.

"Oh, gosh," she said, her face lighting up. "Childhood memories."

Michael turned to the first page and saw a picture of Jocelyn and Andrew playing a board game in a very different living space. The walls were covered in a gaudy wallpaper, a wall he didn't remember seeing during the tour through the living and dining space. It felt smaller and darker than the house he had just seen.

"Wow. Were these taken here?" he asked, unable to mask his shock. "It's so much more open now."

"Yes," she confirmed, then pointed to the wall in the background of the photo. "I helped knock that wall down," she proclaimed proudly.

"You did?" The thought of her working side-by-side with the contractor made him more jealous than he was willing to admit.

"I took down the wallpaper too and repainted the main floor," she said with a smile. "I also helped remove the old kitchen cabinets and did some tiling in the master bathroom."

The memories brought her pride as well as a flood of heat. Her heart fluttered at the thought of the passionate and intimate kiss she and Jack had shared in the shower together. A kiss she had pushed so quickly and so deeply into the hidden corners of her mind that the rush of excitement it delivered was startling.

This house it seemed, held far more value to her than its simple visual appeal, Michael realized. When Jocelyn worked at something, it owned a piece of her forever. Perhaps, he ventured based on her flush expression, the contractor had something more to do with her feelings than the work she'd done on the house.

"That's great," he said sweetly.

He turned the page and scanned the pictures. As he flipped through the pages, smiling at the photos of a little girl he'd seen in pictures Jocelyn had back home, he tried to absorb everything he could.

When he came upon a candid photo of a young boy, he paused. The boy seemed lost in thought as he leaned against one of the support posts that led up to the back of the house. He watched longingly in the direction of a little girl Michael recognized to be Jocelyn as she sat wrapped in a blanket on a lounge chair by the pool. She was immersed in a book and didn't seem to notice the boy's presence. The look in his eyes, though he was only a child, was that of infatuation.

"Woah, this kid has got it bad," Michael said with a laugh. "Who is this? Your first boyfriend or something?"

"Wait, let me see that?"

Jocelyn took the scrapbook in her hands and studied the photo. How had she missed it before? Of course, Jack had told her that he had a crush on her as a child. But it had been an easy remark to brush off and assume that his idea of a crush and hers were very different. But by the look in the eyes of the boy in the photo, she could tell that he had yearned for her. It was a look she had seen in his eyes a handful of times since she'd arrived in Virginia but hadn't deciphered until that moment. With everything she had learned about what he had been through since his mother's passing, it had been easy to believe that his far-off expression had nothing to do with her. Now, she suspected the look *was* in fact for her. A hint that, even now, he might still wrestle with the grief of losing something that might have existed between them.

"Who is it?" Michael asked again, reading the heavy expression on her face.

"It's Jack," she said breathlessly.

The air around her grew impossibly thick. The room felt as if it were closing in around her. Feelings she had suffocated for weeks broke free from their bondage and swirled through her consciousness. How had she managed to convince herself so thoroughly that the tension between she and Jack had been no more than harmless flirtation between a man and a woman? Hardly worth addressing or acting on. He'd kissed her. Like a man starved for something he'd craved for a lifetime. Yet she had still managed to convince herself that it was little more than a mix of lust and convenience.

Jocelyn closed the scrap book, her hands shaking.

"I need some air," she said, pushing herself up to stand. She crossed the room and walked out onto the balcony that overlooked the water.

Michael, knowing full well what he was up against now, followed closely behind.

"Baby," he cooed. "Everything's okay. You're just stressed," he assured her, caressing her arm.

He pulled her closer, angling her face to meet his. He could see the confusion, the fear, and the excitement in her eyes. Glancing down, Michael caught sight of Jack walking up to the house from the dock. He was desperate now. Desperate to create division, to draw Jocelyn's attention to him, and for her thoughts to return to the life they had once shared. The one where he was convinced she was meant to return to.

As Jocelyn looked up into his eyes, lost and apologetic, Michael crushed his lips to hers, holding her face in his hands. He searched her mouth for a response and found little. Polite and familiar, she accepted his kiss for only a moment before speaking his name to separate them.

They stood there for a minute, unspeaking. All at once she knew what she wanted but still wasn't brave enough to say it.

When she heard Jack's truck peel out of the driveway, Jocelyn pressed her eyes closed to shut out the tears that threatened to fall.

Had he seen them? Had she wanted him to? Had she somehow subliminally orchestrated this entire lavish display of dramatic theater all in order to force Jack into doing what he had already done once before? To pursue her. If that's what she really wanted than why had she run when he'd kissed her and agreed that it was best that they remain friends? Why? Because she was scared. And stubborn. And somehow, in an effort to prove herself unphased by the discarded chance to see where things might lead with Jack, she had baited Michael. Who, despite everything she'd denied him by breaking things off between them, was still a true friend.

"I'm sorry," she finally said, shaking her head. "I'm not being fair to you. I'm not sure what I expected you to think this visit meant. I'm not even sure what I thought it meant."

"Jocelyn," he pleaded, placing his hands softly on her arms. "We belong together."

"Michael...I..." Jocelyn hung her head, unsure why she had left so much unsaid between them for so long. "You're an amazing person and any woman would be lucky to have you." Turning her chin up, unwilling to hide from him or the truth any longer, she added "You're just not *my person*."

"It's him isn't it?" Michael said defeatedly.

She nodded meekly.

"Do you love him?"

Jocelyn had fought her feelings every step of the way, but she was certain now that no amount of denial could banish them.

"Yes," she confirmed.

Michael shook his head, exasperated. "I'm sorry...I...I have to go," he said stepping to the side. "I'm such an *idiot*," he added, unchecked, through gritted teeth, then brushed past her to enter the house.

For a moment, Jocelyn was frozen in place. She couldn't reconcile the fact that her effort to prove that she didn't need a man had caused her to push two amazing ones away from her for two entirely wrong and different reasons. As a child, she had fantasized about finding her prince and having him kiss her like Jack had in the shower or even as Michael had just now. In adulthood, after one too many experiences with the wrong guy, she had unintentionally become a cynic.

In real life, she had learned that a kiss was not enough to break a spell, as Jack had shown her weeks before. Nor would it result from true love, as Michael had just proven. But in this very rare case, a kiss had done something that it was often credited for only in the movies. It had woken her up.

"Michael, wait!" Jocelyn called out, bolting through her room and down the stairs.

She arrived at the base of the steps just as he shut the front door behind him, and her heartbeat quickened. As much as she owed Jack an apology, she owed Michael one more, and the one she had just delivered hadn't felt like enough. She hadn't even been thinking of Michael when she'd rattled it off, she had been thinking of Jack.

As Jocelyn followed Michael out across the front yard towards his car, she could feel the eyes of Jack's crew members on her back and she was ashamed, knowing she had brought any speculations they had about her upon herself. As much as she had worked to prevent making a mess of her life by developing feelings for Jack, here she was making a much bigger mess by denying them. And for what? She had successfully nipped any bud of affection that threatened to bloom between them, all the while cutting herself on the thorns of reality.

"Please, wait," she called again weakly.

Michael reached his car and pulled the door open. He paused, his sad eyes meeting hers, unable to command his body to leave without taking whatever it was she intended to offer him as compensation. He couldn't be mad at her for not returning his feelings, but he lacked the discipline to fight off the misery that settled in its place.

"It was unfair of me to invite you here," she reiterated.

Michael shrugged, relinquishing the door handle. "I wanted you to invite me," he admitted. "I wanted to give you another chance to see me in your life.

"I'll admit, I was surprised that you'd extended the invitation so quickly. I guess I took it as your way of telling me that you regretted how things had ended between us. That you returned my feelings.

"I'm not going to stand here and lie to you," he added. "I knew my chances weren't great. But you're not the kind of woman a man wants to lose. You're smart, and beautiful, and you're inspiring in more ways than I think you realize. I *wanted* to be your person. But I see now that I'm not. I guess all I can do is to be happy that at least I was once."

Jocelyn tucked herself into Michael's arms and he fought the feelings that her familiar scent and touch evoked as he tentatively embraced her. His mind knew better, but his heart was still clouded by a hope that wouldn't die.

"Please don't hate me," she whispered.

Michael surprised himself by releasing an involuntary chuckle. "Trust me," he said. "I've tried, it's not possible."

The remainder of the day dragged on as the crew finished up work on the exterior without Jack. All Jocelyn could do was to sit on the porch, petting Lady's head in search of some small comfort and wait for his return as she struggled to come up with the right words to say when he did.

Hours went by and storm clouds crept across the sky, mimicking the growing dread that remained heavy in the cage of her chest. As difficult as denying her feelings had been before, keeping them bottled up now that she accepted them was unbearable.

Just as the sun finished its descent below the horizon, little more than a dark purple haze washing over the scenery, Jack's truck crawled up the driveway. Anxious, Jocelyn made her way from the porch and stood at the top of the steps where she could see around the house to where he had parked. From there, she watched as Jack slammed the door to his truck shut and marched towards the dock, seemingly unaware of her presence.

"Jack!" she called down as he drew closer.

She could see that he hesitated to break stride and suddenly felt intimidated at the thought of a confrontation. When he finally came to a halt a few yards from the base of the steps, Jocelyn descended them to meet him, firm in her resolution to finally address what had been brewing between them since she'd arrived two months earlier. Reading his expression, she stopped at the bottom of the stairs, deciding it was best to respect his apparent need for space. Her own feelings were freshly accepted and vulnerable, and the defensive look he wore made her put up her own guard.

Jack approached Jocelyn, ravenous, territorial, and somewhat unhinged by his primal need to claim her as his own, though he felt less now more than ever that he had the right to do so.

"Where's the Ken doll?" he inquired brazenly. "Picking up some expensive champagne for your night together?"

The words cut her, but she could see that he was hurting too.

"No," she replied plainly.

"I took you for having better taste in men," he hissed bitterly.

Accustomed to slinging fire when his heart had come under careless attack, Jack couldn't keep the venom out of his words. He hated himself for it as Jocelyn looked on, visibly wounded by the slight, but he hated how the thought of losing her made him feel even more.

As eager as Jocelyn had been to open up to Jack, his abrasiveness worked quickly at closing her off to him before she'd managed to do so. Who ever Michael was to her now, at one point she *had* chosen him, and for good reason. The reckless insult didn't fall short of meeting its mark. "I have great taste in men," she countered. "If it's all the same to you, you're my contractor, not my father."

Blinking hard, Jack thought better than to continue down the path their conversation was bound to lead.

"Goodnight," he growled and turned on his heels.

Painfully aware of how unfinished she was with what Jack Evans had to say about her love life, Jocelyn stormed after him.

"Hey!" She called out, angrily.

A gentle rain started to fall from the darkened sky. Still, Jocelyn felt her fierce emotions drawing her out after him.

Jack pushed forward with long strides. He didn't want to face her. He wasn't prepared to confront his feelings or her impending rejection. He'd been tortured enough watching her flirt shamelessly with Mr. Perfect. A man who had clearly claimed her as Jack had waited idly by for a miracle to bring her back to him. When the miracle had come, he regretted, he'd done little with it but to wait for her to return feelings it was not in the stars for her to possess.

Jocelyn jogged to catch up.

"Jack!" She called after him, her feelings shifting rapidly from anger to fear. As much as his words had hurt her, she reminded herself that he hadn't been entirely wrong to build up a defense when she had been so thoughtless with his feelings.

Her heart ached to make him understand something she was still coming to terms with herself.

Whirling around on the dock, Jack squared off with her, panting heavily, soaked through from the rain that fell increasing heavy around them. "Why are you playing games, Jocelyn?"

"Playing games?" She was caught off guard by the accusation.

"Why did you bring him here?" he asked aggressively, his temper growing as he waited for her to meet fire with fire.

"He wanted to see the house," she said, knowing it was a poor excuse, but the only one she had. Her voice wasn't soft, but she remained disarmed.

"Damn it, Jocelyn," Jack lashed out. He placed his hands on his temples, exasperated. "He kissed you, and from my vantage point you kissed him back. You had to know what…no, *who* he came here for."

Jocelyn hung her head, ashamed that she had allowed herself to believe otherwise. *Had* she in fact been playing games all along? Carelessly testing Jack's response to see how it made her feel. She didn't know the answer, but she could see now what she had done unconsciously or otherwise and knew that she deserved whatever he had to say to her.

"Never once did you mention having a boyfriend," Jack went on. "Never once did you think to set up a boundary between us. Can you honestly say that you didn't know how I felt about you? How I've *always* felt about you."

As he waited for the hurricane of emotions he was accustomed to, especially from a woman who had hurt him, Jocelyn remained still, poised, thoughtful. Despite himself, Jack's temper began to cool, and he resented it. If he'd lost Jocelyn to another man, at the very least, he wanted to tether himself to his anger in an effort to keep the pain at bay.

As he watched her through the pelting rain, he detected the lingering innocence of uncertainty. Perhaps, he thought, she truly had no idea how he really felt about her, and maybe now was as good a time as any to make her aware of it.

Shaking his head, he shrugged off the guard that he'd put up between them. "When you walked back into my life…" he began. "I was barely holding onto the hope that things would get better for me. Most days I was poised at the precipice of losing myself entirely. You might not return my feelings, but I can't go on burying the ones I have for you.

"You pulled me from the depths of a darkness within myself that threatened to consume me. Whatever happens or doesn't happen between us, I want you to know that I'll always be grateful to you for that." He shifted in his stance, his posture softening further.

"Seeing you with another man was like having everything you've given me ripped away again. It was a harsh reality that I still have a long way to go."

Meeting his eyes, Jocelyn watched Jack, the full rush of her feelings for him taking a firm hold as his words dismantled any lingering uncertainty. She had never seen this side of him. She hadn't expected for him to fight for her because no man ever had. She couldn't be sure, and she felt guilty at the realization, but that was precisely why she had been so quick to invite Michael up to the house. She was too afraid to make a move towards Jack on her own. Too focused on getting out of this trip what she had viewed as its intended purpose. Now that she had the proof of his feelings, however, she feared that it had come at too high a cost.

"I'm so sorry," she said, her voice almost too soft to hear through the rain.

Jack felt the tug at his defenses as she continued to disarm him.

"You're right," Jocelyn went on, hanging her head. "I came here to escape," she began. "To run away from everything I had built because it all felt wrong somehow. I'm still not sure how I truly feel about my job or about my life in Austin. Some days life there is no better than a prison sentence, other days I see everything I've worked for and it all makes sense. When I came to Virginia and found what I was looking for that scared me too. I'm being pulled in two different directions, but that has nothing to do with Michael." Her stomach twisted to finally admit it out loud. "I'm scared," she said feebly.

"Scared of what?" Jack asked, his voice soft and reassuring. He moved in closer, taking her chin in his hand and angled her face so that her eyes met his.

"Uncertainty?" she said with a shrug. "Of not knowing what I want?" she finally allowed.

"I'm not asking you to know what you want for the rest of your life," Jack said softly. "I'm too afraid to hear the answer. But I think it's fair to ask what you want right now. And we can figure out the rest as it comes."

Jocelyn felt relief wash over her. She had been so careful not to hurt herself by making a choice she couldn't see through to the end. She'd been careful to spare Jack's feelings. Now she could see clearly that she was only causing them both pain as a result.

"I want you," she offered confidently.

Electricity surged through Jack's veins, sending a growing heat throughout his body. He pulled Jocelyn against him, enveloping her in a powerful embrace. He pressed his mouth to hers, elated to find that she was ready to receive his lips, his tongue, his insatiable appetite for her.

Sweeping her up into his arms, careful not to interrupt a kiss he hoped would last forever, he guided them onto the boat and towards the front door.

"Jack," she breathed into him.

"What?" He managed to groan back, fumbling for the handle of the door.

"We're going to get your sheets wet."

Her bold confirmation was enough to unhinge him. "Damn right we are."

As hungry as Jack had been for her, he had managed to control himself enough to unwrap Jocelyn in such a way that she felt both vulnerable and protected. He was claiming something he had waited decades to earn, and he had no intention of rushing it with unbridled lust.

They made love beneath the soft glow of the fleeting storm that had culminated as quickly as it had materialized. The way that Jack studied her, unhurried in his quest to reach the summit of his passion, confirmed everything that Jocelyn had suspected about his feelings for her.

Sex with Jack wasn't simply a deed of physical exploitation, it was a destination. An oasis of feelings, commitment, and a carefree release of her most vulnerable self. Making love to Jack was like being found after a lifetime of being lost.

At one point, he had whispered, "You're like coming home."

Jocelyn had understood his words so thoroughly that the reality of them scared her. She had never known that intimacy could be more than just a physical expression of affection. That their bodies belonged together. His touch evoked in her a peace and a wholeness that nothing and no one else had before, and she feared no one else ever could.

Afterwards, Jack retrieved Lady from the house, insisting that Jocelyn remain in bed, and upon his return, they made love again.

Jack had drawn a curtain that closed off the nook that housed his bed from the rest of the space. Though the windows that surrounded the alcove looked out over the river, the darkness that filled the boat shielded them from view. In truth, Jocelyn hadn't given the room for exposure a thought.

The second time, she let her passion take the lead. Straddling Jack, hypnotizing him with soft brushes of her skin, trailing kisses along his neck, she teased at the very ends of his ability to restrain his appetite for her.

Much time had passed, though they hadn't noticed until the clouds had cleared, revealing a moon that was nearly full as they lay together in contented silence.

"I love you," Jack whispered boldly, incapable of holding the words captive any longer.

Jocelyn propped herself up on her elbow and watched Jack's unabashed expression, his face aglow in the moonlight. How had she not seen it before? How had she allowed so much time to pass before believing a truth that scared her but was no less true as a result.

He might have spent a lifetime loving her, but Jocelyn realized that she had spent a lifetime looking for the kind of love she felt for Jack in all the wrong places. Men who fit into the neat picture she had painted for herself. Those who had come along and fell precisely into place. And no matter how neat the picture had been, she couldn't make the relationships last, because they hadn't been real. Jack made no effort to fit inside a box or a plan, he was unapologetic about who he was, and she felt inspired to do the same whenever she was with him.

She couldn't know what their future together would hold. She had responsibilities that were beyond her control. But what Jack had given her was something no one else ever had. He'd offered her a chance to follow her heart and to let it lead her somewhere her head alone would never have permitted she go.

She leaned into him and traced his lips with a delicate finger before placing a soft kiss upon them. She tucked herself back neatly into his side, reminded of the dream that now paled in comparison to her reality and whispered. "I love you, too."

Chapter Fifteen

Jocelyn hadn't expected the freedom that came with giving in to her feelings for Jack. Nor could she have anticipated the desperation that overwhelmed her to make up for the lost time between them. The past two months of platonic politeness they had shared had seemed to pass by lazily before. Now they felt wasted, their time remaining a trifled offering.

With the majority of the work done on the house, Jack was called away more often to other jobs. Still, he kept his houseboat docked at Jocelyn's place. In an effort to steal as many moments as he could with her, he went in late and ended his days earlier than he would have under normal circumstances. With only three weeks remaining before Jocelyn would be called back to Austin, they both did their best to ignore the harsh reality they would soon face. They were bound to two different worlds and just as hopelessly to each other.

***

"Mmm," Jocelyn moaned, interrupting a particularly steamy kiss. "We should really get set up," she said breathlessly.

Jack had parked his truck—loaded up with odds and ends from the river house—next to the barn. The sale would be starting in an hour and Jocelyn was hoping to use the opportunity to off-load a few pieces from the house as well as to pick up a few new items to use for staging.

Jack let out a groan as he sat back in his seat, putting more distance between him and Jocelyn than he was comfortable doing. "We've got an hour," he reminded her. "There's plenty of time." He raised his eyebrows suggestively.

"One of us has to be the responsible one," Jocelyn said good-humoredly, then pushed her door open and exited the vehicle.

They unloaded the truck bed and staged the pieces Jocelyn had brought in front of the barn. Jack entered the building and retrieved a few pieces to tie the collection together. Among his finds were a large woven area rug, a stained-glass floor lamp and a small storage ottoman. To add a few final touches, Jocelyn placed a decorative basket on the coffee table, a stack of antique books on the accent table alongside an armchair and arranged a few throw pillows on the sofa.

"We make a great team," Jocelyn declared, standing back to admire the display. "I almost don't hate that couch now."

"I like this," Jack said thoughtfully. "Having a showroom out front really draws the customer in. You can see it from the road too," he added pleased as he caught sight of the first car pulling into the parking lot.

"I don't know why you haven't opened this place up on a more regular basis," Jocelyn remarked. "You've said you always have great attendance. Imagine the turnaround you'd have if you held regular hours."

"I've played around with the idea," Jack allowed. "I just don't have the time to run it myself, or to interview people who might be up for the job. Not to mention converting the old barn over to a more permanent establishment. It's little more than a glorified storage shed as it is. I would design a shop differently.

"It's not just a matter of selling pieces either. The shop keeper would have to be able to pair elements together for customers who need more hands-on design assistance and know what the items people bring in for consignment are worth or if they aren't worth anything. There are a lot of great resale and furniture shops in town, but I would need to make sure mine stood out enough to make up for the distance people have to travel to get here."

"Well, one of these days you're going to stop making excuses," Jocelyn said boldly. "And you're going to wish you'd done it sooner." She smiled sweetly then walked over to greet the young couple that was making their way over to view the newly assembled display.

Jack watched on longingly. As she spoke to the couple, showing off the great qualities of the furniture she had placed up for sale, he fought the pull at his heart that told him she fit perfectly into every part of his future. They had agreed to keep their relationship light, given the fleeting nature of her remaining time in Virginia, but he couldn't discern how a relationship built on mutual love could be anything but heavy. This was where she made sense, and Jack couldn't convince himself otherwise.

He refrained from insisting that she consider her options because he knew how crazy he would sound. Giving up a six-figure position that she had earned and worked hard for to run a store in a shabby old barn that still had a long way to go before it could become something more. Living a simple life on a houseboat with a man and his dog. How could he ever, after everything she had already given him, ask her to give him even more?

As the day went on and more customers arrived, Jocelyn moved easily around the space. At first, she stayed outside with the items she had placed up for sale, but she moved inside once the majority of the display had sold. She hadn't been prepared for how eager buyers were to receive her insight on which light fixtures would provide the best addition to a small space in need of a focal point or which chairs could be paired together to make a complete and complementary set. As the day went on, she discovered that she had a knack for retail and a budding interest in interior design to go with it. When a customer came in, searching for the perfect piece to fill the void in their home décor and she was able to pair them up with the right fit, she felt like a merchant and a matchmaker all at once.

While Jocelyn took the reins on managing the sales, Jack helped unload and sort through new merchandise that trickled in for resale. He bartered and traded one piece for another as well as offered a fair price for the pieces that he wanted for his collection.

"Hey, Jack!" Bruce MacDonald, a Farnham local, called from the bed of his Ford F-350. "Mind helping me haul this baby inside?"

Jocelyn was loading a pair of lamps into an elderly woman's trunk when her attention was drawn by Jack's name. With a friendly farewell to the satisfied customer, she made her way over to the scene that began to unfold.

"Sure thing!" Jack called back, jogging over to the truck. "Wow, she's a beauty," he remarked, referring to the Winchester piano and matching bench that were strapped snugly in the wide bed of Bruce's truck. Despite the age of the piece, it was apparent that the instrument had been kept in pristine condition.

Jack hoisted himself up onto the open tailgate and ran his hand over the surface of the piano. Gently removing the straps that secured it in place, he opened the fallboard, and glanced over at Bruce. "Do you mind?"

"Go ahead," Bruce offered.

Jack slipped in expertly, afforded just enough room to sit at the piano and poised his left hand atop the keys.

Curious, Jocelyn moved closer, taking in a scene that seemed just as out of character for a man like Jack as it was fitting for who she knew him to be. A rugged man in well-worn jeans and a tight black T-shirt looked more suited for a motorcycle or a tractor than he did a musical instrument. Yet, as he started stroking the keys thoughtfully, commanding a sweet and elegant sound to infuse the air, the picture of him playing couldn't be more perfect. He brought up his right hand and began effortlessly tinkering in a complementary arrangement. The harmony grew bold and beautifully robust. His fingers danced rhythmically, compelling the keys to create a melody all his own.

Jocelyn watched breathlessly as he played, wondering how many ways one man could surprise her. As many things as Jack was, it was difficult to determine what he wasn't. What it made sense for him to lack, he quickly proved otherwise. He was well rounded and well versed in everything he touched, including her.

Following the sound of the unexpected private concert, customers began to gather around. Jack either didn't notice or didn't care to stop despite the attention he drew.

Jocelyn felt yet another very real and very vital piece of her heart lost to Jack's command. If she wasn't careful, he would claim all of her, body and soul. Despite everything she knew about the reality that stood between them, she was losing the will to stop it.

When he finished, looking up from the keys, as if returning from another place and time, the congregation of patrons all applauded excitedly.

Bashfully, Jack rubbed his neck with one hand and raised the other in modest gratitude to his unintended audience. "I'll be here all week," he said in good humor, then dismounted the truck bed and began helping Bruce lower the instrument to the ground.

It wasn't lost on Jocelyn that a lot of the young women in the crowd watched Jack appreciatively. She imagined some of them weren't even there to make purchases, certainly not as their primary motive anyway. While she wrestled with the urge to make it clear that they were together, she resisted. Afterall, she had no real claim over Jack, because, when everything was said and done, their time together was running out. Without the ability to stick around, who was she to assert her possession over him?

When the parking lot had finally emptied, and the sun was nestled low in the sky, Jocelyn and Jack found a moment to stop and assess the day's sales and new acquisitions.

"You did great," Jocelyn declared excitedly, after counting the money in the black cash box behind the podium.

"*We* did great," Jack corrected. "*You* did great today," he went on. "You're a natural."

"You've got a great business going," Jocelyn praised, unwilling to take any of the credit. "With a few additions like a card reader, some advertising and more hours, I'm telling you, you could really grow this place."

Walking from the building, Jocelyn led Jack outside. "Maybe open up an outdoor section with a covered awning here," she began. "You could take all that patio furniture you've got in the back of the building and display it out here instead. Or maybe," she went on, her vision unfolding quicker than Jack could keep up "you could set up an outdoor dining area. Get a food license and start up a small café and pastry shop. Maybe sell a few signature sandwiches. Or you could partner with some local food trucks. Each day at lunch time you'll have a different one parked alongside your store. People love that kind of stuff, and it's a great way to help support local businesses."

"Woah, woah," Jack said with a laugh. "Easy now."

Ignoring his protest, Jocelyn indulged further as she went on about the endless potential, growing her ideas excitedly as she spoke of the boundless opportunities that might come with the expansion of the establishment Jack had started out of need rather than passion.

Jack marveled at how limitless Jocelyn's vision was, taken aback at how much she could see in a place he had struggled to make sense of himself. He wondered how she had allowed herself to be consumed by a job that was almost entirely void of creativity when it was so obvious to him that that's just what she had been missing.

Jack approached Jocelyn as she studied the space, seemingly lost in thought. He couldn't imagine what she contemplated and thought it too unfair to ask. No matter how much he wanted to insist that she trade her corporate life in Austin for a simple one in Virginia so that they might be together, he couldn't bring himself to say the words. To put it simply, it wasn't his decision to make or to insist upon. He knew that he would fight for her. He would exhaust every effort to keep her there with him forever, but this was not the moment to spark conflict in her heart.

Unable to think about what they couldn't have, he decided, once again, to shift his focus on what they could.

"We've had a full day," he said, wrapping his arms around her.

"Mmm," she cooed in agreement, loving the way he fit naturally around her.

"If I recall," he began, kissing her cheek softly. "You had once dreamed of spending an entire day on the houseboat," he added, allowing his fingers to slide seductively under the edge of her shirt. "How about tomorrow you and I spend the whole day on the boat, ignoring time and responsibilities?" He nuzzled her neck and kissed her sweetly.

"Are you sure? I thought you had a job tomorrow?" Jocelyn countered.

"Jonas can cover for me," Jack replied easily. "That's the beauty of owning your own business."

"I don't know," Jocelyn said with hesitation. "It feels like I'm helping you play hooky."

"I always said that for the right reasons I would slow down," Jack reasoned. "And right now, I have one." he said, planting a deep kiss on her lips.

Jocelyn could tell by the way Jack moved around his small kitchen that he was accustomed to taking care of himself. After leaving the shop, they had stopped at a roadside farm stand where he had selected a few eggplants, fresh basil, ripe cherry tomatoes, cucumbers, and romaine lettuce. From there, they had picked up a few other ingredients at the local market and he now worked expertly to make a meal out of the selection.

"Please let me help," Jocelyn begged.

She was seated in the armchair, her legs reclined on the ottoman while she scratched Lady's head.

"Is it such a terrible thing to have a man cater to you?" Jack teased sweetly. Glancing over his shoulder at Jocelyn, he noticed her free hand strumming absently on the arm rest. He imagined not letting her help might do more harm than good.

"All right," he said in defeat. "Why don't you throw a salad together?" he offered, gesturing towards the vegetables that waited beside the cutting board.

Jocelyn joined him at the counter, relieved that she had something to keep her busy. While she sliced the cucumber and tomatoes and shredded the lettuce, Jack breaded thin slices of eggplant before laying them in a cast-iron skillet to fry. He worked methodically. Breading, flipping, then layering the eggplant with homemade sauce he had retrieved from the fridge, fresh basil leaves, and mozzarella cheese.

"You sure are a well-rounded guy," Jocelyn remarked as she watched Jack move through the rhythm of preparing a meal he knew by heart. "I can only imagine I have your mom to thank for that."

At the mention of his mother, a sad yet sweet smile tugged at Jack's lips. It was still hard to talk about her, but he was grateful that Jocelyn didn't shy away from it. He knew it was something he still needed plenty of practice in doing himself.

"I told you before that my mom hadn't always planned to homeschool," Jack began. "It was a need that presented itself rather than a preference. She noticed that I resisted learning from an early age. Late to walk. Slow to talk. I was in no hurry to impress or show off with my academic skills, to say the least. She took me to get evaluated for just about everything when I became school age. She determined that I just wasn't ready to absorb information simply because it was given to me. Once she started looking into alternatives for traditional schooling, she learned that homeschooling allowed me to work at my own pace."

Jocelyn worked to piece together the pictures of the boy she knew from childhood with the one his mother saw and nurtured. She smiled as she sifted through the few memories she had of Jack and his mother. Faded clips of a petite woman with long brown hair and crisp blue eyes, kneeling to get on his level as she corrected his behavior with a gentle yet stern posture. Other times Jocelyn recalled that Jack would run into his mother's arms, if for no other reason than the fact that too much time had passed since she had held him last. They were the moments of Jack's childhood that she remembered fondly, and she now realized, they were the fleeting glimpses of a boy's bond with the first woman to hold his heart and who would own a piece of it forever.

"Anyway," Jack went on. "It didn't take long for my mom to learn that homeschooling us offered a unique opportunity to make education about more than just academics. She focused a great deal of her time and attention on life skills like budgeting, homemaking, and embracing an entrepreneurial mindset. She didn't want us to see any of those abilities as belonging to one gender or family member alone. She wanted us all to grow in each skill so that we could look after our own families and households one day." Jack glanced over at Jocelyn and noticed, confused, that there were tears in her eyes.

"What's wrong?" he asked, stepping away from his work to place a hand protectively around her waist.

"I…I remember her," Jocelyn struggled to say, swiping at the tears that flowed freely now. "She was always so kind," she went on, determined to get the words out.

"I could tell how much you all loved her and that she loved you like crazy. She joined in on the fun and it came naturally to her to get down on our level. She was always so patient with you, and you tested her patience quite a lot," she added with a smile. "I'm not surprised that you turned out the way you did."

Jack fought the growing tightness in his chest. The memories of his mother that rushed in warmed his weary heart while licking cruelly at the corners of his sorrow. Remembering her, loving her, he was learning would always be a painful mix of joy and sadness. A harsh reminder of a reality he still couldn't face. Jocelyn's desire to go to that place with him, to feel the hurt that raked at his soul, and walk through the coals of hell to feel the warm breeze of heaven on the other side, gave him courage to keep moving in his journey towards healing.

Pulling her in for a long embrace, Jack found himself praying to God for the first time in too long. "God," he said aloud, courageously. "Thank You for bringing Jocelyn back into my life, despite the fact that I deserved no less than abandonment." Jocelyn, sobbing into his chest, quivered at his words. "Thank You for not losing faith in me," he went on "despite the fact that I abandoned my faith in You. I don't know how I'll ever deserve this gift, but I promise to do my best every day to try." He held Jocelyn more tightly in his hands as he waited for his pulse to settle, nearly carried away by the fervent nature of his prayer. "Amen," he whispered breathlessly into Jocelyn's hair.

An immeasurable amount of time passed between them as they held one another, content to stay in place as time and all its constructs went on without them. It wasn't until the oven chimed, alerting them that it had finished preheating, that Jack and Jocelyn finally came out of their embrace. Jack placed a soft kiss on Jocelyn's forehead then returned to the work that remained in preparing the dish.

When Jocelyn finished making the salad, she moved over to get started on washing the dishes. As small as the space was, Jack had laid it out perfectly so that no inch was wasted or slighted where it was needed. While she once struggled to understand how people flocked to the booming trend of tiny homes, she now understood how efficient they could be with the right layout. And the right contractor, she considered with a heavy bias.

A few moments later, Jack popped the meal into the oven and walked up behind Jocelyn, joining her at the sink. Gently, he began massaging her shoulders as she soaped up the dishes and ran them under hot water. She shivered with pleasure as he moved a hand up to knead the muscles of her neck.

"Your hands work magic," she said breathlessly.

Reminded of his impromptu concert at the barn earlier that day, she turned around to face him.

Curious as to why she had stopped, and eager to learn the reason for it, Jack wrapped his arms around Jocelyn and rested his hands on the small of her back.

"You played beautifully today," she said.

"What?" he asked, confused. "Oh. The piano."

"You really are a Jack of all trades."

No matter how hard he tried, he couldn't keep the smile off his face. "Good one," he said with a smirk.

Jocelyn considered her words, only just realizing the pun she hadn't intended to make. "Oh, I hear it now."

They laughed easily together, and Jack stole a kiss from her lips, enjoying the way she couldn't contain the giggles that kept erupting whenever she tried to get a hold of them. He brought his hands up to her face, guiding her closer to his body. Their kiss intensified then simmered and heated up again. As much as the rest of his body was eager to participate in the moment, Jack wanted to delight in the act of letting their lips do all the talking. His body was hungry for her, but he imagined no amount of raw pleasure could satisfy his craving. He tangled his hands in the long locks of her golden hair as she gripped at his shirt, equally practiced in restraining herself. It was as if, together, they had silently agreed it was a torture they both wanted to endure; building up the heat of their desire for one another as the temperature became nearly intolerable.

Chapter Sixteen

Warm light streamed in from the window, forcing Jocelyn's eyes to remain closed and encouraging them to open at the same time. She nuzzled into the sheets, wrestling with the haze of sleep that pulled her back to a dream she could no longer remember. The bedding was cool and crisp, alerting her to the fact that, despite having fallen asleep in Jack's arms, she was now alone.

Unalarmed, though measurably disappointed, she kept her eyes shut for a few more moments before attempting to force them open.

When the welcome scent of Columbian roast permeated her senses, she warranted it a good enough reason to stop resisting the call of morning.

"I thought we were going to have a lazy day. That implies sleeping in," she groaned, begrudgingly opening her eyes at long last.

With no reply, Jocelyn scanned the small space and realized quickly that Jack was nowhere to be seen. Lady, she observed, was also missing. When she noticed a note propped up on the pillow beside her, she took hold of it then dropped back down in her place on the bed to read it.

Took Lady for a walk. I didn't want to wake you. There's fresh coffee in the French press.

Love,

Jack

The word love stuck out, its vicinity to his name making Jocelyn giddy like a schoolgirl. She wondered how long an infatuation like the one she had for Jack could last. More so, she feared what discarding it might do to her. As much as she tried to weigh the options, as eager as she was to try and make a long-distance relationship with him work, she wasn't ready to offer the proposal just yet. Everything was perfect. The time was too limited, too fleeting to focus valuable attention on something as dry and calculated as logistics. That, she was convinced, was better saved for the very end. By then, she knew, they would both have decided what they wanted and would be willing to make it work. Or so she hoped.

With a hot cup of coffee in one hand, Jocelyn trailed her finger absently along the spines of the books on Jack's shelf. The selection, not surprisingly, was all male. *The Great Gatsby*, *Old Man's War*, *Moby Dick,* and *For Whom the Bell Tolls* to name a few. She wondered offhandedly if Jack had read them all or if he merely collected them with the intention of doing so. She continued to browse until one jumped out at her.

Jack walked Lady along the road flanked by corn fields. It was still early; the sun had only just crested the sky and the air was as cool as it would be all day. He had promised her a long stroll in exchange for a lazy day on the boat with no whimpering and minimal demands to relieve herself.

"I can't be sure, Lady," he said absently "but I think she's the one."

Lady, always willing to act as a sounding board for Jack's rare monologues, turned her head up at the sound of her name as if to say, "I'm listening."

"How can I be so sure when so few of the important pieces match up?" he went on. "She's made no mention of turning down the job offer. Which, as far as I can tell, will bring her back to Texas indefinitely. She's continuing to stage the house to sell, and I don't think she'd consider moving in herself. If she wanted to make a remote job work long-term, wouldn't that be the first thing she'd suggest?"

They walked along in silence for a few yards as Jack worked through his thoughts and untangled the feelings they evoked.

"That house has so much of our story built into the foundation," he mused. "Our childhood, and now…" He trailed off. "Well, whatever this is."

He took a deep breath, working to make sense of a picture he wasn't willing to let go of. Unless the pieces fell into place, until he knew where Jocelyn stood at the end of her time in Virginia, what was it worth to torture himself with the what ifs just to be faced with disappointment in the end?

Upon Jack's return, he fetched Lady a fresh bowl of water then made his way over to join Jocelyn where she lie curled up in bed with a book.

"You know," she said, taking a moment to look up from her page. "I fantasized about doing this when you first showed me this place," she said.

Jack lowered himself onto the bed and tucked his arm easily beneath her, kissing her softly. "Bedding the contractor?" he asked playfully.

"No." She laughed sweetly. "Reading in this bed," she replied playfully, burrowing herself deeper into her cocoon of pillows and blankets.

Jack let out a defeated breath. "*Women*." He dropped down beside her and rested his head on her shoulder. "What are you reading anyway?"

"The Hobbit," she informed.

"I've always loved that one."

Jocelyn picked up where she had left off without prompting, reading aloud as Jack looked on. He focused a great deal of his attention on remaining attentive, enjoying the way she read for each of the characters, but eventually the warmth and allure of her body consumed the whole of his thoughts.

Snatching the book from her hands, he abandoned it on the windowsill as he moved over her.

"Hey," Jocelyn protested into Jack's lips as he pressed them to hers. "I was almost done with that chapter," she went on, as he trailed a string of kisses down her body. She shivered at his touch and her attention was lost to him as completely as his was to her.

As he worked to disrobe her beneath the sheets, the sound of a loud foghorn disrupted them. Startled, they both jumped, looking up to see a crabbing boat only a few hundred feet away. On the bow a couple of crewmen cheered as the captain shook his fist angrily from the cabin.

Mortified, Jocelyn scrambled to collect herself, thankful for the small miracle that her body was shielded in blankets and what remained of her clothes. In the heat of her attempt to salvage what remained of her dignity, and with Jack distracted by a fit of laughter atop her, they became hopelessly tangled in the layers of bedding. In his effort to regain his equilibrium in order to help untangle them, Jack mistakenly shifted the bulk of their weight over the lip of the bed frame, sending them both crashing to the floor below.

Now, both laughing and equally ensnared in the web of sheets, Jocelyn straddled Jack who had taken the full impact of the fall. Unable to properly address the pain that surged through his muscles, he laughed as Jocelyn halfheartedly slapped his chest.

"It's not funny," she protested, still working to contain her own involuntary laughter.

"I disagree," Jack replied, shielding himself from the pillow she slung at his face.

"I'm never having sex in that bed again," she insisted.

"It wasn't that bad," he replied with a laugh.

"Laugh it up, Chuckles," Jocelyn warned tepidly, dismounting him.

"Hey," Jack called after her. "Where are you going?"

"I need more coffee," she said, still working to collect herself.

After the dust had settled, and more importantly, the fishing boat had moved well out of view, Jack managed to coax Jocelyn back into bed.

He had pulled a set of sheer curtains closed, providing them a luxurious amount of privacy compared to the formerly undressed windows. Frankly, he didn't care if they made love or not, whether they wore nothing or whether they wore sweats. He simply enjoyed the prospect of staying in bed all day with the woman he grew to love more with each passing moment they shared.

Later, Jack sat propped up in bed with Jocelyn tucked into his arm. They had spent a long moment listening to the subtle sounds of the busy world just beyond the glass, feeling the gentle rock of the boat as they nuzzled closer.

"Can I say something forward?" he probed.

Jocelyn raised an eyebrow with piqued interest. "Go ahead."

"I get the impression that I'm not like most men you've been with. That guy who came to the house the other day...Michael. He looked... expensive. Is that the kind of man you usually date?"

Jocelyn sat up beside him in bed.

"Michael and I did date for a few years," Jocelyn confirmed. "But I haven't been in a serious relationship with that many men. I dated this guy Clint a few years before meeting Michael. He worked at a law firm. So, I guess that makes it look as though I have a type."

Thrown off by Jack's unexpected theory, she considered her track record with men and wondered if she had in fact been unintentionally seeking men of a certain breed. Working in the corporate world, it had felt like the more natural direction, and it had certainly been the class of men she was most commonly exposed to.

Looking back now, she could remember having turned down a blind date once because the guy worked in a bookstore and performed music in coffee shops on the weekends. Had she really been so blinded to what other great men might be out there because she had her mind set on a man who met the same standard of success that she had set for herself? Had her aversion to becoming involved with Jack in fact had something to do with that standard?

Studying his handsome features, his rugged build, and his rough exterior, Jocelyn became consumed with guilt. He deserved so much more than to be seen only at face value. Even still, she knew, his worth to be limitless. He was a skilled craftsman, a mindful and thoughtful steward to the earth as well as a valued member of his community and family. The position he held, the money he made, and his blue-collar exterior only added to his worth. She felt ashamed knowing that a few months earlier, she had easily overlooked him as a romantic prospect and suspected now that might have been a big part of the reason.

She was quickly flooded with relief that she'd taken a chance on Jack despite her undeclared preconceptions. She was glad for the fact that she hadn't let herself disregard the tug of magnetism that pulled her toward him. All at once, she couldn't help but wonder if it was she who was undeserving of him.

Crawling into Jack's lap, Jocelyn kissed him hungrily. Though he seemed more than just a little confused, he happily complied, indulging in a long and sensual kiss as his hands worked to explore her body.

When they finally pulled apart, Jack said, "I'm not complaining… but, what was that all about?"

"I'm sorry I ever left that shower," she offered.

Jack stroked her cheek tenderly, smiling sweetly down at her face. "I still hadn't earned you yet," he offered.

"No," she interjected flatly. "I hadn't earned you."

***

It was well past three o'clock when Jack and Jocelyn finally relented and left the sanctuary of his bed. With the promise of a hearty meal on the other side, Jack insisted that they were both probably due for a shower. It took little persuasion when he suggested they could save time and water if they showered together.

Standing behind her as Jocelyn wiped away the steam from the bathroom mirror, Jack kissed the soft skin of her neck, guiding his hands up the length of her toweled body greedily. It was like a dream. Every moment with her felt fleeting, unreal and stollen. He wanted to take them all and commit them to memory in fear that he would wake up before he was ready.

"Jack," she said half-heartedly, snatching her towel as he worked to pull it free. "I'm starving," she said, feigning protest.

"Mmm," he moaned into her hair. "Me too."

"Jack!" The muffled call from within the house startled them both.

Sobered by the sound of his sister's distressed voice, Jack pulled away sharply as if he'd received an electric shock.

"Jack!?" Sarah called again. "Where the hell is everyone?" she added in confusion.

"Shit," Jack muttered, his heart now racing for a different reason than it had been only moments ago. "Stay here," he instructed through his teeth as he refastened his towel. "Look what you do to me." he groaned, as he adjusted himself in an effort to conceal his arousal.

Jocelyn failed to withhold a giggle and Jack rushed his finger to her lips, shushing her silently as he fought back laughter himself.

"Jack?" Sarah called in confusion again, only just outside the bathroom door.

Jack slipped out of the bathroom, quickly shutting the door behind him. His skin and hair were still wet, his body concealed only by a towel that now felt little better than stepping out in the nude.

"*Ugh, gross,*" Sarah exclaimed in disgust.

Jack rolled his eyes as his little sister averted hers. "You're the one who called me out here, remember?" he reasoned. "What's up?"

"Where's Jocelyn," she inquired suspiciously, noticing that her brother made no effort to move towards his drawers to get dressed. "Do you want put on a shirt or something?" she asked, though it was more of a request than a question.

"I'd be happy to," Jack replied, crossing his arms over his chest. "If you'd just leave, I'll get right on that."

Sarah sneered, discontent with Jack's obvious push to purge her from his home. "You didn't answer my question," she countered. "I came by to see if Jocelyn was okay. She hasn't replied to my texts or calls all day. Why are you still docked here anyway? Didn't you finish up work on the house like a week ago?"

"Her car's still here, but she didn't answer the door..." she went on, increasingly confused.

It was then that Sarah noticed the shift of movement on the other side of the frosted glass of the bathroom door. Her eyes narrowed. "Who's in there?" she inquired suspiciously as the whole picture of what her brother was hiding came into view.

"No one," Jack lied blatantly.

Sarah just raised her brow in challenge. "Jocelyn," she called out boldly. "You can come out now." Her eyes were still locked on her brother.

Jack's expression remained stoic, unfazed, though his pulse quickened as their discretion unraveled before his very eyes.

A moment later, the bathroom door edged open, and Jocelyn ducked out, her eyes shifting down with embarrassment as she stood equally exposed in nothing but a towel.

"Hi, Sarah," she said, unable to meet her friend's eyes.

Looking between the two of them, Sarah assessed the situation and failed to restrain the smile that spread across her face. "Guys!" she exclaimed. "This is amazing!" she declared, excitedly. "Oh my gosh," she went on. "I thought you might have a thing for each other...I mean, of course, I knew you were *obsessed* with Jocelyn," she directed to Jack. "But I can't believe—"

Jack hung his face in his hands. "*Sarah*," he warned in a low growl.

Sarah went on, ignoring her brother's protest, elated at the idea of her childhood best friend and her brother falling for one another. "How long has this been going on?! I want to know *everything*."

Jocelyn giggled, feeling both humiliated and relieved in equal parts.

"Do you though?" Jack challenged.

Sarah thought about it for a moment then shook her head slowly. "No, probably not. But still," she couldn't keep the excitement out of her voice. "This is great. It's wonderful. Oh my gosh, I can't wait to tell Ava. She suspected—"

"Woah, woah," Jack interrupted, putting up his hands to halt her. "We're not looking for that kind of attention," he insisted. "We're just taking this slow, seeing where it goes."

Jocelyn nodded in agreement.

"Yeah," Sarah replied doubtfully. "You're clearly 'taking things *real slow*,'" she mimicked using air quotes. "What was I thinking."

Chapter Seventeen

Jocelyn worked to braid her hair in the mirror as Jack leaned against the door leading into the bedroom. Dressed in a bohemian skirt and a crocheted top, he wondered if she was a mere figment of his imagination. A lingering fantasy created in the lost mind of a desperate man. Reaching out to tug playfully at her finished braid, he reminded himself that his reality truly was better than any dream.

"Are you sure you're comfortable with your family seeing us together?" she asked. "I can always drive myself to Sarah's shower," she offered. "We can arrive separately to eliminate any suspicions."

"I am under no false pretense that we have maintained our secrecy now that Sarah knows," he admitted. "Besides, I've got nothing to hide. You're beautiful, intelligent, funny. I'd be a fool to think it's in my best interest to keep our relationship private."

He tucked himself around her then, drawing in the scent of her as she worked to weave her remaining hair into a second braid.

"That's very sweet," Jocelyn said, making eye contact with Jack's reflection.

Seeing them side-by-side made her heart twist with grief and longing at the thought of leaving in a couple of short weeks. She had yet to find a flaw of Jack's that didn't draw her closer to him. His qualities, be they strengths or flaws, worked collectively to craft a man so imperfectly human that he was inherently divine as a result. His touch was equal parts strong and soft as his hands on her waist held her firmly and the kiss he trailed at the nape of her neck was nearly untraceable in its tenderness. The sensation was just detectable enough to ignite the fire inside of her. A flame that had been a living energy within her heart since she had first seen him round his truck that first morning he'd walked back into her life.

"Do you ever wonder what might have happened between us if my family had never moved to Texas?" Jocelyn ventured, tying off her hair and pausing thoughtfully.

"All the time," Jack replied.

"Do you think we would have dated?" she asked.

"Absolutely," he said confidently.

"How can you be so sure?" she asked, wondering if it would have been as easy a transition on her end had she never left Virginia. Would she have been able to separate the villain of her childhood from the prince he'd become if she'd been present for the transformation?

"I was thirteen when you moved away. After that, I only learned that you'd been in town after your visits had already come and gone. It was a wakeup call that I'd really blown it. Even before you had moved, I'd stopped picking on you, but I'm not sure you noticed.

"I fell back on being shy around you, realizing that without the defense of bullying you, I didn't know how else to get close to you. If I was pulling your hair or cracking jokes at your expense, at least I was getting your attention. When I stopped all that, I'm pretty sure you forgot that I existed."

Jocelyn searched her memories and could recall that her last full summer in Farnham was little more than a blur. She could recall very little of Jack at all from that time.

"So how can you be so sure we would have ended up together?" she ventured.

"I resigned myself to the idea that you would remain the chance I hadn't taken. My unrequited love story. If you had stayed, I think the need to tell you how I felt would have become too much to keep inside.

"I can never know what might have been, but I'm glad that things unfolded the way that they did in the end. Perhaps, some things are written in the stars," Jack offered, turning her gently in his hands to face him.

Cupping her face, he kissed her softly, asserting the affection that his heart had cultivated for her all those years ago. The combination of need, want, and craving his body felt toward her fueled a love he had never experienced before and doubted he ever would again. Jocelyn had been the first true love of his life. Now, he knew with absolute certainty, that she would be his last as well.

Ava hosted the small baby shower at the house for an intimate group of family and a few of Sarah's close friends. Once inside, Jocelyn could see that the home Will and Ava shared was more spacious and grander than it appeared from the outside. With vaulted ceilings and an open floorplan, it was a traditional farmhouse with a modern feel. Though the walls, ceiling, and floor were all a natural wood, soft white couches and a plush carpet tempered the space.

A makeshift clothesline had been fastened in the entryway, adorned with a dozen baby girl outfits, hats, and socks. The back windows allowed a generous amount of natural light in, and the pink hues of the shower decorations softened the room. As a focal point, Ava had created a backdrop wall draped in ivory curtains, twinkle lights, and an array of matte balloons in various sizes and hues of soft pinks and cream to create a whimsical frame.

"You did a beautiful job," Jocelyn praised, bringing Ava in for a hug.

"She shouldn't have gone to this much trouble," Sarah insisted, though she was beaming with pleasure. Her long dark hair had been softly curled, and she was dressed in a flowing pink dress that matched the décor perfectly. "It is just a sprinkle after all."

"A sprinkle?" Jocelyn inquired.

"I already had a shower for Brian," Sarah informed.

"But you're having a *girl*," Ava squealed excitedly. "It's a whole different experience."

"I guess," Sarah allowed.

"I'd have to agree," Jocelyn said with a shrug. "Any reason to throw a party and buy an excessive amount of adorable baby stuff is reason enough to celebrate if you ask me."

"They didn't even make half the stuff they do now when I was pregnant with Brian," Sarah permitted. "It's only been a few years. How can baby stuff be so different in such a short amount of time?!"

Jonas approached then, cozying up to his wife, placing a loving hand on her belly. "Can I get you ladies a cocktail?" he offered. "And a mocktail for the mother-to-be?" he amended, planting a sweet kiss on Sarah's cheek.

"What's on the menu?" Jocelyn inquired. "Hopefully, nothing in the Margarita family."

"Still too soon?" Sarah asked with a wince.

Jocelyn nodded her confirmation.

"Today we have grapefruit mom-osas and pink sherbet punch for the lightweights of the group," Ava said, hooking a thumb in Sarah's direction.

"Joke's on you," Sarah retorted. "The punch is to die for."

"Oh yum," Jocelyn declared. "They both sound yummy. I'll start with a mom-osa," she directed to Jonas.

"Mom-osa for me too please," Ava said with a smile.

"Comin' right up, ladies," he replied.

Once Jonas had returned with their drinks, Jocelyn ventured out onto the back porch where she found Jack and Will facing off in a game of cornhole. Each of them was paired up with an older man. The first, with his hair and beard nearly all gray and his face aged but distinguished, she recognized as Peter, Jack's father. The other man, his skin a beautiful dark chocolate, his salt and pepper hair cropped short, and his build tall and broad, Jocelyn suspected was Jonas's father.

"Impregnated," Jack declared victoriously, drawing Jocelyn's attention as he pumped a celebratory fist into the air.

"It's a boy!" Peter cried out.

With further examination of the game, Jocelyn noticed that each board had been decorated with a large white "egg" around the mouth of the hole. Traditional beanbags had been replaced with sperm shaped sacks in pink and blue.

Taken by surprise by the unexpected humor of the shower game and the animated way in which the men celebrated, Jocelyn erupted with laughter, inadvertently spitting out her drink.

"Dad," Jack called over. "You remember Jocelyn."

Rushing to wipe the drops of mom-osa from her lips, Jocelyn sent a friendly wave Peter's way. She knew that it was only reasonable to be embarrassed, but the humor of the environment only permitted her to laugh again, grateful that at least this time she had nothing to spit out.

"Hello, Mr. Evans," she finally managed once she had collected herself.

"Please, call me Peter," he corrected.

"Jocelyn, this is Emmanuel, my father-in-law."

"Nice to meet you," Jocelyn said with a smile.

Emmanuel returned the pleasantry before lining up his next shot.

It was only the second time meeting Jack's family, but she considered again how unified and inclusive the group was.

Rather than referring to Sarah's father-in-law as a further removed extension of his family, Jack regarded the man as a direct member of his own. It was evident in the way that the group interacted as well that they all felt the same. Lines were blurred, blood was a mere formality, and family was family.

Jocelyn finished her drink outside as she watched the men compete for the position of most fertile. As they faced off, the jokes and laughter the game incited guaranteed that everyone walked away a winner.

Jack draped an arm over Jocelyn's shoulder and stole a sip of her mom-osa. "I was this close," he said, indicating the small margin of defeat with a pinch of his fingers.

"Looks like you're still in for a hefty amount of child support from my vantage point," she retorted.

"Yeah, but I definitely could have fertilized a few more eggs," he proclaimed. "That last shot should have been in."

Pushing the sliding glass door open, he ushered her inside.

"Looks like Ava's getting ready to set up a bottle chugging contest. Now's your chance to redeem yourself," Jocelyn offered.

"Oh, it's on," Jack declared, heading towards the growing congregation of partygoers.

Since they'd become serious, Jocelyn had noticed with each passing day that Jack was much more than the straightedge and professional businessman she had met upon her return to Farnham. He was surprisingly lighthearted as well, fun loving, and well-humored. She couldn't help but wonder, as he chugged a baby bottle full of apple juice with ease, what he must have been like as a teenager or in his twenties. She suspected, without much consideration of the alternative, that he would have no doubt been the life of the party in his youth.

The shower carried on with games, a buffet of playful baby themed entrees, effortless mingling among guests, and the opening of shower gifts. While a handful of guests left around the formal end of the party, Sarah's siblings, and their brood of children—hopped up on cookies and cake—remained.

From the living room, Jocelyn watched as Jack blocked the shots his nieces and nephew took at the cornhole board. Through the glass, she could hear muffled declarations of, "No babies for you!" and "Not on my watch, young man!" The banter had the children in stitches, sneakily trying to home the sperm-shaped beanbags in a game they far from understood the innuendo, let alone the actual rules.

"He's great with them," Jocelyn said, her heart aching reflexively.

"Uncle Jack is the best," Ava confirmed.

"The kids just gravitate towards him," Sarah agreed.

"I don't get it," Jocelyn mused.

"What?" Sarah asked.

"How he's still single," she said. "He seems like he'd be a great husband and father."

"Well, he's technically *not* single," Sarah offered.

"Right," Jocelyn allowed.

"Besides, as you know, it's not for a lack of trying," Sarah added. "In the end though, he has always focused a lot of his attention on the business. I don't even think he realizes when a woman finds him attractive. His thoughts are always on other things."

Jocelyn recalled the scene at the barn sale. She was selfishly relieved at the confirmation that he really didn't notice how alluring he was to the opposite sex.

"But he wants to get married," Jocelyn said, posed more as a question. Though he had said it once himself and she knew he'd intended to propose to Selena, she couldn't help but be baffled by his unhurried approach to life and love. He came off as a man of little regret. A man who knew where he was and enjoyed the ride. It was a trait she envied about him, for she couldn't seem to find the same contentment in her own life without practicing it with intention.

"He does," Sarah confirmed. "And I already know who's got my vote," she said with a wink.

Jocelyn blushed and took a sip of her drink, using the pause to buy herself time in the hopes that she could come up with an acceptable yet honest reply.

"You two are perfect together," Ava added, backing Sarah's insinuation. "I just hoped you'd both eventually see it too."

"We are far from perfect," Jocelyn retorted.

Plagued with the guilt that what she and Jack shared still felt impermanent no matter how much she wished otherwise, she couldn't picture a scenario in which someone didn't get hurt in the end. She continued to struggle in her efforts to rationalize that nothing was important enough to pull her away from the love she had found with Jack. Nonetheless, she was decided in her decision to leave. It almost felt cruel to drag him along, to give either of them more of what she would have to withhold in just a short amount of time.

"I don't think you realize how close he was to fading away," Sarah said softly. "Before you showed up, we were all really worried about him. But Jack has never been one to let on that he struggles. He's always been like that."

"I remember," Jocelyn replied, her thoughts drawn back to the night he had nearly died from appendicitis for fear that others might have to fuss over him. "What do you think makes him that way?"

"Who knows," Sarah said with a shrug. "He's stubborn, among other things."

"I'm still going back to Austin in a couple of weeks," Jocelyn declared, afraid to leave anyone under a different impression for even another second.

"Yeah, I know," Sarah said somberly. "He'll be okay. Whatever happens between the two of you, I know that he's in a much better place now."

Jocelyn certainly hoped so. Leaving would be hard enough without worrying that the act of it might unravel Jack again. He didn't deserve that. It was part of why she had resisted getting involved with him in the first place.

"Anyway, I'm still hoping that the stars will align," Sarah added, reminding Jocelyn of what Jack had said that morning. "Having *two* amazing sisters would really make my life pretty perfect. And, after all, today is still all about me, right?"

Jocelyn laughed. She knew that Sarah was making light, but she too wished that she was brave enough to throw everything she'd built away to make the dream she'd built with Jack a long-term reality.

"Oh geez," Ava broke in. "Would you look at my husband?"

Through the window, they could see Will playing cornhole with a balloon stuffed under his shirt, supporting his baby bump lovingly.

"I can't unsee that," she added with a chuckle.

They all laughed at the sight and Jocelyn found herself grateful for the distraction. Once again, she allowed herself to embrace the present and ignore the impending future, if only to allow herself to enjoy what time she had left in Farnham. No matter what was gained or what was lost on the other side, it had been a perfect day.

Chapter Eighteen

The fire that had ignited between Jack and Jocelyn was all consuming. Jack doubted any length of time together would ever be enough to satisfy his craving for her. It wasn't a simple matter of lust, that much he knew. Jocelyn was part of a bigger picture he had been waiting to complete his entire life. She was the missing piece he had always, in some way or another, known was a perfect fit.

As many times as he tried to consider uprooting his life to join her in Austin, everything pulled him back to the river, back to this house. The home they had created together. While she hadn't said it with words, Jack feared that Jocelyn didn't share his feelings. Or more accurately, he could see that she fought them as her life in Austin called her back.

He had spent the day helping to stage the house for the realtor who would be taking photos for the listing the following day. In a few days the house would be up on the market and the thought of it made him sick. Everything they had shared was unraveling just as quickly as it had begun. He did his best to ignore the fact that they had yet to discuss the reality of what her leaving meant.

Jocelyn allowed herself to be consumed by the details of staging the home. She spent nearly an hour strategically placing the two loveseats and the accent chair in the living room around the coffee table until the placement was just right. She made up the beds in each of the bedrooms with the new bedding she had purchased. Then she took some time adding a pop of color to each room using a stack or two of antique books she had collected from Jack's place. Each room had a different color pallet, brought out with the books, accent pillows and wall art she had picked up at the thrift shops in town. She placed various plants throughout the house that Jack had been more than happy to part with, breathing warmth and life into the streamline space.

They had spent all morning setting up each room and reworking the layout and design several times, and Jocelyn found herself out of excuses to keep moving. She could feel Jack's tension, his need to address the words that remained unsaid between them. She had never been a coward in her life. She had always faced her problems head on but facing Jack and the truth that settled uneasily between them scared her more than anything.

She didn't want to leave, of course she wanted to stay with Jack and live out their fairytale. The time they had spent together in the last few weeks had been nothing short of euphoric, but that didn't mean that she should abandon her life to pursue a fantasy. Where she had once been so ready to leave Austin and abandon her life there, she now clung to the security and certainty that it brought her. Everything would make sense once she returned. It just had to.

From the kitchen, they took in the finished layout of the main floor. Jocelyn had finally run out of adjustments to make and had pulled herself up to sit on the counter to scan the room, hoping to find something else to move or change. In all the time she had been at the house, she'd remained busy. Being done once and for all brought with it the sad ache of farewell.

"I can't believe it's almost time to say goodbye," she remarked somberly.

"You don't have to go," Jack offered, placing himself in front of her, hoping to close any distance that threatened to come between them.

"Please," Jocelyn said timidly. "Not now."

Jack knew that it was Jocelyn's way of putting off the inevitable. The truth that they had both carelessly ignored in the previous weeks. Now, only days away from her scheduled departure, he felt the rude awakening of reality rattle the dream he had been naive enough to believe could be his life.

He looked down at his watch, noticing that the morning was all but spent. "I should get going anyway," he said with some relief.

He gazed up into Jocelyn's eyes as she placed her arms around his neck. He took her face in his hands and kissed her as if it might be the last time. When their lips parted, she brought him into an embrace protectively. He could hear her heartbeat quicken and he knew that she was just as scared of losing everything they had made as he was.

No longer able to stay with the unspoken words that hung between them, Jack pulled away and Jocelyn leaned in for another soft kiss. He brought her into his arms and lowered her from the countertop, wrapping her in one final embrace. He kissed her forehead and stroked her hair absently, drumming up the will to leave.

"I love you," he whispered, hoping that the three little words were enough to leave her with.

Jack busied himself on the job, grateful for a bathroom demolition to remain distracted with. It was a task he could complete in his sleep, but it kept his attention off Jocelyn's pending departure. Tearing down, ripping out, and hauling off the contents of the bathroom consumed the remainder of his day. It was physically exhausting work and by the time he returned home, he had just enough energy to shower and little else.

When he and Jocelyn made their way out onto the screened-in porch to watch the sun set that evening, it was easy to imagine that they could let another day go by without addressing the truth that grew between them, creating a space that Jack could no longer ignore.

Jocelyn sat in a rocking chair, settling in easily as she always did. Jack, however, remained restless. Unable to sit, he walked up to the railing and gazed out over the landscape. Below, the cool blue water of the pool reflected the changing colors of the evening sky. The lawn that stretched out between the home and the beach had been cut, filling the air with the crisp scent of freshly mowed grass. Waves lapped lazily on the sand, the gentle sound adding to the quiet evening symphony. Beyond the shore, a handful of fishermen coasted over the surface of the water. It was a scene Jack never tired of. A sight he knew Jocelyn looked forward to starting and ending each day with.

"We can't keep putting off this conversation," Jack spoke at last, breaking the silence between them. He turned to face Jocelyn, not surprised to see the uneasy way she shifted in her chair. "What happens to us once you leave?"

Jocelyn felt assaulted by the directness of his words and wished that she had posed the question first. The last thing she wanted was to feel responsible for providing the right answer.

"Why does anything have to happen?" she retorted evasively.

Jack leaned on the post at his back, his hands dug deep into his pockets. "Come on, Jocelyn," he said softly. "You know as well as I do that everything is about to change between us."

"Not everything," she countered.

Jack let out a heavy sigh. "Enough," he said firmly. "Enough will change. I'm not being unfair in wanting to know exactly what that means."

"I know," Jocelyn allowed.

"My question to you is, why does it have to?" he asserted. "Don't go back," he offered again boldly. "Stay here with me."

"You say that like it's so easy," Jocelyn said, trying to control her unexpected temper. "Because, for you, it is. I change everything and you change nothing."

Jack crossed his arms over his chest, forcing himself to remain calm. "I'm not trying to compete with you," he said curtly. "I understand that it's not a small request, but that doesn't mean I won't have to make changes too."

"It's not that simple," Jocelyn said pointedly.

"And why is that?" Jack asserted. "I love you," he said firmly. "And you love me. I don't care about the rest."

"So, you would move to Austin for me?" she asked brazenly. She could feel her temper flaring as she prepared for his reply.

"You know I can't do that," Jack declared. "My life, *our* life, is here," he reasoned.

He moved towards her, and she pushed herself out of her seat, needing the space to remain between them so that she could stand firm in her defense. Women upend their lives for men all the time. Was it so hard for him to consider being the one to uproot everything he knew for her instead? If not, then why was it presumed she would bend to the will of his needs, his convenience?

"I have a life in Austin," she argued stubbornly.

"What life?" he retorted.

"A career for starters," she shot back. "I have a beautiful condo and my parents are there," she went on. She was exasperated that she had to prove that she had any skin in the game simply because they had sparked up a romance on his turf. "What's so terrible about a long-distance relationship anyway?" she challenged. Just because she wasn't ready to gamble everything on their love story, didn't mean she didn't still want it to continue it.

"Oh, come on, Jocelyn," Jack said exasperated. "We're not teenagers. I want to make you my wife, not a pen pal."

Momentarily stunned at the mention of marriage, Jocelyn was lost for words.

As her silence carried on, baring more meaning than any words could, Jack shook his head, exasperated.

"I'm not sure how I managed to convince myself that you would stay." His heart sank and he realized quickly how much he had invested in the hope that Jocelyn wouldn't leave after all.

"Why is that the only alternative you'll accept?!" Jocelyn pressed on.

It wasn't Jocelyn's job to fix him, Jack knew that, but he was working to piece himself back together. His life had suffered great loss the previous year and he had managed to ignore it up until only very recently. She was a big part of that. She was the anchor in the storm that he had desperately needed and still did.

Jocelyn would return to Austin and a life that had no place for him. She would go back to working with a man who clearly maintained feelings for her and fit neatly into the life she had chosen. With everything he was still unpacking in his own life, Jack didn't trust that he could handle what a long-distance relationship would undoubtably require of him. The last thing he wanted was to push Jocelyn away because of jealousy or insecurities that were agitated by his baggage.

"I don't want us to put our life on hold," Jack reasoned. "I don't want to wish every day away that we're not together. I won't be content living a half-life, Jocelyn. I'm sorry. I wish I could see it differently. I've tried. But the truth is, I'm not built for texting and long phone calls to make up the majority of our time together until I can see you again. There's no room in my life for a relationship full of insecurities and jealousy. I don't want to worry about where you are or who you're with when I can't reach you. I don't want to pine for you, I want to spend time with you, and invest actively in our future and in building a life together. As long as you're there and I'm here we are living two separate lives."

The picture in his mind of their life together in Farnham was so clear. He couldn't understand how she couldn't see it. Why she refused to see it.

"Long distance relationships work out all the time," Jocelyn argued. "After a few months or a year, I can look into working remotely part-time. I'll visit you once a month, you'll visit me. It won't be that bad. We haven't even tried it."

Jack shook his head, his emotions threatening to consume his ability to respond with more love than hurt. He wished that he could be flexible, that he could agree to her terms, but he couldn't see the sense behind it. Consumed by the clear picture he had built of them together, he wondered how Jocelyn could be so blinded by a life that her heart had no affection for.

Spend more time together in a year? He wanted to make her his wife in a year. He wanted to start a family with her in a year.

"There's no rush," she insisted, interrupting his thoughts.

Jack had been looking at engagement rings earlier that week. He had started designing the blueprint for a permanent shop to replace the barn. A suggestion Jocelyn had made. A business venture he couldn't imagine without her. Maybe she refused to see it, maybe she was too afraid to jump, but that didn't mean she was right.

He considered her words and the more he did, the more hurt he felt. *No rush?* He couldn't believe what she was saying. It wasn't a matter of rushing. He was simply unwilling to bring their relationship to a screeching halt.

Patience had never been Jack's strongest attribute. Selena had given him room enough to prove that throughout their fiery relationship, but Jocelyn had just barely scratched the surface of his untamed heart. She grounded him more than anyone else could, but even she couldn't have controlled the storm that churned inside him now.

"You're driving me crazy!" Jack barked; his throat raw with emotion. "I don't have space for this, Jocelyn!"

Jocelyn recoiled; her heart physically wounded by the shards of his words. "It's not that easy," she disputed, her voice a mixture of anger and sadness. "I can't just leave my life for some guy!" She could tell that she had succeeded in delivering her own blow and instantly regretted it.

Jack took a few involuntary steps toward the door, her reply fueling the distance between them. As he tested words on his tongue, they all tasted of poison and he thought it better not to speak them.

Defeated, he let his guard down long enough to say, "I was lost when I found you again. I won't let myself go back to that place."

Before Jocelyn could respond, Jack let himself out.

She watched him walk towards the houseboat and disappear inside. Without the words to confirm it, she knew that he would only accept one answer. She knew that he waited, fuming, for her to go after him and agree to make a life together in Virginia. Stubbornly, she felt herself drawing further away from a willingness to do so.

She made her way inside, busying herself with mindless cleaning, unsuccessfully distracting herself from the unspoken ultimatum that hung between her and Jack. Her heart ached at the thought of losing him, and she worked to build a wall to protect herself from the pain it caused. Jack Evans was a great many things, but *everything* was not one of them. And everything wasn't something she was willing to give up for a love she had no guarantee would last. In all her life the one thing she had been able to rely on was her work ethic. The thing she could count on the least was her record with men.

**

Jack had left in the dead of night, fueled by an ache in his heart so deep he chose numbness over feeling. In the early morning hours, he had called Jonas to bring him by the house to pick up his truck and he was gone from her life before Jocelyn awoke for the day.

Jocelyn hadn't been surprised when both Jack's houseboat and truck were gone, but that didn't stop her from glancing periodically out the window all the same. She imagined he was as mad at her as she was at him. More than anything, she was mad at the fate that stood between them. It was the only thing that kept her from breaking down. If she was mad, then she didn't have room to be devastated. With a full day ahead of her, the last thing she needed was to wrestle with her feelings and the doubts that threatened to dismantle every aspect of her life.

The realtor arrived just before noon, providing a much-needed distraction from the pain that Jocelyn was working hard to ignore. She gushed over the home and the many intricate details that she *just knew from experience could only be the work of Jack Evans*. The staging, Jocelyn had done, would make for a quick and competitive sale. The property would be under contract, the realtor promised, by the end of the week.

As happy as the positive feedback made Jocelyn, she struggled to rein in the conflicting emotions the reality of it left her holding. Had it been so easy for Jack to walk away? Leaving her to carry the burden of their dismantled love story alone?

When Sarah arrived unannounced that afternoon, it took every fiber of Jocelyn's being not to come undone completely. Despite herself, she fell, sobbing, into her friend's reassuring embrace.

"I'm so sorry," Sarah said warmly. She rubbed Jocelyn's back, soothing her as she quivered under the weight of her sorrow.

Jocelyn fought to maintain her anger. She was unwilling to ask herself if she had made the right decision. She was equally unwilling to picture her life on the other side of her flight back to Austin.

When they finally made their way to the living room, Sarah helped herself to the kettle and made them each a cup of tea. Jocelyn sat cross-legged on the sofa, working to collect herself.

"He can be really bullheaded sometimes," Sarah said, placing a cup of tea in Jocelyn's hands. She lowered herself into the loveseat opposite Jocelyn and went on. "He loves you. I've never seen him this in love."

"Then why isn't he willing to make it work?" Jocelyn asked, defeated.

Sarah shook her head. "Jack has a very specific idea of what love looks like," she began. "Mom and Dad were like two sides of a coin. Different in almost every way, but together they made sense. Together they were whole. Dad worked, and Mom took care of the house and raised us. She was smart and capable in many things, but she put her plans on hold to raise a family. There wasn't anything my dad wouldn't do to keep her happy, to fill her cup, to provide her with the lavish things he felt she deserved."

"I can't be your mom," Jocelyn said gently.

"He knows that," Sarah replied with a sigh. "But he also believes that you're not supposed to leave."

"That's easy for him to say," Jocelyn retorted.

"Of course, it is," Sarah agreed. "The weight of that choice falls solely on you. He needs to be more considerate of that. He hasn't given you much of a chance to make the decision for yourself either."

Jocelyn nodded.

"Jack's still hurting," Sarah offered. "He likes to think that he's acting rationally, but he's got a long way to go still, and it shows in how easily he pushes people away."

Jocelyn was no stranger to pushing others away to protect herself. Unlike her, Jack had already chosen someone to spend his life with once. She could only imagine what getting that close to someone again just to lose them too might feel like. To have it happen only a year later, she could understand how hesitant he probably was to gamble with everything he had spent his life building. In that, they were alike.

Jocelyn let out a heavy sigh. "I'm not afraid of leaving my life in Austin," she admitted. "I'm afraid of doing it for the wrong reason. Of course I've thought about what a life with Jack might be like. How could I not? These past few months have been amazing. But the opportunity I have in Austin has been years in the making. I would be giving up so much."

"Absolutely," Sarah agreed. "I can't imagine having to make a decision like that."

"I'm struggling to see why I have to," Jocelyn said firmly.

"You don't," Sarah confirmed. "Jack is very black and white when it comes to matters of the heart. He can't see the gray areas, and it wouldn't be the first time it's left him wounded as a result."

Jocelyn shook her head and studied the mug in her hands. She felt her feet planted firmly in her belief that she had made the right choice, but she had no idea if it was because she had or if she was just as willful as Jack was.

"Can you just promise me something?" Sarah asked.

Jocelyn met her friend's eyes and smiled, hoping it was a promise she could keep.

"When you get to Austin, if you find what you're looking for, don't look back," she stated plainly. "But if you don't…please, don't let your pride get in the way of going after it."

It was a bold promise to make. Both options felt impossible, but Jocelyn knew that she would have to face one.

She nodded firmly, knowing that one way or another she had a difficult decision to make.

***

Jocelyn could no longer stay in the house that she and Jack had brought back to life and she was about to lose. She turned the realtor's contact information over to her parents and booked a flight back to Austin the following day. She couldn't see the house go, but the thought of staying made her sick. The bungalow was no longer hers—in truth, it never had been—and it now represented memories that hurt too much to think of.

In contrast, the thought of returning to her condo and to Austin for good no longer felt like returning home. It was a return to emptiness, loneliness, and uncertainty. The heartache she fought against corrupted her every thought and she worked tirelessly to remind herself that this was just part of the healing process. She had seen the end of other relationships, but she had always been ready for them. This wound would take longer to heal, but that didn't mean it never would.

It felt too late to make a different choice. The words she and Jack had exchanged, along with his abrupt withdrawal, confirmed what path she was destined to travel down. All fairytales ended eventually, she reminded herself. Reality was harsh and unforgiving, and infatuation rarely weathered the storms that inevitably crashed upon it.

Was that all she and Jack had shared in the end? Infatuation? Lust? A summer fling like teenagers destined for a life bigger than the one they had built together. Or had it been something more? Was love truly not enough? Had their romance been doomed from its trepidatious beginnings?

As much as she wanted to wish the months they had shared together away in an effort to spare herself the pain of seeing it all come to an end, she was reminded that they had been the most beautiful moments of her life, and for that, she had no regrets.

Chapter Nineteen

Jack sat parked outside of the liquor store, hands braced on the steering wheel. The lights from the neon signs flashed, beckoning him and mocking his weakness simultaneously. The hurt he fought lay just below the surface, threatening to consume him if he didn't find a way to suppress it.

It had never been a question of what Jack was willing to give up to keep Jocelyn in his life. In truth, there was nothing he coveted more than her love. He would sell his business, sell his boat, sell everything he owned and move into her Austin condo. He regretted not making that clear to her. He believed that their life was in Virginia, but more than that, he believed that he wasn't ready to uproot his life. Even at the cost of pushing Jocelyn away. His foundation from one day to the next was still unstable at best. He had far more work to do on himself. Far more healing to undergo before dismantling the remainder of his life as he knew it.

In the year since his mother's passing, Jack had come to understand a few foundational truths. The value of time for one. That no amount would ever be enough when it came to those you love. But he realized also that no matter how connected two people became, everyone had to go through life fundamentally alone. No one had the ability to carry and unpack anyone else's burden, they were too weighted down by their own. It was an unfair thing to ask of anyone, especially the woman he loved. To carry him through the trials of his life that were far from over. Not just the loss of his mother, but the loss of a relationship he had fully invested himself in. He couldn't even begin to compare Selena and Jocelyn, but he had entrusted her once with his heart. In many ways, he was still learning to trust another woman with that kind of power over him.

When Sarah had called to tell him that Jocelyn was leaving early and laid in on him about driving her away, Jack had unloaded the remainder of his anger and hurt on her. He knew it hadn't been fair, but she fought with him, toe-to-toe and the truth of her words cut him like a straight razor. He hadn't intended to discard Jocelyn or the love that existed between them so carelessly. He could barely stand the thought of spending a day without her in it, but he had loved and lost before.

While he knew that Jocelyn was different, it felt inevitable that the result would be the same and he was ill equipped to handle it. In fact, he was willing to admit that he wasn't prepared to love her like he should even if they stayed together. Not long term anyway. He couldn't fight for her while a battle still waged on inside of him. How could he expect her to stay when he was still so broken?

The feelings that rushed in, the ones tied to losing every woman who had ever held a place in Jack's heart, became suffocating. He wanted to quiet the ache, numb the pain, and drown out the thoughts that threatened to consume him. He couldn't go after Jocelyn. He couldn't start a new life because he had left the one she had entered into in shambles. If he hoped to gain any chance of deserving a woman like Jocelyn, any promise of building a life with her, he would have to start by rebuilding himself. With intention this time.

Jack kicked his truck into reverse and tore out of the liquor store parking lot, leaving behind a demon he had let feed on his wounded soul for far too long.

When Jack arrived at his father's house, he felt the uncomfortable rush of dread wash over him. As much as he avoided talking about his mother for his father's sake, he knew he wasn't being fair to say that it was the only reason. Jocelyn was the only one he had talked to openly about her since she had passed. He was coming to realize that in an effort to protect himself, he had done more damage instead.

Peter opened the door, surprised to see his oldest and most independent child looking as lost as he'd ever seen him. "Jack," he said in surprise. "I'm sorry, I must have forgotten—"

"No," Jack interrupted. "You didn't forget. I…" He rubbed his neck, buying time to collect his nerves. "I just came by to talk," he offered.

"Oh." Peter, pleasantly surprised, welcomed his son inside.

Jack crossed over the threshold and the weight of his sorrow fell to the floor. The home he had grown up in had changed little since his childhood. Fishing magazines were stacked on the coffee table and a few stray dishes lay forgotten in the sink, but his father had worked tirelessly to honor the home that he'd shared with the love of his life.

Photos from Jack's childhood decorated the walls. His mother's most recent collection of family portraits hung proudly in the entryway. Floral throw pillows, doilies, and vases Jack noticed his father kept fresh flowers in offered a feminine touch that said the home had been well loved by a woman.

"The place looks great," he offered.

"I do what I can," Peter allowed.

"Don't sell yourself short," Jack insisted. He shook his head, disappointed in himself for taking this long to see his father clearly. "I don't know what I would do in your position," he began. "I've run so far and so fast from feelings I haven't wanted to face."

"You thought you had more time," Peter offered, fighting the emotions that constricted his chest.

"So did you," Jack retorted. "You lost your lover, your best friend, your other half and you've still managed to face the reality of it better than me."

"Your mother was slowing down," Peter said, sinking into an armchair.

Jack took a seat on the couch beside his father, no longer able to stand.

"She didn't have the same vigor that she used to. She took more naps. She became exhausted more easily. Sometimes the idea of getting out of bed was just too much. The diagnosis came shortly before the end, but I always suspected that we didn't have as much time as the doctors said," Peter admitted, a tear falling absently down his face.

"I didn't see it," Jack said, angry with himself.

"You had your own life. Your own love," Peter reasoned.

"But I should have paid closer attention."

Peter shook his head. "Don't blame yourself. Your mother wouldn't want that any more than I do."

Jack's jaw clenched involuntarily, unable to free himself of the guilt, but knowing it wasn't his father's baggage to unpack. "Can you tell me more about her?" he asked, sitting forward in his seat.

Peter smiled. Jack had made Margaret a mother. Though he had been the first to move out and to build his own life, full of plans and independence, he was such a big part of who she had become in adulthood. He had paved the way for the kind of mother she had become. Where she had once wanted a great many things out of life, she easily decided after looking into her firstborn's eyes, that if she couldn't succeed at motherhood, she wanted none of the other trimmings that the world had to offer.

"You sparked a fire inside of her," Peter began. "Of course, she always knew that she wanted to be a mother, but she never knew how important it would be until you came along."

Jack smiled, the ache in his heart soothed by the potent reality of his mother's love which remained very much alive. He realized that in shutting out the acceptance of her passing, he inevitably shut out so much more.

He listened to his father speak of the woman who had shaped every life she touched. He enjoyed the fond memories and the new details of a life he had yet to see completely. He vowed in that moment to stop running. From his sorrow, from the truth, and from his heart. He still had plenty of work to do on himself, but he knew now more than ever what it would take.

***

Returning to Austin had felt like waking up from a dream that had ended too soon. Jocelyn went through the motions of reentering her daily routine determined to heal from the hurt and to start fresh. While she promised Sarah that she wouldn't let her pride get in the way of making the right decision, she hardly had time to think about the life she'd left behind since her return.

Using a rainy day to unpack the boxes she had shipped back to Austin from the river house, she found herself surrounded by childhood memories once again. She had ignored the small pile that sat untouched in the corner of her bedroom for nearly a week. With no remaining excuses to put off sifting through a past long gone as well as one that she was still fiercely tied to, she opened the first box.

At the top of the pile sat the plaque with the mounted green shovel. She considered the childhood memory attached to the keepsake. Determined and headstrong, she had searched in vain for the beach toy. It wasn't until she had stopped looking that she'd finally found it.

As much as Jocelyn had grown apart from the symbol that had come to define her as a child, she now found herself looking to it for answers. Had she managed, yet again, to find what she was searching for once she'd finally stopped looking? Had she designed her life so completely, so intricately, only to discover that it had all been a diversion from what she truly sought out of life? Had she led herself away from happiness, from love, from simple pleasures in exchange for the promise of success and career advancement?

Jack's face flashed across her mind. His easy smile, his thoughtful stare. He was a man undefined by any one thing. He wasn't just a contractor who could build something from nothing, he was a thoughtful musician who could coax a beautiful melody from an old piano. He had a love for family that exceeded mere obligation. He was hard working, and in contrast he was effortlessly fun loving. He was stoic and reserved, and yet vulnerable in a way she had never seen in a man she admired so completely. As much as she fought the thoughts of him from surrounding her, calling her back, the pull of his energy was overwhelming. Yes, he had pushed her away, but hadn't she also run?

***

Jocelyn sat at the bar, hesitant to join her co-workers as they celebrated with tequila shots and shrimp cocktails. Not only had the proposal gone well, but the company they had been working with had also extended their contract with the firm for another five years. Jocelyn knew that she should be elated, and she convinced herself almost completely that she was. It had been a busy month since her return to Austin, and she was still settling back into her life, not to mention into a new position at the firm, but she couldn't shake the hollow feeling that threatened to consume her. The feeling that she had made the wrong choice.

She was mad at herself for the effort that was required to carry on conversations with her coworkers that would have been effortless only four months earlier. Why did everything in Austin suddenly feel so foreign to her? She was excited about her new position. She had earned it. She was happy. Why did it require so much effort to convince herself of that?

From across the room Michael studied Jocelyn. She plastered on a fake smile and acted as if nothing was wrong during office hours, but he could tell that it was far from the case. Sitting at the bar, stirring her martini with a skewered olive, she stared vacantly in the direction of their coworkers seated at the bar top tables a few feet away, and he wondered how much longer he could bear to see her this way.

Answering his own question, Michael rose from his seat and strode over, claiming the seat beside her.

At his arrival, Jocelyn smiled half-heartedly. "Hey."

"What are you doing here?" he asked bluntly.

Taken aback by his question but disarmed by the gentle way in which he spoke the words, she shook her head in confusion. "What do you mean? We're celebrating," she stated, as if it were obvious.

Michael gestured towards their co-workers who laughed freely at a joke Greg had told that probably wouldn't have been very funny three drinks ago. "They're celebrating," he said matter-of-factly.

Jocelyn raised her glass and plastered a phony smile on her face. "*So am I.*"

"What, is that your...first sip?" he chided.

"What's it to you anyway?" Jocelyn challenged.

"What's it to me?" Michael retorted. "We may not be together anymore. You may not return my feelings, but that doesn't mean I can't tell when you're miserable or that I want you to stay that way."

Jocelyn's face contorted into an expression that challenged him to accept her as she was.

"Wow," Michael said, laughing incredulously. "You really are *that* stubborn, aren't you?"

"What's your problem anyway?" she shot back.

Michael disengaged, giving himself pause before confronting Jocelyn further. He studied her and took a sip of his drink as she absently did the same. It wasn't easy watching the woman whom he had loved for years falling so helplessly in love with someone else. He couldn't help but be torn up over it, but he wasn't about to let her know it. That was his cross to carry.

In the months that followed their breakup, Michael had remained hopeful that they might reconcile. He was ready to settle down, ready to start a family. Jocelyn had fit so easily into his proverbial five-year-plan. Now, he was willing to admit, he had noticed years ago that she hadn't felt as sure about the direction of her life as he did.

No matter how hard he had tried over the years to remain a supportive partner in her life, he realized he had only managed to satisfy the façade she had built up rather than her truth. Now, watching her stare off blankly past her drink, he knew he could never be what she needed no matter how much he wished otherwise.

"*Why are you here?*" Michael repeated, more sternly this time.

His words pierced her indifference, dismantling her weak resolve. Caught off guard by the emotions she had been suffocating since returning to Austin, Jocelyn began to openly weep, and she wondered if she would ever find the will to stop.

Michael moved in closer and pulled her into his side. She didn't know how long she sat there, crying uncontrollably over her drink, but when she finally stopped—her face red and tear soaked—she laughed at how pathetic and relieved she felt all at once.

"Is that better?" Michael asked warmly.

She nodded, though she knew the small breakdown wasn't even the tip of the iceberg. "I don't want to be the girl who gives up everything for a guy," she muttered half-heartedly.

"What exactly are you giving up?" Michael challenged. "You've been miserable here for easily a year or more."

"I haven't been *miserable*," Jocelyn denied.

"You haven't let your misery get in the way of your work," Michael corrected. "That's not really the same thing."

"I love it here," Jocelyn countered.

"You *live* here," Michael amended boldly. "I'll allow that at one point or another you probably really did love it here. The woman I fell head over heels for certainly did. She loved her job. She loved everything she had worked hard for. Maybe for that reason alone. But by the time you had grown tired of me, I knew that you had lost your affection for this city and your job at the firm. I like to tell myself that our relationship was collateral damage in a war you've been waging long before I entered the picture."

"Why didn't you ever say any of this before?" Jocelyn challenged.

"Because you would have denied it," Michael said plainly.

"No, I wouldn't have," she bit back.

Michael raised a challenging brow. "You needed to see it for yourself before you would even consider believing it."

"Then why did you want me to stay?" she asked, crushed by the weight of the reality she now faced. "Why did you come to Virginia? Why did you kiss me?"

Michael leaned in and placed a hand over Jocelyn's and waited for her to meet his eyes before he spoke. "Because I love you," he said flatly. "I would be a fool not to fight for you. It took me far too long to realize that, and now it's too late. Now I know what you want and who you want, and I can't, in good conscience, claim that I can offer you a life that would compare."

"He's not fighting for me," Jocelyn said flatly.

"He's not falling for the lie you've been telling yourself," Michael corrected.

In the two years they had been together, Michael had never been confrontational. He had never challenged her. He had never forced her to face her own reflection. Now, at the defense of another man, he held nothing back.

Jocelyn studied their hands. She had never wanted to love Michael more in her life than in that moment. He had done for her what she had always wished he would, and she realized it still wasn't enough to earn the love from her that he deserved.

It would be easy to stay in Austin, to spend the rest of her life learning to love Michael the way he loved her. She wouldn't have to change anything. She wouldn't have to leap into uncertainty and doubts that clouded the path that chose her while she'd been trying to stay on track with the one she had picked for herself. But it would be a lie. And as hard as taking the risk to follow her heart might be, she knew that she would be committed to a lifetime of purgatory in ignoring it.

"What now?" she asked, knowing full well that Michael was more attuned to her than she'd ever given him credit for.

"I can't speak of your taste," Michael began coolly. "You've clearly got some wires crossed in that department, but that's not really any of my business, is it?"

Jocelyn shrugged, flashing a teary smile.

"The way I see it, you have two options. Keep everything you've ever worked for and be entirely miserable for it, or give it all up, get on a plane to Virginia and be happy without it."

Jocelyn let out a shaky breath, surprised to hear herself laughing. How was Michael more willing to see what she was too afraid to admit herself?

"What if I get there and he doesn't want me anymore? I hurt him," she said, ashamed. "I thought that staying on course was the right thing to do. I was wrong." She hung her head.

Michael cupped her chin in his hand, and she met his eyes again.

"If he turns you away then he's an idiot," he offered boldly. "I don't know a lot about the guy. He seems a bit primitive to me, but what I do know is that you love him. You're an intelligent woman, Jocelyn. The smartest person I've ever met." He peered over his shoulder. "Don't tell Bridget," he added in a whisper.

"The way I see it, if you love the guy, then you see something I don't. That's enough confirmation for me that he's worth taking the risk. But I imagine after leaving like you did, he's going to need the whole deal this time. So, the question is, what do you choose? Your job and everything you know in Austin, or some guy in Virginia who has apparently loved you since you were kids."

Jocelyn flung her arms around his neck. "Thank you, Michael," she said, feeling the weight of the decision continue to lift.

"Don't mention it," he replied, enjoying the sweet scent of a woman who no longer had a place in her heart for him. "Let me know if there's anything else I can do," he added, confident that helping Jocelyn find true love was the best way to profess his unrequited love for her. "I know a great realtor. She'll have your condo sold in a day."

"How can I ever thank you enough," Jocelyn beamed.

"Just promise me if things don't work out, you'll come back and find me," he said sweetly.

Jocelyn smiled. Though she knew she would fight for Jack every day for the rest of her life, Michael no longer felt like a consolation prize, but a true friend. How she had managed to find two great men in one lifetime, she didn't know.

"Deal," she agreed easily before planting a friendly kiss on his cheek and leaving the bar without looking back.

Chapter Twenty

The easiest part of leaving Austin had been making the decision to do so. Though Jocelyn knew it had come much later than it should have. It had taken returning to a life she no longer recognized and the candid advice from Michael to dispel the illusion that this was still hers to claim.

Everything else about the move had been far from effortless. Bridget, unlike Michael, hadn't taken the news well. Not only had Jocelyn's choice to leave the firm come as a complete shock, but it had also delivered a fair amount of insult. She had only just received a prestigious promotion, one in which Bridget had fought hard for her to get. Turning down the position had built, sealed, and buried the coffin that contained any chance Jocelyn had of staying with or returning to Bradford and Bend. It was a fact that made following through with her plan both easier as well as more terrifying.

Michael, as promised, had put her in contact with an excellent realtor. The sale of her condo, however, was little more than a glaring reminder that, for all intents and purposes, she was now homeless. She wondered off-handedly if she would be able to adjust to life on a houseboat that had little room for her personal belongings. That was, of course, if Jack didn't slam the door in her face.

The river house had sold before an official listing had even been posted. She felt the returning pang of remorse in knowing that she could have avoided the loss of the property forever by offering to buy it from her parents instead.

While she worked to completely dismantle her life, Jocelyn was faced with the reality that she had no idea what she would find when she returned to Farnham. She couldn't bring herself to reach out to Jack. Though she stayed in contact with Sarah, they didn't speak of her brother. When she informed Sarah that she would be returning, she had begged her not to tell him. She still didn't know what she would say to him and the last thing she wanted was for him to be more prepared than she was when they were finally face to face again.

***

Jocelyn had spent two days driving her silver Mazda from Austin to Farnham. The beautiful fall foliage made for a scenic drive that managed to distract, on occasion, from the nerves that settled painfully in her chest. With a brief overnight stay in Tennessee and a few pit stops for food and fuel along the way, she had arrived in Virginia.

Everything she owned, apart from two suitcases stuffed full of her clothes and a few boxes of her most prized possessions, had been packed up in a storage unit or sold. How she had managed to swap familiarity for chaos so completely was still a mystery, but now it fueled her.

A few hours later, Jocelyn pulled her car into a shady curbside motel on the outskirts of town, certain she would need a good night's sleep before facing Jack. Her need for him had only grown stronger as she drew closer to the memories they had made together.

Lying in bed, imagining what it might be like to see him again, she tossed and turned all night, plagued by doubts and the weight of her decision to uproot everything she knew to start a life together in Virginia.

What if he didn't return her feelings? Where would she go if he had moved on? Had she thrown it all away for nothing?

As sleep finally worked to win over her busy mind, Jocelyn conceded to the fact that, despite all that still remained unknown, she had no regrets. She had leapt without thinking and she didn't need anyone to catch her, she simply needed to open her wings to fly or fall on her own.

***

The next day Jocelyn checked out of her motel and headed into town. Drawn by an overwhelming, almost magnetic pull, she turned down the road that led to the river house. She wanted to face Jack, she wanted to confront what had happened between them, but fear—or something else she couldn't name—took over and she sought out comfort instead. She hoped that the buyers wouldn't be there when she pulled up the drive. Just in case, she worked to form a weak excuse as to why she had come.

She had left in such a hurry, she felt suddenly deprived of a proper goodbye. She had been so eager to get away, that she had neglected to acknowledge just how much the place meant to her. Turning down the driveway, she was relieved to see no cars parked out front.

Exiting her Mazda, Jocelyn pulled her chunky cardigan closed, warding off the chill of the breeze that swept in from the river. Paired with a black pair of leggings and boots, it was the most bundled she'd been at the river house in decades. She had forgotten how cold it could get in October.

The foliage, a lush green when she'd left, was now a mix of auburn, crimson, and gold. Leaves danced on the wind as it swept through the trees, plucking them from their branches and littering them across the lawn. On the porch, she could see a large collection of pumpkins and gourds of every size and variety spilling thoughtfully down the steps in a carefree cascade.

Though the seasons changed, and time continued to pass without permission, the house looked just as she had left it. The sense of returning home overwhelmed her. It was more than just a home for her childhood memories. The bungalow had marked a transition in her life she might never have been brave enough to make without it. She felt a pit in her stomach knowing she had no right to feel that way.

Jocelyn walked around the side of the house and found the pool covered and the lounge chairs tucked against the ivy laden lattice in a neat stack. She noticed a few dozen hearty plants arranged along the perimeter of the patio. Her heart ached as she was reminded of Jack. She suddenly felt foolish, faced with the magnitude of what she had done. Exposing the nerve that bound her to Jack, she suddenly felt weak and uncertain. She was returning to a place and feelings she now questioned whether she had a right to feel.

The world around her spun mercilessly out of control and she made her way to the beach in search of fresh air and refuge. With it, she hoped to also find clarity. Anything to stop the fear of a harsh reality from closing in around her.

On her way to the shore, she noticed the houseboat, parked at the dock as it had been most of the summer. It was little more than an illusion, she told herself, she was almost certain she was experiencing a mirage brought on by what she could only suspect was a panic attack. Closing her eyes, working to dislodge the vision from her mind's eye, she heard the rumble of an engine coming down the driveway.

A deeper seated panic set in and Jocelyn questioned how she had convinced herself to unravel everything that made sense in her life as completely as she had. The series of events since her return to Austin two months earlier had been carried out with reckless abandon. Now, she found herself faced with the fruits of that seemingly delusional labor.

While the nerves that coursed through her veins told Jocelyn to return to her car and deliver her sincerest apologies to the new owners, her curiosity planted her feet as the sight of Jack's houseboat refused to fade from view. When she heard steps approaching, she turned around, alarmed for the second time.

Jack walked towards her, his steps sure and his expression unreadable. Wearing a thick flannel and jeans, he was a softer version of the man she remembered from only a couple months before. His formerly cropped hair had grown out, revealing a gentle wave and his chiseled jawline was softened with fresh stubble. He was as handsome as she remembered, though she was willing to admit more so now.

The burden he had once worn on his face like a mask was replaced by a calmness that told her that he was finally at peace with his grief. As he drew closer, she also noticed that his blue eyes were soft, gentle, not the harsh daggers of guarded protection she had anticipated.

The silence that stood between them was measured. Jocelyn could feel the shift in the air as she perceived that the house was no longer her home, but his. The reality that he might seek to buy it hadn't even occurred to her until she put the pieces into place now. She'd never even thought to inquire about the sale from her parents, nor had she spoken to them of her relationship with Jack. It was no wonder they hadn't thought to connect the dots or make mention of it.

She hadn't intended to abandon the river house so easily. She'd simply followed the plan that she had set out for herself. Now, as she could see Jack positioned protectively, comfortably in the place they had built their foundations on, it all made sense.

"I didn't take you for a festive guy," Jocelyn said flippantly, eager to break the silence, but unwilling to address the weight that hung between them.

Jack squinted, briefly confused, then turned to acknowledge the array of pumpkins that decorated his home. He shrugged then replied plainly. "I'm not."

"Sarah," Jocelyn guessed knowingly.

"She's nothing if not consistent," he confirmed.

Silence threatened to grow between them again as Jack's stance tensed and he dug his hands deep into his pockets.

"Did you come here to talk about pumpkins?" he asked.

In that moment it all felt terribly confusing to try and explain. Her reason for leaving in the first place and her subsequent reason for returning seemed to fall short of the answers that Jack deserved.

As Jocelyn struggled to provide an explanation she knew would satisfy, she pictured the green shovel of her childhood. An image that continued to resurface when she thought of her relationship with Jack. An object that had come to symbolize the future she wanted. The future she was willing to fight for, but knew she no longer had to work to find.

"You are my green shovel," she heard herself say.

"I'm sorry, what?" Jack's expression was unguardedly confused.

"All I've ever really wanted was to live a life with meaning. A life with purpose, happiness…true love. I thought that was a life I had to build for myself. That I would only find it if I worked really hard and earned it. Then you came back into my life and you gave me everything I've ever wanted. It was effortless." She paused as she considered it. "I found you once I had stopped looking for what I wanted."

Jack watched Jocelyn from guarded eyes.

"I'm sorry," she offered. "I should never have left, but, if I'm being honest," she allowed. "I needed to face this crossroad head-on, and in order to do that, I had to go back." She felt her heart constrict as she awaited Jack's response. "Please forgive me."

Jack moved closer, leaving only a breath between them.

"I wasn't ready for you to leave," he admitted. "But I won't lie and say I didn't need it too." He took hold of her in a posture of surrender. "I needed to lose you to realize that I wasn't ready to deserve you."

"Are you ready now?" Jocelyn asked breathlessly.

Jack's lips grazed over her forehead, her closeness once again grounding him like nothing else could.

"I'm afraid I may never be," he whispered.

Jocelyn let herself melt into his tentative embrace. "Even if it takes a lifetime," she murmured. "I'll be right here."

Jack wrapped his arms around her, instantly filling the holes that had been left vacant in her absence. He felt undeserving of her grace. Of her love. Despite how much work remained in his own journey, he didn't have the strength to let go.

After an immeasurable amount of time passed, Jocelyn glanced up, meeting Jack's gentle blue eyes.

"I can't believe you bought the house," she said.

"I wanted to hate you," he admitted. "Even as I clung to whatever I could to keep you close, but I couldn't. The more I tried to forget you, the more I began to question if I had ever truly loved before you."

"Well," Jocelyn said firmly. "I'm not going anywhere."

Jack considered her words, remembering that the Mazda parked out front had Texas plates. "What about your job?" he asked. "The promotion. Your condo."

"Austin has given me a great many things," she offered. "For that I will always be grateful. But it's not where I belong. I know that now."

Jack pressed his lips to Jocelyn's, the hunger inside of him fueled by her words. He tasted her as if for the first time. She matched his appetite, craving what they had both been denied since they had last held each other. Her soft gentle curves fit perfectly in his hands as he claimed her once more. Pulling his lips from hers felt like an impossibility but he managed it all the same.

"Welcome home."

Epilogue

(One Year Later)

Jocelyn worked to unload a shipment that had been delivered to the shop that morning. She rested a free hand absently on her growing belly as she unboxed the inventory. Bohemian throws, handcrafted jewelry, and a selection of Aztec rugs were among the collection of merchandise she had ordered for the store's new "small business" section.

She had taken the seed of the shop that Jack had envisioned and grown the space to become a brand all its own. Separate entirely from his contracting business, the store she ran was much more than just a place for consignment and repurposed home design elements.

The sign out front read, "The Green Shovel." The name had been Jack's idea. As for the rest, together they had come up with a design for a new building. They had torn the barn down and two shipping containers were placed at either end of a concrete foundation, a nod to Jack's industrial design style. Between them, the main structure had been erected, creating an expansive showroom between the two containers with a vaulted ceiling. Large front windows and French doors allowed natural light to flood the space. The containers had been covered in stained wood paneling and the trim had been painted black to match the office nestled on the other side of the lot. Large windows were mounted at either end of each container, allowing more natural light in.

In the center of the structure, along with the checkout counter, were a collection of neat displays of flatware, cutlery, accent pillows, eclectic finds, and other home décor accents.

Each display represented a different room of the house, offering a cohesive selection of items that complimented the overall industrial and bohemian feel of the shop.

Off to either side, were access doors leading to each of the storage containers. On one side was a quality selection of consigned furniture and collectables and on the other was a variety of architectural salvage pieces. Old doors, shutters, countertops, cabinetry, and structural items were neatly organized by section.

Jocelyn moved through the main room, adjusting each display as she incorporated the new merchandise. She could never have known how at home she would feel working in the shop she and Jack had once spoken of in passing, nor could she have imagined how much the endeavor would exceed her expectations. In addition to running the shop and selecting the design elements and the products they sold, she also managed a small staff. With a baby on the way, she would happily run the shop from home and check in a few times a week when life allowed. She already knew that she wanted to offer to her family what her mother and Jack's had offered them. While she had once thought that being a wife and mother meant having to choose between family and having a career, she was learning that balance was achievable in all things.

With the store momentarily free of customers to greet, Lady, the shop's honorary mascot, returned to the dog bed that had been set up behind the checkout counter. Jocelyn smiled after her, knowing full well that she was moping.

"Don't look so sad," she consoled. "This is the first lull we've had all day."

Lady let out a quick snort in reply.

Just then the door opened, and Lady's ears perked up. When Jack entered, she settled again.

"Lunch is served," he announced, holding up two plates loaded with Turkish doner kebabs.

Jocelyn's eyes grew wide, and she left the display she had been organizing. "I'm starving," she announced.

"Let's eat outside," he suggested. "It's a beautiful day."

Once outside, Jack selected a picnic table away from the other customers that congregated around the food trucks that filled the air with their robust flavors and humming business. It was an image they had dreamed up together. A business built on the foundations of their two worlds colliding.

Jocelyn had once thought that by leaving Austin she would be giving up her independence and her natural skill for business, when in fact staying would have denied her the opportunity to put her talents and motivation to work for herself. With some tactful marketing and good old word-of-mouth advertising, the shop became the success she had once insisted it could be. Not only were Jack's customers loyal, but the tourists who came through seasonally enjoyed having a unique place to stop for food, shopping, and small-town charm.

Jack had worked mostly on the business side of his company since Jocelyn's return, unwilling to spend the majority of his day away from her, and Jonas took over as lead contractor. In addition to promoting a couple of his strongest workers to help lighten the load, Jack also took steps to expand their customer base, reaching out to local businesses in need of upgrades and expansions at a reasonable cost. Jocelyn provided fresh ideas and an appetite for expanding the company.

They had come a long way, not only in the business but in their life together. Jocelyn glanced at Jack's hand and the wedding ring proudly displayed on his finger. Not even a month had passed after her return to Virginia before Jack had proposed. A few months later, they were married at the river house, surrounded by family and a handful of close friends.

Jocelyn had no doubt that she had made the right decision to return. Jack proved to be a man of his word, eager to build a life alongside her that they both came to realize had, in fact, been written in the stars.

The River House | S h a w n   M a r a v e l

Acknowledgments

This novel is my green shovel. It is the book that found me when I wasn't looking to start writing again. On the current of the Rappahannock River, one of my children's toy shovels threatened to drift away. As I retrieved it, I was reminded of the green shovel story of my own childhood that I had always intended to build a story around. And so, *The River House* was born.

Thank you first and foremost to my husband David, for being my true love story and a constant inspiration in my life, writing, and personal growth. I've grown up with you and in our lifetime together we have managed the delicate balance of supporting one another as individuals while nurturing the love we've built together. You are my true and only love story and for that God has blessed me beyond measure. Thank you for your constant encouragement, support, and willingness to read fifteen pages of sexual tension at a time.

To my parents, Barbara and Walter Baumgarten, for instilling both a love of reading and storytelling as well as the love of wordsmithery (if it's not a word already, it is now!) Together, your individual talents and passions have helped to inspire my own journey in writing and a love of fiction. Though I wish, Mom, that you were still here to read my latest novel as you always did with such pride, it gives me great joy to know that your legacy has provided me with a hunger to write again.

This story in many ways is my love letter to you and all you have given me as my mother and friend. Dad, your infinite capacity for passion and drive have fueled me in my own life, unafraid to stumble and fall and eager to rise again. As you once said, "Life is like ice skating. Sometimes you fall, but you get right back up." Pursuing my passion and love for writing has always come down to that core value. I think it is safe to say that you've also passed down your ability to use words as an artform. Though I've dabbled in many forms of artistic expression over the years, writing is by far my favorite. You also took on the task of helping with edits in the last stages of finishing this novel. It's a job that Mom usually took on, and while romance is far from your genre of choice, you didn't hesitate to offer help where you could, and you came to love this story and these characters as I do.

To my twin sister Erika, my confidant, my best friend, and my greatest support in my writing journey. No one has quite the ability to be as excited about my stories, characters, and vision as you are. You are the only one I can trust to read along as I write without throwing me off course because of your ability to see inside the world that exists only in my mind. While you are happy to offer suggestions and edits along the way, you never steer me away from the world that I have created. Writing is such an intimate and vulnerable process, and it is something you understand and respect without question. Without your support and excitement, I'm not sure I would have the fuel I need to complete a single novel, let alone six.

To my mother-in-law, Diane, for your gracious support while reading and providing edits and insight for this story. Your help means the world to me.

To Lisa, a dear friend who was placed in my life, as it is my belief, to inspire my writing again among a great many other things. As a wife and mother, I have always been fulfilled in my roles at home, but when you took to reading my previously self-published novels (in all their flawed glory,) gushing over the characters and stories, you helped to awaken a part of me I had happily let remain dormant for eight years. Your unyielding love and support since my mother's passing as well as your hunger for my writing provided me with exactly what I needed to turn sorrow and loss into a beautiful new life. It's not often that I meet someone who finds me interesting, exciting, or thought provoking. As a supporting role in the lives of those I love most, it is easy for others to see past who I am as an individual. But you reminded me that I am the main character in my own story, as much as I am the loving mother and wife in the stories of those I hold most dear. For that gift, I can't imagine how I'll ever be able to thank you enough.

To Fahn and Jeff, for your generous invitation to your beautiful river house that created the spark of inspiration as well as provided the setting for this story. During a time in my life where I needed to heal and reflect, you both opened your arms to my family and I in a way that I can never thank you enough for. Fahn, our conversations about personal growth, career aspirations, and what we all have to offer the world helped remind me that I was long overdue for pursuing my passions and using my gifts to create again. When my mother passed, I teetered on the edge of falling and maintaining my balance in the face of sorrow I hadn't expected to come up against. With your help, nurturing, and generosity, I found healing I could never have anticipated and for that I am eternally grateful.

To Liz Eitel, you were an unexpected gift in the process of creating, perfecting, and telling this story to the world. Your feedback, enthusiasm, and intuitive understanding and affection for this book provided me with the exact brand of insight and support I needed to polish this project to meet its full potential. I feel truly blessed to have reconnected over our shared love of reading and I look forward to having you as a member of my beta reader group going forward.

To Heidi Seebohm, thank you for falling in love with my book and these characters and for all your wonderful insight and input upon discovering your copy in a Chester, New Jersey *Little Free Library* (thanks of course to the wonderful Liz mentioned above!) When it comes to self-publication, it really does take a village. You are the newest member of that village, and I cherish your readership immensely. Thank you for your exchange of Russian novels back and forth, gushing over the pages of this novel, as well as your technical help, and for being the one to light the spark that showed me that these characters were far from finished telling their stories.

To the family members and friends who have offered their support and advice as I dove back into writing again, thank you. Without readers, writing is a hollow experience. It is one I enjoy sharing with as many people as I can, and I am grateful to be surrounded by loved ones who are excited to join me on this journey.

To my children, Landon and Evelyn, thank you for teaching me about what it means to grow, give and receive grace, and to never stop learning. For every lesson I've taught you over the years, you've taught me a hundred. You've given me a reason to put family first, but to chase my dreams and reach for my goals along the way. You both inspire me more than you could ever know.

Finally, thank you to the doors that closed, and the people who closed them. Thank you for the polite rejections from the people who were looking for something else and didn't find it in me. You gave me pause to consider where I had room to grow, made me adopt a skill for craftsmanship, and pushed me to find what I was looking for in myself. I might have walked through a door of my own construction, but without the support and influences along the way, I would have never developed the grit and ability to build it in the first place.

The River House | Shawn Maravel

Manufactured by Amazon.ca
Bolton, ON

24720149R00164